YOU MAY BE WRITE

MY SO-CALLED MYSTICAL MIDLIFE BOOK 2

ROBYN PETERMAN

Copyright © 2021 by Robyn Peterman

All rights reserved.

No part of this book may be reproduced in any form or by any electronic or mechanical means, including information storage and retrieval systems, without written permission from the author, except for the use of brief quotations in a book review.

This book is a work of fiction. Names, characters, places, and incidents either are the product of the author's imagination or are used fictitiously. Any resemblance to actual persons, living or dead, businesses, companies, events, or locales is coincidental.

This book contains content that may not be suitable for young readers 17 and under.

Cover design by *Cookies Inc.*

Edited by *Kelli Collins*

ACKNOWLEDGMENTS

Writing Paranormal Women's Fiction rocks. Bring heroines my age to life is fabulous. LOL I love writing the **Good to the Last Death** series so much, I'm diving into a new one! **You May Be Write: My So-Called Mystical Midlife** book 2 flew from my fingertips and was a blast to write. It's action packed, snarky and my mom says it's hilarious!

As always, while writing is a solitary experience getting a book into the world is a group project.

The PWF Fab 13 Gals — Thank you for a wild ride. You rock.

Renee — Thank you for all your support, your friendship, your formatting expertise and for being the best Cookie ever. You saved my butt on this one. Forever in your debt. TMB. AND the freaking cover rocks. You are brilliant.

Wanda — Thank you for knowing what I mean even when I don't. LOL You are the best and this writing business wouldn't be any fun without you.

Kelli — Thank you for saving me from scary grammar and timeline mistakes. You rock. And thank you for letting me be late… again. LOL

Nancy, Jessica, Susan, Heather, Mom and Wanda — Thank you for being kickass betas. You are all wonderful.

Mom — Thank you for listening to me hash out the plot and for giving me brilliant ideas. You really need to write a book!

Steve, Henry and Audrey — Thank you. The three of you are my world. Without you, none of this would make sense. I love you.

DEDICATION

This is for the real Ann Aramini. I love you more than words could ever express and I miss you everyday.

MORE IN MY SO-CALLED MYSTICAL MIDLIFE SERIES

BOOK DESCRIPTION

YOU MAY BE WRITE

No one in their right freaking mind ever said midlife was magical.
Apparently it is.
Or at least mine is...

Once upon a time there was a paranormal romance author who caught her husband in a *compromising* position. One divorce later, she's free and ready to start her new life at forty-two.

Right?
Wrong.

Divorced idiot ex: Check
Saved idiot ex from getting murdered by his new nasty gal pal: Check
Idiot ex accused me of trying to kill him: Umm check

Still seeing my fictional characters: Check
Teeny tiny crush on my lawyer: Check check
Town under siege by dark forces: Of course
Crazy enough to try and stop it: You bet

With the darkness on the horizon, I need to clear my name and get to work. Forming a Goodness Army is on the top of the list. Shockingly, my army consists of my wacky tabacky smoking aunt, my high school counselor who can shift into a house cat, the town gossip who turns invisible after downing five beers and a few fabulous others with nefarious talents. And of course, a cast of fictional characters… who I created and definitely have an opinion on how I should proceed.

What could possibly go wrong?

I'm going on pure gut instinct at this point, and I can't wait to see how the plot turns out.

I may be wrong. I may be *write*. Either way, I'll just keep turning the pages until I find my happily ever after.

PROLOGUE

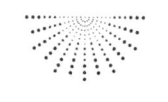

YESTERDAY

"Wow, you look beautiful," Seth said as I ran smack into his broad chest in the reception area.

I was afraid my knees might give out from the compliment or the sheer impact of slamming into his rock-hard chest. "Because I normally look like a train wreck?"

Seth's eyes widened. The light caught the blue of his irises as he backpedaled. "Oh my God, I mean... I'm sorry. I meant... I meant I didn't mean... It wasn't exactly... you know, appropriate."

His struggle to find the right words was amusing. "You want to take it back now?" I asked with a laugh.

Seth chuckled and dropped his chin. "No. I stand by my first statement, but the timing might be a little off."

I inhaled deeply and nodded. "It kind of is," I replied, glad that Nancy wasn't sitting at her desk. I didn't want to have to explain anything to anyone. Nancy was a fabulous human, but she was a talker.

Seth nodded. "Right. Of course. I figured."

"Right," I repeated, not knowing what to say. The crazy part of me wanted to take it back and ask him out on a date. However, the sane part knew that was a very bad plan. Jumping into something when I still had to figure out who I was on my own had disaster written all over it. As a newly divorced woman of approximately five minutes, I was nowhere near ready to complicate my life, no matter how pretty Seth Walters was... and he was.

Seth ran his hands through his blond hair and smiled. I realized I was jealous of his damn hands. I wanted to touch his hair.

"You know," he began casually—too casually. "There's no reason we can't be friends. Everyone needs friends, right?"

I pressed my lips together. I'd been out of the flirting and dating game for so long, I had no clue if friends actually meant friends.

"Define that," I said, knowing that I had to leave, but *really* wanting to stay.

"Friends," he said, looking up the word on his phone. "A person whom one knows and with whom one has a bond of mutual affection, typically excluding sexual or family relations." His gaze met mine and his mouth quirked up at the corners before he continued. "Terms subject to change when the time becomes right."

I laughed. This was fun. "That addendum at the end was ballsy," I pointed out.

Seth shrugged. "I'm a ballsy kind of guy."

I stared at him. He stared right back. Could it hurt to be his friend? I adored his little girl, and even though he didn't know it, Cheeto needed me and the other gals. Of course, it could hurt a whole hell of a lot if I let my heart get involved, but a future concern was not a right now problem. I had no plans to fall in love with anyone ever again. It hadn't ended well the first time.

"What the heck? Why not? Yes," I said. "I'll be your friend."

His smile made my heart skip a beat.

"Excellent," he said. "Friends we will be."

"Friends who wear muumuus every other Tuesday," I informed him.

His eyes narrowed playfully. "And every third Thursday… in public. Preferably at the bowling alley."

"You drive a hard bargain," I pointed out.

"I'm good like that," he replied. "Have to get to a meeting. Talk to you later, *friend*." He winked before he turned and headed toward his office.

I rolled my eyes as my pulse kicked up with giddiness. "Friends don't wink at friends," I called after him.

I heard him chuckle as I watched him walk away. To be more specific, I watched his ass as he walked away. I was in so much trouble.

"Leave now," I told myself, moving toward the front door of the office. "Jumping a *friend* and sticking your tongue down his throat is a crappy plan."

"Clementine," Nancy said, entering the reception area in a tizzy. "Have you seen Cheeto? She was with me and then she was gone."

"Cheeto?" My stomach tightened and I felt light-headed. Was Jinny Jingle aka *the black and decker pecker wrecker* after

7

Cheeto? My ex's new overly enhanced gal pal was out to get me. Was that why I was so antsy? If the horrible woman had indeed recognized the magic in me, could she see it in the others? Was I concocting shitty plots because I was on edge? Hopefully.

"Yes. Cheeto," Nancy said, looking under her desk. "She likes to play hide-and-seek, but she usually tells me where she's going to hide."

"Cheeto talks to you?" I asked.

"A little bit," Nancy said, looking in the supply closet. "I offered to watch her while Seth took a call."

It didn't surprise me that Cheeto talked to Nancy. Nancy had the woowoo juju—like me, my best friend Jess and a motley crew of old gals including my aunt Flip. However, it did surprise me that Cheeto would take off. "Does she do this often?"

"Never," Nancy said, sounding frantic. "She normally sticks right to my side."

Warning bells exploded in my head. "Do you think she went outside?" I asked, getting on my hands and knees and checking under the furniture.

"Possibly," Nancy said, wringing her hands in distress. "Can you walk around the building and I'll keep looking in here?"

"Yes," I said, back on my feet in a flash. "Get Seth and tell him."

Nancy nodded and took off. I was out of the door in a hot sec. My heart raced and I thought I might puke. Why would Cheeto run away? She was only seven and adored her dad. Was I nuts to think the Weather Hooker took her?

Seth wouldn't make it if something happened to his daughter. I was certain of that. Hell, I wasn't sure I would make it either. Cheeto had weaseled her way into my heart and set up a permanent place for herself in a very short period of time.

"Calm down," I told myself. God, I wished my book characters were with me. Up until a week ago, I thought I'd lost my mind. Turned out I was indeed nuts, but my mind was still intact. According to Aunt Flip, the circumstances around my humiliating divorce had brought out my woowoo juju. I could see and talk to the fictional characters I'd created in my novels. They would come in handy right now. Clark Dark, my lovably frumpy werewolf detective, could find a needle in a damn haystack. "Cheeto?" I called out.

"Beautiful Clementine!" she answered.

She was standing next to my car in the parking lot, smiling and waving. Her blonde curls blew in the wind and her red cowboy boots, yellow tutu, and purple and pink shirt were a beautiful sight to see. My relief was visceral. Running in stilettos was not fun and I was pretty sure I looked like I was about to go down, but my adrenaline was pumping and my instincts took over.

"Baby," I said, squatting down and checking her over for injury. "You can't take off like that. Nancy's very worried."

"I'm sorry," she said, touching my dark curly hair. "I want to go home with you and play with Flip."

My heart still beat irregularly, but I was so relieved, I laughed. "In the future, before you make big decisions like that, you need to ask a grown-up."

"You're a grown-up," she pointed out with a giggle.

At that moment, the skies opened and the rain began to fall. Quickly opening the car door, I put Cheeto in the driver's seat so she wouldn't get soaked. Popping open my umbrella, I stood next to the open door and searched my purse for my cell phone to call Nancy.

"I'm a grown-up, but you need to check in with the grown-up who is watching after you first."

"Okay," she said, putting her little hands on the steering wheel and pretending to drive.

"You were supposed to get me the damn house!" a shrill voice screamed.

It was a sickeningly familiar voice. The sound cut through the rain like a bolt of lightning. My ex and the woman he'd been banging while we were married were having a lover's tiff. The low-rent piece of trash wanted my house. It was on a ley line. I was pretty sure Jinny Jingle thought the house would give her magical power. She didn't get it. What I'd learned recently was that some had the woowoo juju and some wanted the woowoo juju. The have-nots who were aware that the magic existed would do anything to get it. I wasn't even sure I wanted the woowoo. Too bad, so sad. I had it. It was now part of my identity and the Weather Hooker wasn't going to get it.

The argument grew louder and uglier.

Whatever. Darren and Jinny were a match made in Hell. Actually, she'd done me a favor in poaching my husband. Although, it would have been lovely if my humiliation hadn't hit the national news, but what was done was done. Good riddance to crappy rubbish.

"Baby. Come on, baby," Darren said. "I tried. You know I'll give you anything you want. I'll buy you a house. I'm your boopy."

"I wanted *that house*, you useless piece of shit," Jinny Jingle snarled. "We're done."

They were on the other side of the parking lot. The parking lot wasn't large. It could hold about twenty cars and was only half-full right now. However, I couldn't physically see them, which hopefully meant they couldn't see me.

"You don't mean that," Darren whined. "How about we go on over to the jewelry store and I'll buy you something expensive?"

"How about you keep your word?" she demanded. "I told you what I wanted, and you failed."

"Not my fault," he insisted, sounding pathetic.

The conversation was one I didn't want to hear. It further convinced me that Jinny did know about woowoo juju and that she might very well be the elusive darkness I was searching for. I needed to get to Aunt Flip and the gals ASAP. However, I needed to get Cheeto back to Nancy first.

While a small part of me got some satisfaction out of eavesdropping on Darren and Jinny Jingle's imploding relationship, the reality of it was gross and unsettling. They deserved each other.

"Here you go, sweetie," I said, grabbing my tablet from my purse and quickly opening Candy Jelly Crush. Cheeto didn't need to hear this crap. I turned up the volume and hoped it would block out the ugly sound of the voices while I called Nancy. "Do you know how to play this game?"

"Yes!" Cheeto said. "It's my favorite." She began to play and seemed oblivious to the outside world.

Cheeto and I had more in common than I'd originally thought.

"I've wasted months on you!" Jinny shouted.

"Try decades," I muttered, digging for my cell phone.

"What are you doing?" Darren shrieked, sounding alarmed.

"What does it look like?" she asked in a tone that sent shivers up my spine.

"Baby, put the tire iron down," Darren said. "Quit playing around. Let's go to the jewelry store."

The sound that came next made me ill. My imagination was creating something that couldn't possibly be happening.

"Oh my God!" Darren cried out as I heard the grotesque noise of something hard connecting with flesh. "What the hell are you doing?"

"What I should've done weeks ago," she hissed. "Bye-bye, Darren."

I felt the bile rise in my throat as the sounds of a physical beating went down. Darren's shouts grew frantic and Jinny's grunts grew crazed. What the hell was happening? Was she hitting him? With a tire iron?

Instincts I wasn't aware I possessed took over. I felt like a character from one of my novels. Grabbing the stun gun from beneath the driver's seat, I kicked off my stilettos.

"Cheeto, I'm going to close the car door so you don't get wet," I said, hoping I sounded calm. "I need you to stay here."

Cheeto nodded without looking up. She was so engrossed in the game she'd barely heard me.

The door clicked shut and I ran like I was running from a murderer. Only, I was running *toward* the murderer... not away.

Darren looked like hell. They were behind his car. The trunk was open. He'd backed into the spot like he'd always done for as long as I'd known him. He was on the ground and Jinny Jingle stood over him with a tire iron raised over her head. Rain fell from the sky as heavily as the blood poured from Darren's face. It was horrifying.

His eyes were swollen, his nose was definitely broken and there was an open, oozing wound on his forehead. Thick red blood streamed from his slack jaw. Darren grunted in agony as the tire iron connected with his neck. She was trying to kill him.

"Back off," I shouted, holding the gun and aiming it at Jinny. Aunt Flip had said point and shoot. I hoped she was right. "I said, BACK OFF. NOW."

Her head jerked to me. Weather Hooker's eyes grew wide with delight. She was out of her freaking gourd.

"Back away from Darren," I yelled as the rain began to come down in torrents.

"Make me," she snarled, raising the tire iron in preparation to strike him again.

I wasn't even sure he was alive. And if he was, he couldn't take much more.

"Fine," I said calmly, even though my insides were churning. "I will."

Pulling the trigger was easier than I'd thought it would

be. Watching Jinny fly backwards into a car with a loud thud was shockingly satisfying. I was sure Clark Dark would be proud.

I, on the other hand, thought I was going to vomit.

Jinny was out like a light. Darren was moaning, which meant he was alive. My damn purse was in the car. Calling an ambulance was going to be a little difficult.

"Are you okay?" I asked, kneeling down on the ground next to my seriously wounded asshole ex. The question was absurd, but it was the first thing that came out of my mouth.

Darren looked at me. His eyes were almost swollen shut. The tire iron, covered in his blood, was on the ground next to him. I'd fantasized about beating him up a few times, but the reality of seeing him in this state made me sick to my stomach.

"I think I might have made a mistake," he choked out with effort. "Let's not get divorced. What do you say we give it another shot?"

If he hadn't been possibly dying, I would have punched him in the head. "Umm... that would be a hard no," I said, wondering if I should try and move him to a sitting position so he didn't choke on the blood gushing from his mouth.

I needed help, but I was afraid to leave him alone in his condition.

"Finally," Jinny grunted with satisfaction, getting to her feet with effort. "Fucking finally!"

The shock of her voice and the fact that she could stand up terrified me. Thankfully, the stun gun was still in my hand and the tire iron was out of her reach. Standing up on shaking legs, I aimed the gun at her. This time, I was prepared to stun the living hell out of her.

"What is wrong with you?" I shouted. "You almost killed him."

"He's still alive?" she asked, disappointed.

"No thanks to you," I snapped. "Attempted murder isn't a good look. You're in a lot of trouble."

"That's where you're dead wrong," Jinny shot back with a smile so ugly, I winced. "You just handed me my *external disaster* on a silver platter."

What was she talking about? Had she been concussed when she slammed into the car?

"Are you confused, Clementine?" she inquired with a sneer.

"Enlighten me," I said.

"With pleasure, *old lady*. When one loses their magic and happens to remember it, they need a bitch who still has the enchanted power to cause the external disaster. It certainly took you long enough," she informed me with a laugh that made my skin crawl. "I screwed your husband. I set up the film crew to catch us. I threatened to take your new boyfriend. I terrorized you. You were a hard nut to crack."

"You're insane," I said.

"Maybe," she replied with a shrug. "But I always get what I want."

I stared at her. She wasn't nearly as stupid as I'd thought. There was now a slight golden glow around her, but it was marred with a grayish-black mist. I hadn't been wrong about the darkness. My vision had been correct—partially. But I also hadn't known the full extent.

This was bad.

Darren moaned and spit up more blood. Jinny Jingle laughed. She was a soulless horror of a human being.

"Watch your back, Clementine," she warned. "I wouldn't want to be you right now. It's going to get ugly."

A crack of lightning and a rumble of thunder punctuated her parting words. With another laugh that would live in my nightmares, Jinny Jingle turned and ran from the parking lot.

"Help me," Darren begged.

"I will," I said as Nancy and Seth came tearing out of the building. "Call an ambulance! Darren is hurt."

"Did you find Cheeto?" Seth asked, glancing around wildly for his daughter.

"She's safe," I said quickly. "She's in my car. She wanted to come to my house and play with Flip."

"Hi, Daddy," Cheeto said, standing in the rain. Her wet blonde hair clung to her face as she stared at Darren with an undecipherable expression.

I hoped she hadn't seen what had just happened. If she had, she was going to need therapy. I was pretty sure I was going to need some therapy too. I also needed to tell Flip and the gals that Jinny had gotten her magic back and was on the loose.

"Cheeto," Seth said gruffly, scooping the little girl into his arms and holding her tight.

"What the hell happened?" Nancy screamed, taking in Darren's state and pulling her cell phone from her pocket.

"Jinny Jingle beat him to a pulp with a tire iron," I said. "Call the cops and tell them to send an ambulance. Now."

"On it," Nancy said, shaking like a leaf. "The station is right around the corner. They'll get here fast.

That was good. Small towns had their advantages.

Kneeling down in a puddle of rain and blood next to the man who had been my husband for most of my life, I gently put my hand on his arm. "It's going to be okay, Darren," I promised. "The ambulance is coming."

"Give me the house," he whispered.

"I'm sorry, what?" I asked, sure I'd heard him wrong.

"Give me the house," he repeated, even softer.

"Have you lost your mind?" I asked, shocked to the core.

His lover had almost just beaten him to death and he was still trying to get her what she wanted. My fury rose, but outwardly, I stayed calm.

"You have thirty seconds to make a decision," Darren warned as a cop car with lights flashing pulled into the parking lot.

"You are not getting the house," I ground out. "Give it up."

Darren smiled through all the blood. It was not a pretty picture.

"What happened here?" a cop I didn't recognize asked, standing over me.

"Darren Bell was beaten with a tire iron by Jinny Jingle," I said, still thrown by what Darren had just asked for. "She ran that way." I pointed in the direction Jinny had escaped.

"No," Darren said, trying to sit up. "She's lying."

My head jerked to him and my eyes narrowed dangerously.

"Clementine Roberts tried to kill me. She's devastated

that I divorced her. She begged me to take her back. I said no and she tried to kill me. I want to press charges," he said, glaring at me with sadistic victory in his eyes.

My blood ran cold at his chilling accusation. I had half a mind to pick up the tire iron and finish him off.

"That's a lie," I ground out, standing up and backing away from the vile man I'd wasted years of my life on. "I did no such thing."

"Beautiful Clementine is telling the truth," Cheeto said. "I saw it."

My heart lodged in my throat. As thankful as I was that there was a witness, I was horrified it was Cheeto.

Darren's laugh was deranged as it gurgled in his throat mixed with all the blood. "She's a child," he choked out. "And everyone knows she's not right in the head. The word of a brain-damaged child is proof of nothing. I'm pressing charges against my ex-wife for attempted murder."

It took everything I had not to dive for the tire iron and kill him dead. He'd crossed the line of decency for the last time. Cheeto was off-limits.

"I didn't do this," I said as the rain picked up even more.

"Put the stun gun down, ma'am, and raise your hands over your head," the cop said.

"I didn't try to kill Darren," I repeated as Seth moved immediately to my side and I followed the officer's direction. "I didn't. I used the stun gun to stop Jinny Jingle from killing him."

The cop nodded. "Step away from the woman," he advised Seth as he put his hand on his weapon.

How in the hell was this happening?

Seth slowly moved away, but his eyes held mine. "I believe you," he said softly.

I was so relieved, I almost dropped to the ground like a sack of potatoes. The EMTs pulled up, immediately put Darren on a stretcher and into the ambulance. I despised Darren, but sent up a quick prayer that the bastard didn't die. I'd be screwed if he did.

"We're going to have to take you into the station for questioning," the cop said.

Nancy was texting like a madwoman on her phone. I hoped to hell and back she was alerting the ladies. I might need bail money shortly.

"I'm her lawyer," Seth told the cop. "She won't be talking to anyone until I'm with her at the station."

The cop nodded curtly.

One of the best days of my life was quickly turning into the worst. I'd thought the viral video of Darren balls-deep in the Weather Hooker was horrible... this beat it hands down.

Seth leaned into the back of the cruiser after I was placed inside. "I believe you," he said again. "My dad and I will meet you at the station. Do not speak to anyone until we're with you."

I nodded, terrified. "I didn't do it."

"We know," Cheeto said softly. "I will save you. I'm not brain damaged. I'm just different."

Seth closed his eyes for a brief moment, then smiled at his daughter. "Different is good, munchkin."

"I know, Daddy. Clementine's different too."

Seth gazed at me with an intensity that made me feel raw and exposed.

"I can see that," he told Cheeto. "Like I said, different is good. It's beautiful."

My breath caught in my throat. I wondered how much he actually *saw*. "Thank you for believing me and helping me," I whispered.

"You're my friend, Clementine," he said. "That's what friends do for each other. We'll work this out. I promise."

Seth's words warmed me and brought a small amount of comfort as the officer of the law ushered him aside.

"I'm going to have to ask you to move," the cop said to Seth, putting the tire iron into a plastic evidence bag.

"Not a word," Seth reminded me as he backed away. "We'll be there soon."

I nodded and tried not to cry. He was probably regretting wanting to be my *friend*. However, I was thanking my lucky stars. As Albinia had warned me, *a friend in need is a friend indeed*.

∼

"Well, this is certainly a mess," Cassandra muttered.

"A definite twist I didn't see coming," Clark agreed.

They had appeared in the back of the cruiser the moment the cop closed the door. I'd never been so happy to see imaginary people in my life.

"Am I screwed?" I asked, as the cop walked around the car to get in and drive me to the station.

"Remains to be seen," Cassandra said. "The plot has

gotten quite messy. It's sad you're not a demon. You could have incinerated both of them to ash and the rain would have washed the worthless pieces of dreck away."

"Not helping," I muttered.

Clark said nothing. That didn't bode well.

"I didn't do it," I told them. "I despise Darren, but I would never try to kill him."

"Affirmative," Clark said. "We shall just have to prove it."

"Will it be easy?" I asked. My head pounded and my mouth felt like sandpaper.

"Nothing worthwhile is ever easy," Clark said cryptically, much to my sinking disappointment.

I was seriously hoping for a succinct yes.

"Are you ready for the adventure to begin?" Cassandra inquired.

"Do I have a choice?" I asked.

She laughed. "No. You most certainly do not."

I closed my eyes and let my head fall back on the cracked leather seat. I was sitting in a place where criminals had sat. I wasn't a criminal. I was a forty-two-year-old romance author in a soaking-wet, ruined Chanel dress. Being charged with attempted murder was not going to help my career or my mental health.

My ex-husband was a lying asshole with a greedy black heart and revenge on his mind. Jinny Jingle now had woowoo juju mixed with darkness, thanks to me. That alone could be disastrous. Cheeto had witnessed something no child should ever see. Flip and the woowoo gals were going to flip. I was flipping. My BFFs Jess and Mandy were going to freak. The plot to my life was hellish and rewriting it wouldn't help. I wasn't in charge of the storyline.

"Fine," I said, opening my eyes and watching the rivulets of rain run down the windows of the cruiser. "I'm ready." I wasn't sure if I believed my words, but if I said them enough, they would come true. They had to. "There's always sunshine after the rain. Let the adventure begin."

CHAPTER ONE

"Hell to the no," I muttered, wincing at the bright sunlight pouring through my window. The golden glow mocked my state of mind. I needed a hurricane to match my mood. Since I was landlocked in Kentucky, that was doubtful. "Maybe it was a dream."

Peeking over at my waterlogged Chanel dress on the floor, I groaned and quickly shut my eyes.

"Not a dream. Crap."

Of course, the day *after* one of the worst days of my existence had dawned blindingly sunny and in complete juxtaposition to the circumstances of my life at the moment. Yesterday had fallen into the category of *a day to block out for the rest of time*. Sadly, that wasn't possible.

After I'd signed my divorce papers, I'd spent seven hours at the police station doing my best not to lose my shit. Having Seth and his dad there as my lawyers was good. The fact that I needed lawyers to defend myself against a crime I didn't commit was not good. The rancid icing on the poisonous cake was that Jinny Jingle now possessed woowoo juju and I'd handed it to her with Aunt Flip's stun gun.

Again, crap. Actually, that one merited a much stronger word, but I'd settle for the semi-tame "shit".

"I want a do-over," I told my popcorn ceiling, refusing to glance over at the alarm clock. It was better not knowing that it might be noon. Sleeping late made me feel icky—like I'd wasted the day. Loading anything else on my plate was not smart. Hence, avoiding the actual time. "Invert," I commanded my ceiling. If I stared really hard at the pattern above, it looked like the bumps were indented. The mind could play amazing tricks—no magical woowoo juju needed at all.

My life felt like an unending fictional nightmare from Hell. If I'd written the last few months into one of my novels no one would buy it—literally or figuratively.

Basically, it had sucked. I needed therapy. My dated, 1970s popcorn ceiling would have to do.

"Soooo," I told the white plaster as I stared hard and tried to un-invert the bumpies. "In a very short span of time, I've been busy… I caught my husband banging the Weather Hooker on our kitchen table with a local film crew trailing me for my latest paranormal romance novel. It went viral." I sighed dramatically and waited for my inanimate head shrinker to say something nice. Didn't happen. Kept talking. Maybe getting it all out would take the onus off of it.

"You know, Sigmund… may I call you Sigmund?" Unsurprisingly, Sigmund didn't answer. Sigmund wasn't the most original name for my make-believe shrink, but I was worn out. After the week I'd had, I half expected my damn ceiling to answer me. "I'd always dreamed of notoriety for one of my novels, not for throwing a bucket of dirty mop water on my husband's naked ass while he was making the beast with two backs with the black and decker pecker wrecker. You feel me?"

Sigmund was very neutral.

"Good times," I went on, ignoring Sigmund's lack of empathy. "But then, after a few months of wallowing in self-pity and questionable hygiene, I thought I'd lost part of my debatably sane mind when I started seeing and talking to the characters from my novels. Turns out I'm not crazy. My characters have walked right off the pages and into my reality. Apparently, I unloaded my cheating assbag of a husband and gained woowoo juju. I'm now part of a sorority of magical crazies, and I'm the lead nutbag by default."

Sigmund's qualifications as a therapist were lacking, but his nonjudgmental attitude was working for me.

"Of course, getting questioned for an attempted murder that I didn't commit makes everything else I just overshared pale in comparison." Since Darren hadn't formally pressed charges, after a five-hour wait where I spent most of my time trying not to freak out, I was fingerprinted, photographed, and questioned for two horrifying hours. Ultimately, the police let me go after giving me the standard "don't leave town" speech. I stared up at my imaginary therapist. "Would you like to say anything, Sigmund?"

Sigmund had nothing to say. Honestly, there wasn't much he could say. It was not looking good for me. Jinny Jingle was on the loose with God only knew what kind of powers. Darren was in the hospital and I was looking at possible jail time. Not to mention, according to my characters, I was supposed to form a Goodness Army to ward off the darkness.

When the cops finally released me, Seth had driven me home from the station. I was so darn exhausted, Seth walked me inside and stayed with me while I went back over the events of the day with Aunt Flip. Flip's tail was tied in a complete knot over what Darren had done. She'd been right to have worn black to my wedding all those years ago. Hindsight was twenty-twenty. In my case, my lack of vision had kicked me in the rear end... and could get me ten to thirty in the state pen. I'd literally fallen asleep in the middle of a sentence as I'd told her my hideous tale.

If I wasn't mistaken, and I don't think I was, Seth had carried me up to bed. The man had to be regretting the day we met. Not that I was on the market, but my life was enough to scare even the bravest potential future suitor away. I was a hot mess of trouble.

"Your life is a fucking shitshow," an unfamiliar voice grunted.

Awesome. All I wanted to do was sleep for another hour or five, but apparently someone wasn't cool with that plan. I groaned. It felt like the buttcrack of dawn. I didn't do mornings—especially this morning.

"Sigmund?" I asked, refusing to open my eyes. I was pretty sure seeing a talking popcorn ceiling would give me nightmares.

Maybe my ceiling was a smoker because a coughing fit

ensued. Or maybe I'd jumped the shark and landed in Insanity Land.

"Do I sound like a Sigmund, nardass?"

"Umm... possibly," I said. Sigmund might be a little feminine...

"Get your sorry fat ass out of that bed," the voice commanded with a barking cough that made me feel a little phlegmy myself.

The hacking cough was alarming. The fact that an unknown person was in my bedroom had become surprisingly normal as of late. My characters didn't have good boundary skills. Of course, the fact that I thought it might have been my ceiling talking was not going to be discussed. I should make my bedroom off-limits, but was pretty sure no one would follow the rule. My fictional characters seemed to have minds of their own... even though I'd created the freaks.

I didn't even open an eye. My ass wasn't fat and I wasn't in the mood to deal with a person who might need the Heimlich. Last week, I might have screamed and grabbed a pair of scissors. This morning... not so much.

The voice was female—condescending, rude and breathy. It was definitely a new character. It didn't belong to Mina, the fabulous badass, sexy witch; Cassandra, the demon stepmother from Hell who was growing on me daily; Sasha, the amazing demon stepdaughter and all-around kickass gal; or Albinia... the Regency heroine who I probably never should have written. Albinia was a disaster. I barely understood a word of her Regency-speak, but I felt protective of the kooky woman who I'd created in my freshman attempt at a novel.

Suffice it to say, *Scandalous Sensual Desires of the Wicked Ones on Selby Street* was not my finest work. In my defense, it had been my first book... and it was terrible. Live and learn. My happy place was in paranormal romance. Although, magical fiction was fast becoming my real life.

"Are you deaf?" the female snapped. "I told you to get your bony carcass out of the bed."

"Make up your mind," I grumbled, burrowing deeper into the covers. "My ass can't be fat *and* bony. Pick one."

"Fine," she huffed. "Neither. It's saggy. Get your saggy bahookie out of the bed."

I rolled my eyes. My bahookie was not boney, saggy or fat. For a forty-two-year-old divorcee, it looked darn good. "Nope."

"Yesssssssss," she hissed, then hacked.

Interestingly, the tone and cadence didn't ring a bell—neither did the coughing fits. I'd written a good handful of books, but I'd never imagined this particular voice inside my crowded brain.

"Not happening," I told whoever had shown up as I pressed the heels of my hands into my eye sockets to block out the sun. "Who are you?"

"Wouldn't you like to know," the woman said with a grunt of laughter and another yack that should have caused the dummy to burst a blood vessel in her face.

I sighed and racked my brain. I was obsessed with the guessing game. Since real life was headed towards Hades in a handbasket, I may as well get lost in my imaginary world and have some fun. Fun being the relative word right now.

"Which novel are you from?" I asked with my eyes still clamped shut.

It was kind of like when I played my electronic Yahtzee game and made deals with myself. If I got a large straight and four sixes, it would be a good day. Since my Yahtzee game was in the bathroom, I'd improvise. If I guessed which new character had invaded my life, I wouldn't get charged with attempted murder. If I didn't...

"That's cheating," the woman said with a strange slurping sound. "You can't ask what fucking novel I'm in."

Who in the hell did I write that had a slurping speech impediment and a filthy mouth? God, had I written someone with excessive saliva and the plague?

"Mmmkay," I mumbled, tempted to open my eyes and peek. Cheating would get me incarcerated. I would not look. My future depended on it. I had a penchant for writing werewolves, vampires and demons. If I had to guess, I'd put the woman into the shifter category. "Will you tell me what species you are?"

"Nope, douchecanoe," she answered. "And you'll never figure it out."

"I will."

"Won't."

"Will."

"Won't."

I laughed. As gross as the character was, she was amusing in a teeth-grinding way. "I don't think I like you."

"Feeling's mutual, Clementine," she informed me, then gagged excessively.

She was trying to make me open my eyes and end up in the pokey. I wasn't going to fall for that crap. The sound was awful. My own gag reflex kicked in. The character was disgusting.

On a final cough where I was certain she'd hocked up a lung, I almost caved and looked. While I was fairly sure my characters couldn't actually die unless I killed them on paper, this sounded pretty dang bad.

"You okay?" I asked, pulling my comforter over my head so I didn't look at her before I guessed who she was.

"Great," she said sarcastically. "And if my polite requests for you to get your hairy sphincter out of bed don't work, then maybe informing you that your batshit crazy aunt Flip is calling people to invite them to a BDSM party at your house might set a fire under your poop shoot."

"WHAT?" I shouted, ripping off the covers, jumping out of the bed and falling flat on my face.

"Graceful," the woman said with a cackle.

Glancing around wildly, I scanned my bedroom for a new character. I'd changed my mind about the species. It had to be a demon. Shifters were generally nice. Demons? Not.

"Wait. What?" I muttered, getting to my feet and tossing the comforter and sheets back onto the bed. No one was in the room with me. Just me and my fat evil cat, Thick Stella.

Peeking under the bed then in my closet, I searched for the owner of the voice. I was not in the mood for games.

And I was not in the mood for a BDSM party. What the hell was Flip thinking?

"Show yourself," I demanded.

"Up yours, candy ass," the voice grunted.

My head jerked to the left. Thick Stella was having a go at her hoohoo, completely oblivious to the invisible intruder. Whoever was in here had an ass fixation.

"Crap," I said, backing myself up against the wall so nothing could sneak up behind me. I'd written too many werewolf detective novels to leave myself open to an enemy. "Are you a ghost?"

Had I written ghosts? I didn't think so, but none of my characters could render themselves invisible... so it had to be a ghost or spirit of some kind. Whoever it was didn't answer. Maybe the character left after she'd clued me in on the scary shenanigans that my eighty-five-year-old aunt was up to.

After a quick text to Seth to check on Cheeto, I pulled on some clean sweatpants and a t-shirt. He assured me she was doing fine. Fine could have many meanings. I was fine for the most part, but I wasn't fine at all. Seth said he would be by in the evening to chat. I hoped with all my might he would have some good news. I'd just have to wait and see. Didn't love that, but I would learn to deal with it.

Moseying to my bathroom while still keeping an eye out for the cougher, I brushed my teeth, then splashed some cold water on my face. "Not good, but better," I told my reflection. "Today is a new day and it can't be worse than yesterday. There's always sunshine after the rain."

Please let that be true. There was only so much a perimenopausal gal who saw imaginary people could take.

∼

"Everybody will be here in a few, Clemmy-girl," Aunt Flip informed me as she hustled around the living room putting out unidentifiable breakfast concoctions.

Her muumuu was a blinding lime green, and she had slapped on so much blush she looked feverish. She was beautiful. My aunt loved me, crazy and all… and the favor was returned tenfold.

"If you're hungry, you can go on ahead and eat," Flip said, placing bottles of catsup strategically around the room. "You didn't eat no dinner last night. You gotta eat or you're gonna waste away."

"Hardly," I replied with a pained laugh. I was hungry, but the casserole closest to me was so loaded with cheese, barbeque sauce and French-fried onions, I gagged. "Who is *everyone* and why are they coming here?" I asked, sitting down on the chair farthest away from the odiferous pans of mystery.

Aunt Flip slapped her hands on her boney little hips and eyed me. "Did you forget what's goin' on?" she demanded, racing over and shoving a brownie into my hands.

Normally a brownie for breakfast—or brunch, since it was noon—would be a treat. Not this particular brownie. Flip was known for her pot brownies—very strong pot brownies.

"Nope," I said, putting the brownie on a coaster on the side table. "Answer my questions, please."

"Alrightyroo," she said, plopping down on the couch and fluffing up her perm. "The woowooers are on their way. We're gonna have a little party and make a plan."

The woowooers consisted of me, Aunt Flip, Ann Aramini, Sally Dubay, Joy Parsley, my BFF Jess, and Nancy from the law firm. Cheeto also had the woowoo juju, but she was just a child. Whatever Flip had up the sleeve of her muumuu would not include Seth's little girl.

"A plan to do what?" I asked, feeling a little queasy.

The myriad of bizarre powers amongst the group was enough to give me indigestion. Aunt Flip could light objects on fire by staring at them, along with being able to detect illnesses in people. Ann Aramini was a tiny Mack Truck of a woman who had no filter at all. She'd abandoned it the day she'd turned seventy. The nutty woman had been my high school counselor. She'd terrified me back then… and kind of still did. Ann could move things with her mind and shift into a house cat, or so I'd been told. As of this moment, I'd never actually seen her shift into a house cat—not sure that I ever wanted to.

Sally Dubay was as sweet as they came. She was pushing ninety and could fly. I'd seen her do it. I'd also seen her crash land. 'Nuff said. Nancy, who I'd cheated off of on a spelling test… once… in elementary school, knew the characters from my novels better than I did. She could also see and talk to dead people. In fact, she had a difficult time discerning who was alive and who was deceased. Cap that with the sweaty truth that she was deep into menopause and you had a hot mess. Literally.

My BFF, Jess, thought she was losing it for a few years. She'd dealt with the woowoo juju on her own. Thankfully, that was no longer the case. She'd joined the club. Jess could transport herself short distances and knock trees down with her bare hands. I'd seen her do both. It was impressive.

But the gal who took the cake was Joy Parsley.

No one in their right mind would call Joy a joy. She was in her later sixties and had a sour expression on her mug twenty-four seven. The somewhat hostile gal had a habit of reporting everyone to the town council on a regular basis. Aunt Flip told me I'd get used to Joy. I didn't believe her. The town menace loved to review each of my books after they came out. She hated every bit of every book I'd ever written... except the sex scenes. She liked those. As for her *power*, Joy aka Joyless could touch objects and tell their story. She could also drink five beers and render herself invisible.

That one had left me speechless.

"Plans to do what?" I repeated as Aunt Flip grinned like a nutball.

"Make sure that you don't end up in the pokey," she said.

"I didn't try to kill Darren," I reminded her. "The Weather Hooker did."

"Got that," Flip said. "You ever see *Hannibal* or *Saw III* or *The Usual Suspects*?"

"Umm... most of those. Is there a point here?" I asked, thinking she had some pretty gnarly movie-watching habits.

"Yesirree," Flip said, nibbling on one of her brownies. I waited for the rest. It didn't come.

"Mmmkay," I said, eyeing my brownie and thinking a little bite might help me get through the woowoo gathering. "Would you like to be more specific?"

"Sure thing, darlin'," she said. "The villain can win. Proof is in the DVDs."

I nodded. I needed to buy my aunt some new movies. "Those are fiction."

Flip rolled her eyes. "As far as you know they're fiction."

Pressing my lips together, I said nothing. If I was about to find out that Anthony Hopkins really was Hannibal Lecter, I would commit myself. It was terrifying enough that I saw imaginary people and that Flip could burn down the house she and my granny had given me by staring at it. My God, I was now insanely thankful that I wrote about fictitious species like vampires, werewolves and demons. It would suck all kinds of butt if I wrote about true crime. If those people showed up, I would be screwed.

"I'm not gonna touch your last statement," I told her, moving on to something potentially more alarming. "Is this a BDSM party?"

I held my breath and waited for the answer.

"That was supposed to be a surprise!" Flip yelled. "How'd you find out?"

"Not the point," I said with an eye roll. "But if you really want to know, a new character showed up and tattled on you."

"Which book?" she asked.

I shrugged. "Not a clue. She had a hacking cough, a foul

mouth and a slurpy speech impediment. It was disgusting. She left before I could see her or get her name. However, that's not important."

"Maybe you can write a speech therapist for that poor gal," Flip suggested.

It wasn't a bad idea. Wait. Scratch that. Flip was making me lose my train of thought. Plus, if I'd written the awful character, it was far better to not remember her. "Look… I… umm… I have no issue with what consenting adults want to do in the privacy of their… you know, bedroom, but I have to draw the line at watching you handcuff and whip Joy Parsley."

Flip threw her hands in the air and laughed so hard I thought she might choke. "That ain't a bad idea! Joy Parsley could use a good whoopin'. She reported me to the town council and I don't even live in town. Can you believe that malarky?"

"What did she report you for?" I asked, so shocked that I forgot what the heck we were talking about.

"Jaywalkin' when I was doin' my flower deliveries," she explained, still grinning.

"Oh my God, she reported you for dealing pot?" I couldn't believe the sourpuss old bat could be so horrible. Joy was a big lover *and* indulger of Flip's *flowers*.

"Hell to the no!" Flip yelled, falling back into another laughing fit. "For jaywalkin'. Joy might make my butt itch occasionally and she could start an argument with an empty house, but my gal is loyal. She knows I don't charge for my flowers and I'm helpin' people who need a little blossom or two in their lives."

Heaving out a sigh of relief that the two of us weren't going to end up in the big house, I ran my hands through my hair and tried to remember the point of the conversation. "So, you're not into floggers and butt plugs?" I asked with a wince. I couldn't even believe the words had come out of my mouth in a conversation with my aunt.

"What's a butt plug?" she asked.

Closing my eyes, I laughed. "What exactly do you think BDSM means?"

"Sally Dubay said it means bagels, drinks and scrambled meats. Said she read it on Facebook. Why?"

"First off, I would suggest not getting facts off Facebook," I told her, taking a small bite of the brownie. A little wouldn't hurt and was clearly necessary. "Secondly, that's not what it means."

Flip looked confused. "Burgers, daiquiris and soul music?"

"Nope."

"Bacon, doughnuts and sausage McMuffins?" she tried again.

"Nope."

Flip scratched her head in confusion. "Is it a breakfasty kind of thing?" she asked.

"Definitely not," I said with a smile pulling at my lips. The collection of old women I was in cahoots with were right out of their minds. "Do you wanna know?"

"Do I?" Flip asked with a giggle.

"Probably not," I said with a laugh. "But I'm telling you so you don't have any more BDSM parties."

"Shoot, Clemmy," she said.

"Bondage, domination and sadomasochism," I told her.

For the third time in five minutes, Flip laughed so hard I thought she'd have a dang stroke. "Well, I have never," she gasped out between peals of laughter. "Sally is just gonna poop her Depends."

"TMI," I said, taking another tiny bite of my special brownie. I needed it. If this was the way my morning was starting, there was no telling what was coming next.

CHAPTER TWO

"Stay with me, gals," Ann Aramini said, marching around the living room and checking out the array of gas-inducing casseroles. "We get Joy wasted and she turns her tattling ass invisible. We drive her to the hospital and she enters Darren the jackhole's room."

"I'm liking it so far," Joy announced, piling a plate high with mystery meat covered in bright orange cheese.

"If we need to get there faster, I can fly her over," Sally Dubay offered with a mouthful of something that resembled vomit.

"Umm... no," I said quickly, more terrified of that plan than what was in her mouth. I'd seen Sally's flying skills. Plus, I was pretty sure Sally flying into the hospital carrying an invisible and drunk Joy Parsley wouldn't end well. Woowoo juju was a secret. Visual proof could end in disaster, especially since we needed every woman on deck to fight back the impending darkness.

I wasn't sure exactly what defeating the darkness meant or what it would entail, but the more woowooers the merrier. My lovable and sloppy detective character, Clark Dark, had said we needed eight for a Goodness Army. We had seven. It was better than none.

Ann Aramini gave me a covert thumbs up in agreement of putting the kibosh on Sally's airborne plan, then kept spewing more horror out of her mouth. "Alrighty, now that we got Joy in the room, we have Sally fall down and start screaming in the hallway. That'll distract the nurses."

"What if I zoomed around a little and crashed into the nurse's station?" Sally asked.

"While that is a wonderful suggestion, I'm gonna go with a no," Flip said, handing Sally an open bottle of catsup. "Might cause more trouble than it's worth. We don't want you really getting hurt."

"I see where you're going with that," Sally said sweetly. "My bad."

"No worries," Ann Aramini told her. "Teamwork is imperative. No idea is bad."

"Seriously?" Jess muttered under her breath, echoing my sentiments exactly. Jess, Nancy and I were new to the group of crazies. Right now, I couldn't believe they were still alive if this was the kind of *plan* they were used to making.

Joy spit out a chewed wad of food onto her plate, wiped her mouth with the sleeve of her sensible beige cardigan, and took a swig of Mountain Dew. No one batted an eye. I just shook my head.

"So, I'm in the room. What am I gonna do?" she asked.

Ann cackled and rubbed her little hands together. "I'll

shift into a house cat, then you'll pick me up and move me all over the room—like I'm flying. I'll hiss and throw a damn fit like I'm in heat and haven't banged in twenty years—which is unfortunately accurate. Once Darren the douchebag is freaking out, you put me down and start rearranging all the furniture. I'll double up on the effort and start moving crap around the room with my mind. Bing bang boom, the son of a bitch has a heart attack."

"Does he die?" Nancy asked, concerned. "I mean, I might not be able to tell. I'd hate to run into him and not know if he's deceased."

"Dead as a doornail," Ann Aramini assured Nancy.

"Thank you for the clarification," Nancy said, munching on some burnt toast and mopping her sweaty face with a napkin.

"Welcome," Ann told her.

"Not working for me," I announced, pressing my temples and not knowing whether to laugh or scream. I'd wished death on Darren too many times to count over the last few months, but never in a million years would I want to be personally responsible for his demise.

"It sounds solid to me," Joy Parsley countered with a raised brow.

Last week Joy's arched brow might have unnerved me. This week, there was very little that could throw me. Well, going to jail might qualify, but that wasn't going to happen. I hoped.

"There are holes all over it," I pointed out. I wrote books. I recognized plot holes a mile away. "Plus, we don't want Darren to die."

"We don't?" Ann questioned, confused.

"No." I let my head fall back on my shoulders. "He needs to be alive to refute his statement that I tried to kill him. If he's six feet under, he can't do that."

"Unless Nancy has a chat with him," Sally volunteered. "You know, when he's dead."

Sally was too nice to yell at. "Okay," I said, doing my very best to reach deep down for my Southern polite roots. "While that might be true, it's not going to hold up in court."

"Smart and beautiful," Aunt Flip crowed. "My Clemmy is a real leader."

"The bar is kinda low," Jess muttered.

I laughed. Thank God I had my bestie along for the roller coaster ride from Hell.

"I'd like to add something," Sally announced with catsup all over her mouth.

"Does it have anything to do with flying?" I asked.

She thought about it for a long moment. "Nope."

"Shoot," I told her.

"Bald Gene Herman is blind," she shared with a nod and a smile

I looked around the room to see if anyone had followed Sally's convoluted line of thought. The answer was no. "Does that pertain to the plan?" I asked.

"No, no, no, dear," Sally answered as she slathered her scrambled egg concoction with catsup. "But I wanted to put that out there in case Ann Aramini wants to fornicate with someone."

"Much appreciated and I'll keep that in mind," Ann said.

"Do you know if he has a Viagra prescription? The old geezer has to be in his late eighties."

"He does," Joy Parsley assured her.

"And you know that how?" I asked, then slapped my hand over my mouth. I didn't want the answer to the question. My stupid author brain had a mind of its own. I wasn't one to let well enough—or in this case, appalling enough—alone.

"Joy snoops in people's mailboxes," Flip chimed in casually as if it was no biggie.

"That's illegal," Jess said with a groan.

"Your point?" Joy inquired.

Jess shook her head and laughed. "Just an observation."

The meeting had derailed. "Plan A is a no-go," I told the gals, deciding to ignore Joy's felonious hobbies. "Does anyone have a plan B?"

Flip cleared her throat. "I say I make a batch of weed brownies that knock him into the middle of next week lookin' for Sunday. We get the coppers over there and have him make another statement. Hard to lie when you're pickled."

I wrinkled my nose and stared at my beloved nutjob of an aunt. "While creative, not realistic."

"Why's that?" Flip asked.

"Umm… so many reasons," I said with a sigh. "One of which is how you're going to get the *coppers* to the hospital to hear a new statement."

"Joy?" Flip asked with a sly smile. "Would you like to field that concern?"

"With pleasure," she replied, downing the rest of her

Mountain Dew, then letting a loud burp rip. "I've got something on most of the idiots on the force."

"Legally?" Jess asked with a wince.

"Define legally," Ann Aramini chimed in.

"I'll pass," Jess said with a groan.

Nancy giggled. "I'm curious."

Joy popped open another can of Mountain Dew, seated herself on the couch with a grin and made herself comfortable. "Captain Lewis wears women's underpants. Tough old Sergeant O'Malley collects Beanie Babies and sings show tunes in the shower. Officer Lang has one testicle. Officer Brady has a secret second family. Officer Shakley has four nipples. Officer Willis searches out his ex-wife's car all over town and leaves parking violations on it even when she's legally parked. Officer Kinter enjoys eating dog snacks, and Officer Peters's real name is Pete Jerpants."

"Petejerpants!" Sally squealed with delight. "I could loan him some Depends!"

My mouth was open. Jess was shaking her head and giggling. Nancy's hands were over her mouth and she was bright red, she was laughing so hard. She'd gotten far more than she'd asked for. We all had.

"Mmmkay," I said, wondering what the heck Joy Parsley had on me. "While that was horrifyingly illuminating, I'm not sure that's going to help our cause. Not to mention, a statement under the influence of weed probably isn't admissible."

"Damn shame," Joy said. "Would have loved to let Lewis know I'm onto him and his pink panties."

"Nothing wrong with a man wearing lady's panties—not

against the law," I pointed out diplomatically. "I wear men's boxer briefs."

Joy eyed me for a moment. "Yep. I know that—went through your drawers when I was pretending to go to the bathroom last time I was here. However, Captain Lewis likes to call other men girly—including my Harry, God rest his lazy soul. I'd be right delighted to call out the fat ass on his mean bluff and put that lacy panty-wearin' fool in his place."

Reminder to self... don't leave Joy unsupervised. Joy was awful but she wasn't all bad. Captain Lewis was a dick. He'd been the one up in my face yesterday, along with the polygamous Officer Brady and kibble-loving Officer Kinter. All three had been Darren's buddies when he was on the force fifteen years ago. I'd never liked any of them. However, parading their personals wasn't going to get us far.

"Look," I said, running my hands through my hair in frustration. "I love that you gals are trying to support me. It means the world. However, killing, maiming or getting Darren high isn't going to work. What we need is for Darren to take a lie detector test or something like that. Not sure the asshole will retract his accusation."

"Question," Jess said, pushing her glasses up on her nose. "Does Darren of the mini-weenie know why the black and decker pecker wrecker wants the house so badly?"

I shook my head. "Doubtful. As far as I know, he knows nothing about the woowoo juju or that my home is on a ley line."

"That loser is a suppressor of magic," Flip said with a

shudder. "I think that's one of the reasons Clemmy's woowoo came out so late."

"Where is the Weather Hooker?" Nancy inquired. "Have the police questioned her yet?"

I shrugged. "I have no clue. Has anyone seen her?"

"Nope," Ann Aramini confirmed. "But we haven't been lookin'. That can be remedied."

"Not so fast," I cut in quickly. "She has magic now laced with darkness. No one goes near her without me. Clear?"

"Told y'all," Flip said smugly. "My Clemmy has balls and smarts. She's gonna lead us to victory! We're gonna beat the heck out of the darkness. Just you wait and see."

Flip's words were terrifying. The vote of confidence was lovely, but the reality was sobering. I had no idea what I was doing.

My chin fell to my chest. I tried not to cry. Normally when I felt like this, I'd lose myself in my writing. It was an escape that kept me whole. Right now, I couldn't even do that.

There was silence in the room. I could feel all the eyes on me. None felt judgmental. All the gazes were loving and hopeful. That was far worse.

"Are any of your people here?" Ann Aramini asked, gently patting my back.

I glanced around the room and looked for the people only I could see… well, Nancy seemed to be able to see them too. I figured it was because she was such a big fan of my books. "No. No one is here right now. They usually show up when they want to. But speaking of my characters, Nancy, do you recall a female character with a hacking cough and a slurping speech impediment in any of my novels?"

Nancy's brow wrinkled in thought. "No, I don't. And I'm pretty sure with that description I'd remember."

I nodded. Who the heck had been in my bedroom? Did it matter? If she showed up again, I wasn't closing my eyes. The blind leading the blind was a disaster waiting to happen.

"I have an idea," Flip said.

"Is it a good idea?" I asked with a tired smile.

"Define good," Ann Aramini said with a chuckle.

"It's good," Flip promised. "Very good. Has nothing to do with that no-good lyin' sack of poo."

"I'm all ears," I told her. "What's the idea?"

Flip grinned. "How many people can you fit in your SUV?"

"Eight. Why?" I asked suspiciously.

"We're goin' to the cemetery to see Jumper," she announced.

My tummy tingled. A smile pulled at my lips. Just as quickly, it turned to a gasp. "We're not digging my granny up, are we?" I asked with a horrified expression.

Flip slapped her skinny thigh and laughed. "Hell no! We're just gonna visit and commune with her spirit. Might lead us in the right direction."

"You can talk to her?" I asked, feeling strange and excited. I missed my granny something awful. Woowoo juju would be worth it if I could have one more conversation with her.

"Not in the normal sense of the word," Flip said, wrapping her arms around me and hugging me tight. "I just get feelings when I'm close to where Jumper was laid to rest."

I nodded jerkily. Earlier I thought my ceiling might be talking to me, and now, I thought I might be able to talk with my dead granny. I needed to stop thinking. It was getting me nowhere fast.

"Let's go," I said, ignoring the feeling of disappointment.

"That's my girl," Flip said, grabbing the platter of brownies.

I smiled and rolled my eyes. My life could not be any more insane than it already was.

Or could it?

CHAPTER THREE

The late afternoon sun beat down on our motley crew. It was a scorcher for May. Poor Nancy looked like she'd taken a shower with her clothes on. She was chowing down on Aunt Flip's brownies for some relief from her hot flashes. Before we'd all piled into my SUV, I'd quickly changed out of my sloppy sweats and pulled on a cute sundress and sparkly flip-flops out of respect for my granny. Plus, everyone else looked presentable. I'd almost mismatched my flip-flops in honor of my little buddy Cheeto. I was worried about her. And Seth. And me.

Cheeto had witnessed something no child should see. Honestly, I wasn't clear how much she saw. Everything had happened so fast. The police had opted not to question her. However, my brave little buddy had insisted on making a statement. I didn't get to hear what she'd said. She'd been with Seth when she'd spoken with the cops. His dad, Mr. Ted, had stayed with me.

Seth had insisted that Cheeto was fine when he'd driven me home. At the time, I was so frazzled, I'd believed him. Today? I wasn't so sure. One thing at a time. If I overloaded, I'd lose it. There was no time for that.

"I wanna be cremated and spread out on Main Street," Joy Parsley announced. "Graveyards freak me out—too quiet. I need to be where the action is."

"Good luck with that," Jess said with a laugh. "Not sure the town council will let that happen."

Joy grinned. It was scary. "I have so much on those cockroaches, they wouldn't dare defy me. Flip, Sally and Ann all have sealed letters with incriminating evidence to go out to the newspaper if they disobey me in death."

With a mouthful of brownie, Nancy tapped Joy on the shoulder. "What if the gals all bite it before you do?"

Joy Parsley was stymied. "Well, crap. Never thought about that," she admitted, then lit right back up. "Tomorrow, I'll hand deliver sealed letters to you, Jess and Clementine."

"Great. That is just awesome." Jess took a deep cleansing breath and grabbed a brownie. The only way to get along with Joy was to be slightly impaired.

"We should have brought flowers for Jumper's grave," Sally fretted. "Not respectful to come empty-handed."

Flip held up the platter of pot brownies. "We ain't empty-handed. I'm gonna leave my sister some of my special flowers, if you know what I mean."

I did. Flip was nuts. "We can't go to the grave yet," I whispered.

"Sure we can," Flip said as she began to walk toward her sister's headstone.

Gently grabbing her arm, I stopped her. "No, we can't. There are people standing at her grave who I don't recognize."

Flip squinted her eyes and looked across the rows of graves. "Don't see nobody."

"Two people. A man and a woman," I told her, thinking I needed to make an eye appointment for her.

They were as clear as day. It would be incredibly difficult to miss a woman in an antebellum gown and a man in an old-fashioned tuxedo. They were the only other people here. The cemetery was actually a lovely place. I'd sat on the bench near my granny's grave many times over the years and just let my mind wander. There was a simplicity and peacefulness that I couldn't find in other places.

Flip glanced over at me with concern. "Clemmy, there ain't no one there."

"I don't see anyone," Sally added. "But I need cataract surgery, so don't listen to me."

Joy Parsley pulled a pair of binoculars out of her purse and aimed them at Jumper's grave. "Nope. I don't spot anyone."

I rolled my eyes. Of course Joy Parsley carried binoculars. However, I knew what I saw.

"Jess?" I asked, knowing she had good eyesight and wasn't right out of her ever-loving mind.

She shook her head. "I don't see anyone. Is there a chance it's some of your characters?"

I stared at the duo. Their backs were to us, so I couldn't make out their faces, but I'd never written a novel set in antebellum times. The closest I'd come was the shitty Regency, but the clothes were very different.

"No," I said, then glanced over at Nancy. She had seen my characters at my house. But I wasn't sure if that was because the house was on a ley line or if she would be able to spot my characters anywhere. "Nancy, do you see a man and a woman?"

She stared hard, then shook her head. "I don't see anyone, but I'm a little high."

"Not to worry," Flip said, patting her back. "I'm high too."

I rolled my eyes. Maybe some of my characters had gone to a costume party in one of my books and I'd forgotten about it. That was a somewhat logical possibility to a seriously illogical situation. But when one was grabbing for straws, any straw would do.

"What are they wearing?" Joy Parsley inquired.

I was still amazed that no one in our crew found it odd that I saw people who weren't there. The situation was treated as if it was normal. I was treated as if I were normal. But, then again, they weren't exactly normal.

"Well... umm... the woman has long, shiny sable-brown hair. From the back she looks dainty and lovely—small waist, must be cinched. She's wearing an emerald green-satin gown over a hoop skirt and carrying a matching parasol in a lighter shade of green. The man is in what looks like a tux or possibly a formal morning suit. All black. His hair is dark too—slicked back—and he's tall."

"Well slap my ass and call me Veronica," Flip yelled, doing a little jig.

"I'd rather not," Ann Aramini said with a grunt of laughter, joining Flip's impromptu dance.

"Do you think?" Sally asked, clasping her hands together in excitement.

"Yeppers!" Flip sang. "I do think."

"Think what?" I asked, pressing the bridge of my nose.

"Guess," Flip challenged.

My aunt knew me. I *loved* guessing. I couldn't resist. It was one of the reasons I was more of a pantser author than a plotter author. The joy for me was in not knowing what came next. I was as surprised as anyone where my stories would lead me and what my characters would do. When it all clicked together it was a feeling that verged on orgasmic.

"Are they my characters?" I asked.

"Nope," she said.

"Okay." They were clearly fictitious if no one could see them except me. But why could I see people I didn't create? That wasn't how it had played out so far. If I started seeing *all* fictional characters, that would suck enormous butt. Hell, maybe the coughing, profane gal who woke me up this morning wasn't one of my characters at all. That would actually be a relief. She was foul.

"Are they from a book?"

"Yep," Flip said.

"A book I've read?" I asked.

Flip thought about it, then nodded. "I'm gonna go with a yes on that. It's kind of a classic. You always had your nose in a book when you were a little girl."

"She still does," Jess added with a wink.

"Guilty as charged," I replied, looking at the couple and

trying to figure out the mystery. Why would they be at Jumper's grave? Were they here for me or for my granny? And why would imaginary people be here for her? They would have to have known her. "Holy shit," I gasped out.

"Did you get it?" Flip asked with wide eyes.

"Possibly," I said, moving quickly toward the people.

My posse jogged right behind me. We must have made an interesting picture. Three gals in their forties followed by a foursome whose ages ranged from late sixties all the way up to ninety, running through a cemetery in broad daylight. Nancy and Jess had no clue what was going on, but Ann Aramini, Joy Parsley, Sally Dubay and Aunt Flip were positively giddy.

"Just glad it's not two old bats in nightgowns," Ann Aramini huffed out. Surprisingly she was able to keep up with me. "That would have been bad."

I was now positive I knew who was standing at the graveside. Granny had minions. I had characters. The old bats in nightgowns would have been Baby Jane Hudson and her sister Blanche. From the stories I'd heard, those two gals were whacked. Granny had also chatted with Dorothy Gale and Glinda the Good Witch. None of those were the ones standing at her grave. It was her main minions.

At least I hoped it was. If it was just weirdos in costumes, I was going to be bummed. Flip had shared that Granny used to listen to her minions and then spread the word on how to make the world a better place. Clark Dark was worried that he and my crew might not be as good as Granny's crew. I didn't believe that. I wasn't Granny. I was me. My characters and I were finding our own way together. We were lost at the moment, but that was beside the point.

The other point I needed to remember was that I was not running towards Vivian Leigh and Clark Gable. Nope, I was headed right for Scarlett O'Hara and Rhett Butler.

I came to an abrupt stop about six feet away. This threw off my girls, who all slammed into my back and sent me flying at the iconic duo. I closed my eyes. If I couldn't see Rhett and Scarlett, maybe they couldn't see me. I was fully aware how ludicrous my theory was, but one could hope. It was definitely not one of my best entrances.

"My goodness," Scarlett O'Hara exclaimed, raising a perfectly arched brow. "You certainly know how to wake snakes."

I scanned the area around me in alarm. If I'd landed in a nest of snakes, I was going to lose my shit for real. No snakes. I had a sneaking suspicion chatting with Scarlett and Rhett might be like conversing with Albinia. I barely understood her Regency-speak… and I'd created her. I was pretty sure I was about to get a lesson in antebellum-speak from a stunningly beautiful couple.

Getting to my feet and brushing the grass and dirt off of my sundress, I extended my hand. "Hi, I'm Clementine. Jumper was my granny."

"Yes," Rhett said with a smile that made me swoon as he took my hand and kissed the back of it. "We've known you since you were a baby. Nice to see you've turned into a huckleberry above a persimmon."

Unclear if I'd just been complimented or insulted, I smiled. Southern manners were ingrained in me. I figured since they were Southern too, they'd appreciate it. "Thank you, Mr. Butler."

"Call me Rhett," he said with a gallant bow. "Mr. Butler is my father."

Scarlett looked me up and down. With a curt nod of satisfaction, she smiled. It was as entrancing as Rhett's. "I'm quite pleased you found us. You are being honey-fuggled," she informed me in an ominous tone.

"And that's bad?" I questioned.

"Depends," she replied. "You must make the jackanape acknowledge the corn."

I was screwed. I felt the sweat break out on my brow and drip down my face. Soon I'd be rivaling Nancy in the soaked-to-the-skin department. They were giving me clues and I had no freaking idea what the heck they were saying. Shitshitshit.

Glancing over at a grinning Aunt Flip and the gals, I begged for some help. I knew they couldn't see or hear Rhett and Scarlett, but maybe they could translate for me. "Does anyone speak antebellum?"

No one said a word. Awesome. There was a chance that my vampire character Stephano might understand the conversation, since he secretly read romances and understood Regency- speak, but Stephano wasn't here.

"Scrap that," I said. "Does anyone have paper and a pen?"

"I have my grocery list in my purse," Nancy volunteered. "Will that do?"

"Yep, can I borrow it?"

"Might be damp," she said, digging it out and handing it

to me along with a purple crayon. She giggled. "Had my grandkids over. Sorry about the crayon."

"If it writes, I can use it," I told her gratefully, jotting down all the strange terms I'd just heard. Turning my focus back to Rhett and Scarlett, I smiled. "Can you tell me more about the jackanape?" I inquired politely.

"What would you like to know?" Rhett asked, leading Scarlett over to a bench and making sure she was comfortable.

"Umm... not sure since I'm not real clear on what a jackanape is."

Rhett's expression went from surprised to concerned. "I see. Are you not the biggest toad in the puddle?"

Pressing my lips together, I tried not to giggle. His tone was pleasant, so I was pretty sure he wasn't being rude.

"Yes," I replied, guessing he'd just inquired if I was in charge.

He smiled with relief, as did Scarlett. God, they were pretty people.

"To see the elephant, you must open your eyes," Scarlett advised.

"Right," I muttered, taking notes. "Anything else?"

"There's always something else," Rhett pointed out. "The landscape is always backing and filling. Keep that in mind."

"Will do," I said, more confused than ever. I was either going to have to reread *Gone with the Wind* or find a freaking translator.

"Oh!" Scarlett exclaimed, fanning herself with a hanky. "It's best to avoid come a cropper."

Both of them stared at me, waiting for a response. Crap.

I forced a pleasant expression. I was pretty sure I looked constipated. "Croppers are just terrible."

"I couldn't agree more," Scarlett confirmed with a nod.

"Won't get an argie out of me on that one," Rhett agreed amiably.

Scarlett giggled and batted her lashes at her charming man. "Not by a full jug!"

They both laughed. Rhett then laid a smackeroo on Scarlett that made me blush. My mouth fell open and I wasn't sure what to do.

"What's happenin'?" Flip asked.

"They're umm... making out," I whispered.

"They always did that," Sally confirmed with a wide smile. "Jumper used to throw buckets of cold water on them when they got too frisky."

"Mmmkay," I muttered, hoping I wasn't about to watch them bang. There was no water in sight. "Excuse me." I waved to get their attention.

They kept tangling tongues.

"Umm... excuse me," I tried again.

Nothing. Rhett was now lying on top of Scarlett.

"Rhett? Scarlett?" I asked. "Do you guys have anything else to share... other than what you're doing?"

"Can you see his penis?" Ann Aramini asked.

I resisted the urge to smack her in the head. "No," I hissed.

"Damn shame," she said. "I'd love to see his penis."

"You really need to get laid," Joy Parsley pointed out.

"Tell me something I don't know," Ann agreed.

Scarlett's hoop skirt was up over her head and Rhett was

unbuckling his pants. This was getting out of hand. There was no way in hell I was going to watch imaginary people have sex.

"Rhett Butler," I shouted in my outdoor voice. "Do NOT take off your pants."

"Let him," Joy grunted. "You might see his penis."

I shot Joy a glare that rivaled the glares she'd shot me over the years. She was impressed. I almost laughed. "I do not want to see Rhett Butler's penis," I snapped.

"It's quite impressive," Scarlett yelled from underneath her hoop skirt.

I rolled my neck and tried to figure out how to be diplomatic. Nothing came to me.

"Be that as it may," I said, marching over to Scarlett and adjusting her skirt so her bits weren't on display. I pointed to Rhett's pants. "Zip that back up. You two can get a room somewhere after we're done here. You feel me?"

"Where?" Scarlett asked.

I shrugged. "I don't know. Don't you guys live somewhere?"

"I'm lost," Scarlett said. "I was under the impression that you would like us to feel you. Which part of you shall we feel?"

"This sounds like an enjoyable pastime," Rhett concurred.

"Okaaaay," I said, twisting my hair in my fingers. Apparently, all fictional people were very literal. I'd run into this exact issue with Albinia. "I don't actually want you to feel me."

Scarlett began to pout. "I find it quite rude for you to make the offer then rescind."

Oh my God, they were literal *and* incredibly oversexed.

"My apologies," I told the disappointed pair. "I didn't mean to... umm... lead you on."

Jess's explosion of laughter behind me was the perfect sound to pull me back into reality. This was hilariously ridiculous.

"Apology accepted," Rhett replied with a wink. "If you ever change your mind, we shall be delighted to comply."

"Good to know," I said, trying not to laugh. "So, before you guys go get a private room, can you help me out with the impending darkness or what to do about Jinny Jingle?"

Rhett and Scarlett exchanged wary glances. That did not bode well.

"I do not know of a Jinny Jingle," Scarlett said.

"Nor do I," Rhett added. "However, I do have some advice. The author of the story controls the action... the players... and the outcome."

I quickly wrote it down. The cryptic message didn't help one bit.

Scarlett sighed dramatically. "But you must remember, there are always consequences—and some will be grave."

"Would you like to be more specific?" I asked.

Both shook their heads sadly.

"We wish we could," Rhett told me. "We have shared all that we know."

I nodded and scanned the notes, hoping like hell that once I deciphered them there would be some real clues.

"Thank you," I said, then paused for a long moment. "Do you still speak to Jumper?"

Scarlett smiled. Rhett glanced down at the headstone with great fondness.

"No," Scarlett whispered. "We come here to remember her."

My heart pounded in my chest. I did the very same thing. They clearly loved Granny too. Rhett kissed the tips of his fingers, then pressed them to the headstone. Scarlett draped her lace hanky on top of his placed kiss.

"Will I see you again?" I asked softly.

"I don't know," Scarlett said. She walked toward me and daintily air kissed each of my cheeks. "One can only hope."

Rhett bowed gallantly, then kissed my hand. "If Flip could leave a few chocolate delicacies that would be wonderful."

I grinned and shook my head. Walking over to Flip, I grabbed a couple of brownies off the tray and handed them to him.

"Much obliged," he said with a wink. "Take care, Clementine. The darkness draws near."

"Can I beat it?" I asked, desperately needing a vote of confidence.

Rhett and Scarlett began to speak at the same time. The sound was fast and staccato. I couldn't understand a word they were saying. Their lips moved so quickly it was like they weren't moving at all.

And then they faded away.

Squatting down in defeat, my chin dropping to my chest, I stared at the well-manicured grass.

"Did Rhett Butler show you his penis?" Ann Aramini asked as she squatted down next to me.

"Nope. No penis," I told her.

"Damn shame," she muttered, standing up. "Well, I say it's time to summon some spirits. What do you say, girls?"

"Not so sure about that," Nancy said, worried. "I'm afraid they might like me and stick around."

"Nah," Flip said. "Spirits are different from the dead."

"How?" Jess asked.

Flip thought about it. "Don't rightly know. They just are."

"That's as clear as mud," Jess said with an audible sigh. "I think we have enough on our plate without conjuring up spirits."

Sally Dubay giggled. "Not to worry, dear," she told Jess. "We've never successfully conjured anything. Jumper used to say it was a good bonding exercise."

"Fine," I muttered, still staring at the grass. If Granny had thought it was a good idea, then we would do it. I wasn't doing very well as the woowoo leader on my own. "Let's bond. Then let's go home. Seth is coming over this evening and I'm hoping for news—preferably good."

"Only takes a half hour to conjure," Joy Parsley announced.

"Oh my God… what the hell are you doing?" Jessica asked, shocked.

"Gettin' topless," Flip explained. "Gotta be boobs to the wind to conjure correctly!"

My head jerked up. I gasped, then started to laugh. I was staring at four saggy pairs of knockers—Flip's, Ann's, Sally's and Joy's. I was going to need therapy to wipe the image away.

"Nope," I said, scooping up shirts and bras and handing them back to the crazy old bats. "It's broad daylight and this is a public place. There will be no boobs in the wind today... or ever."

No one would take their clothing back. I chased half-naked idiots around the graveyard and tried to put their shirts back on them. It was a shitshow. Jess and Nancy tried to help me catch them. We were all screaming and laughing. It was absurd... and absurdly beautiful.

After a half hour of crazy, the old gals finally let us dress them. I was sure they were going to have sunburned boobs later this evening, but they had no one to thank but themselves for that.

"Unreal," Jess said, still giggling as we piled into my SUV.

"Word," I replied with a chuckle.

"I thought it was fun," Nancy said, climbing into the back.

It was. It was silly, appalling and fun. I actually kind of liked Joy Parsley now. It had been alarming when Sally Dubay decided to fly and crashed into a crypt. We all held our breath as she slowly got to her feet and proceeded to laugh like a loon. The old gal clearly had good bone density. It had been a bonding experience like no other.

"You're a sneaky old broad," I told Aunt Flip with a grin as I checked to make sure her seat belt was secure.

"Thank you, darlin'," she replied with a thumbs up. "A little bonding never hurt no one."

She was right.

Glancing back at Granny's grave, I blew a kiss. "I miss you, Granny. I'll try to do you proud."

I wanted her to answer me.

She didn't.

I was going to have to answer for myself. There was no other choice.

CHAPTER FOUR

"What a freaking day," I muttered as I put Thick Stella's food on the floor and narrowly missed getting gouged by the violent furball.

The cat was an asshole. I loved her anyway. Occasionally, I wondered why I adored the vicious monster, but I appreciated that she never pretended to be something that she wasn't. She was an asshole through and through and owned it. The fat feline also had a hairball issue. She'd hocked up quite a few gelatinous globules as of late. I watched to see if she would like the new hairball-control food. She gobbled it up. I shouldn't have worried. Thick Stella ate everything... hence her name.

"Someday I'm getting a dog," I told her.

She extended her back leg and continued eating. The damn cat flipped me off with her haunch. I could swear the hairy hellion understood English.

"Seriously?" I asked with a laugh.

She ignored me and continued to inhale her food. Taking a page from Thick Stella's book might be a good idea. Nothing seemed to bother the pudgy terror. Ever.

The gals had finally gone home after a few hours of lively chatting. We'd made no headway on deciphering the clues. I needed my characters' help—specifically Stephano's. They hadn't shown up, but I had my fingers crossed they soon would. There had been a long and passionate debate on Rhett Butler's penis. I didn't participate. Ann Aramini definitely needed to scratch an itch. She'd announced that she was going to call Bald Gene Herman and *get her some*.

When the chat had degenerated into a discourse on Bald Gene's junk, I almost lost my cookies. I was also chastised several times for not letting Rhett remove his pants. It took Sally Dubay falling asleep midsentence while waxing poetic about the meaning of different-sized testicles to make them realize that it was time to head home.

Jess had offered to stay and wait for Seth, but I told her to go. She'd played hooky from work today. Granted, she was her own boss, but I knew she'd have to play catch up this evening.

I had a little free time on my hands since I was waiting for my edits on my recently finished book. My agent, Cyd, had loved *Exclusive*—read it in one sitting. She'd even loved that I hadn't killed off the evil stepmother, Cassandra. Cassandra was a little put out that I'd redeemed her, but she'd get over it. I was terrified if I killed off a character in a book, I'd never see them again in real life—real being an insanely relative word. Cassandra and her not-so-evil ways had weaseled her way into my heart. She was still incredibly bitchy, but that was part of her charm.

"You hungry, Clemmy?" Flip asked. "Got plenty of leftover casserole from this morning."

"I'm good," I said quickly. I was hungry, but there was no way I was going to eat mystery meat covered in cheese. "I'll grab something in a bit.

Flip stretched her skinny arms up over her head and yawned. "Think I'm gonna ice my boobs and take a little nap."

I grinned. They were all suffering from their *boobs to the wind* stunt this afternoon. "You do that," I told her. "I'll let you know when Seth gets here."

"Sounds like a plan, baby girl. Oh, and how would you feel about me keepin' a room here at the house?"

"I would love it." It was on my list to beg her to stay. The house was large and could be lonely. Having Aunt Flip with me made it feel like a home. "You can move back in permanently if that would make you happy. It would definitely make me happy."

"Nah." Flip walked over and kissed the top of my head. "Soil is crap here for growin' weed. Can't live here all the time, but I'll set up my room the way I like it."

"Works for me." I hugged her close. "Go ice your knockers."

Flip giggled. "On it. Next time we conjure, it needs to be cloudy outside."

I rolled my eyes. "There will be no next time."

Flip just grinned. "You never know, little girl. Boobs in the wind is a mighty powerful statement."

"Understatement," I shot back. However, she might be correct. While the visuals had been hilariously appalling, the bonding had been brilliant.

∼

Fifteen minutes after Flip went for a nap, my people showed up. Well, two of them.

"I'm quite sure I can be of assistance," Albinia announced. "Together we can cut through the fudge and unravel the quiz. And if we can't, we shall locate the dandy and grand lady and offer them a pony."

I needed an interpreter for my interpreter. Thankfully, Stephano had shown up with her.

They'd poofed into my office and scared the crap out of me. It would be a whole lot less heart-attack inducing if they would use the front door, but I didn't complain. I was just happy they were here.

Albinia wore a bright yellow Regency gown. It was loud and so was she. For a brief moment, I wondered what Albinia would look like in jeans and a t-shirt. The thought made me grin. As usual, she was dressed like she'd walked off the film set of *Sense and Sensibility*. Her blonde hair shone to the point of absurdity and was twisted into an elaborate up-do with pearl-encrusted combs. Wispy tendrils framed her perfectly heart-shaped face and her lavender eyes sparkled.

"I didn't understand most of that," I told her, sitting down behind my desk and hoping that Stephano knew what the heck she'd meant.

The vampire was in his usual black Armani. He was ridiculously beautiful, not too bright, but very sweet. He was, also, the antihero in my Good to the Last Bloody Drop series. Basically, Stephano was my undead asshole with a heart of gold. I was pretty sure he and Mina, my badass witch from a different series, might have a little *thing* going on. I refused to ask. That was their business.

"What's going on in your bone box?" Albinia demanded, pulling a lemon-yellow hanky from her ample cleavage and fanning herself. "We mustn't be bamboozled. Time is of the essence, Clementine."

"Right," I said, running my hands through my hair and hoping we'd get through this before Seth arrived. "I'm aware of that."

There was no easy way to explain to someone who didn't have the woowoo that I could speak to imaginary people. Or that they spoke back. But it was true. Magic was real. And Seth was in for the motherload of real truth, considering Cheeto definitely had woowoo juju, and he would need to know about it in order to help her. I hoped telling him wouldn't blow up in my face or in Cheeto's. It was clear that Seth knew his beautiful seven-year-old little girl was different... he just had no clue how different.

One thing at a time.

"Stephano, can you interpret for Albinia?" I asked.

"Of course," Stephano replied as he sat down on the couch and scratched Thick Stella behind the ears.

The cat didn't gouge him. The bulbous little asshole purred. If I had done that, I would have lost a finger. I was struck for a moment that the mean little feline could see my characters and even feel their touch. No one else but Nancy could see my people. And I had no clue if she could physically touch them like I could.

"Alhoohundra stated that she could help you cut through the crap and solve the riddle. And if that doesn't work, she suggests that we find the gentleman and lady and offer them money," Stephano said. "Personally, I call bullshit."

I squinted at him. "Why?"

"Alhoohundra is broke. She doesn't have a pony to offer."

"Whippersnapper!" Albinia, who I guessed was going by Alhoohundra now, hissed at Stephano. "I am not cucumberish! The costermonger paid me handsomely for short sheeting Horace Skevington's bed and telling anyone who would listen that Horace likes to wear a cravat on his member whilst pleasuring himself. Apparently, I am not the only one Horace Skevington has bamboozled. And I most certainly *do* have a pony to bribe the scoundrels who spoke in an undecipherable language to poor Clementine."

Pot, kettle, black.

"Wait," I said, fascinated by Albinia's mess of a life—not the part about Horace Skevington's self-pleasure practices, but the rest of it. "Horace Skevington cheated on Dudley Albon Stopford? After he cheated on you with Dudley Albon Stopford?"

Apparently, the characters from *Scandalous Sensual Desires of the Wicked Ones on Selby Street* were creating their own narrative and it was wildly out of control.

"Alas, yes," Albinia admitted. "Horace has now fornicated with a Bond Street beau along with a saucy wench. It's quite the scandal. Horace is rumored to be a male adventuress."

"Man whore," Stephano clarified just in case I'd misunderstood.

I hadn't. "Got it." I gave him two thumbs up. "While the news is interesting in a train wreck kind of way, I need help that has nothing to do with Horace Skevington's sexual peccadillos."

"Agreed," Albinia said. "We shall not speak of the bacon-faced baggage further. But I'd like to add that his joy stick curves abruptly to the left when in a state of arousal."

There was two minutes of silence after that revelation. Stephano was doing his best not to laugh and I was trying not to scream.

I glanced over at Albinia. She had no clue that what she'd told us was a massive overshare. Karma was a bitch. I'd created her and now I had to deal with her. "Are you done?" I asked.

"I don't have to be," she answered. "There's oh so much more to tell. Shall I go on?"

"Nope," I said quickly. "That's about all I can handle right now."

Albinia graced me with a smile. Every time she smiled, I heard freaking birds chirping happily in the background... I was nuts.

"Very well, then," she said. "I shall continue at another time."

"Awesome," I said with the tiniest eye roll possible, pulling out Nancy's grocery list with the antebellum-speak on the back. "Stephano, have you read *Gone with the Wind*?"

The vampire clasped his hands together. "But of course. I find Scarlett O'Hara quite bangable. I had many delightful visions of a vigorous, sweaty shag with the Southern belle when I read it. My guess is that her bosom would be bouncy. I adore bouncy bosoms."

I promised myself I'd write Stephano new pickup lines since his sucked. He definitely needed to put a lot less emphasis on describing female body parts... as in *no* emphasis. Part of that was my fault. I hadn't written him less-offensive lines.

"And Rhett Butler seems like a man's man," Stephano continued. "Bizarrely, I found him quite attractive as well. Unusual for me as I prefer vaginas."

This was going off the tracks fast. Rhett and Scarlett would probably be delighted by Stephano's assessment and would gladly take him up on a threesome. I was not going to share that with the randy vamp. I needed his full attention on the problem at hand—not focused on banging other imaginary people.

"Okay," I said with a wince. "A little more than I was asking for."

"Whoops," Stephano said. "Too much?"

"Yep, but let's keep moving," I told him. "Do you understand antebellum?"

He shrugged. "I can certainly give it a shot. I don't recall a lot of antebellum terms in the novel, but I read it back in 1937."

I glanced up at him, stunned. I'd written his series in the last fifteen years. He didn't actually exist before the 2000s. But... he was ninety years old even though he didn't look a day over thirty. Did my giving people a certain age mean they had experiences from before they actually existed in my imagination? Holy cow, the thought was intense. My brain raced as I tried to understand the physics of it all.

I froze.

I slapped myself in the forehead.

Putting science behind magic was an attempt at futility that would send me down a rabbit hole that I wouldn't return from. I just needed to accept everything my characters said at face value. There was no sense to be made.

"Okay," I said, jerking myself back into the moment as Thick Stella hocked up a particularly unappetizing hairball. Without missing a beat, I grabbed a wad of tissue and cleaned it up. My fat cat kept coughing for a few minutes. We all waited for another gelatinous glob to come flying out of her mouth. It didn't come.

"Is she quite alright?" Albinia asked, scooping Thick Stella into her arms and cooing at her like she was a baby.

I held my breath and waited for Albinia to lose an eye.

Didn't happen. The cat simply purred. Unreal.

But while we were on the subject of coughing… "Do either of you recall a female character in any of your books with a filthy vocabulary and a hacking cough?"

"You mean like Thick Stella's cough?" Albinia asked, still fussing over my killer cat.

"Well, sure," I said. "But it was a person, not a house cat."

Stephano shook his head. "I recall no such person in my series."

"Nor do I," Albinia echoed. "Why?"

I laughed and pressed my temples. "There was someone in my bedroom this morning. Rude as all get out and I thought she was going to cough up a dang lung. I couldn't place her."

"What did she look like?" Stephano inquired. "Was she stacked? Juicy?"

Groaning, I closed my eyes. It wasn't going to matter if I wrote the vampire new lines. He was a lost cause. "I didn't get a look at her. She just cussed at me and left."

"We shall keep our eyes open for a woman with a foul mouth and the plague," Albinia assured me.

"Thank you. Back to business. I'm going to read each section I need translated. Cool?"

"I am ready!" Albinia announced in her outdoor voice, waltzing around the room with a hacking Thick Stella.

"You might want to put her down," I suggested. "Unless you want a phlegmy ball of hair on your gown."

"Not to worry," she sang. "My closet has many frocks for me to choose from."

I shrugged. If Albinia wanted to get puked on, who was I to tell her no? "Okay. Here we go. What does honey-fuggled mean?"

"I would have to say that means fornicating covered in honey," Stephano announced, pumping his hands over his head in victory.

It took a herculean effort not to throw a book at his head.

"Wrong!" Albinia shouted, startling all. "It means cheated. What was the context?"

"Scarlett O'Hara told me I was being honey-fuggled," I told her. "Then she added that I have to make the jackanape acknowledge the corn."

Stephano raised his hand. "Since I failed so miserably, I would like to give this section a shot."

I was scared, but I let him go for it.

"Speak," I instructed.

"I believe Alhoohundra was correct about being cheated," he said with a nod to a preening Albinia. "And the rest of it means that in order to get your money back from being swindled, you must eat a pumpkin and some corn… and then tell everyone that you did so."

"Wrong again!" Albinia announced, sticking her tongue out at a confused Stephano. "It means that you must make the scoundrel confess! I'm WINNING!"

Stephano laughed. I did too. I was shocked that Albinia was all over it. I'd expected the vampire to come through. I was wrong. Didn't care. I was just grateful that someone could decipher the mess and that it made sense.

"Albinia, you are definitely winning," I told her with a grin.

"Please call me Alhoohundra," she said. "I'm in the process of finding the real me. Is there more to the message? I'm feeling quite lucky at the moment."

"There is," I told her. "And luck has nothing to do with it. You're smart."

Her expression was shocked. "I am?"

"Yes," I said firmly. "You're very smart. Don't let anyone tell you differently."

"Are you saying there is more to me than my distracting beauty and heaving milky-white bosom?"

"May I field this question?" Stephano inquired.

"Absolutely not," I told him.

"Let him," Albinia insisted. "I would like to hear what my friend has to say, please."

I gave Stephano a look that meant business. He simply grinned.

"You are very clever, Alhoohundra," the vampire told her as I grabbed my pencil in case he said something stupid and I needed something wooden to stab him in the heart with. "Not many women of your time would have had the gumption to leave such a slutty scoundrel as Horace Skevington when he cheated on you with the costermonger. Not to mention you left Onslow Bolingbroke to bang the constable, Horace Skevington. Very progressive. You know your own mind. And while I find your beauty and your enormous jugs that bounce delightfully when you walk riveting, they are the least of what I admire about you. You are a strong woman who deserves the very best. I'd suggest a man whose dong doesn't harden at an angle next time. And I do have a few vampire buddies who would definitely be interested in a sweaty shag with you. Let me know. But back to the main reason I wanted to speak. I think you are intelligent, quick-witted and very well-dressed. If a man ever tries to make you feel less than wonderful, please point him out and I will happily kill him for you."

I was speechless. While part of it was wildly inappropriate and socially unacceptable, it was lovely at the same time.

"Did I do well?" Stephano asked me with a shy smile.

"You did great," I told him.

"I am wonderful!" Albinia said. "Stephano, you are a true gentleman. I value your friendship. I shall consider the offer of banging one of your friends at another time. I'm taking a break from men for the foreseeable future."

"Ahh," Stephano said. "You're going to fornicate with women now?"

"No, silly," she said with a giggle. "I do enjoy a nice rod, so the fairer sex is not my thing."

"Alrighty then," I interrupted before it degenerated further. "Alhoohundra, can you tell me what 'to see the elephant, I must open my eyes' means?"

"I can," she said, gently putting a sleeping Thick Stella on the couch. "The elephant usually means battle. So, I would surmise that it means you must be ready for the battle."

"Or possibly, you should ride an elephant into the battle," Stephano added, not wanting to be left out.

Albinia and I stared at him. He shrugged.

"Or not," he said with a laugh.

"What else?" Albinia inquired.

"I'm supposed to keep in mind that the landscape is always backing and filling."

She took a preemptive bow. "It means everything waffles and changes," she explained. "Do not count on what you knew prior to the battle. Look for what is happening in front of you."

My God, Albinia was smart. And so were Rhett and Scarlett.

"More?" Albinia asked, excited and delighted that she was helping me.

I nodded and glanced down at the paper. "I'm supposed to avoid come a cropper."

"Ah! They want you to avoid any serious setbacks," she

informed me. "Did they happen to tell you what the ruination could possibly be?"

I sighed and rested my forehead on my desk. The wood was cool and my head was a hot mess. "No. It was cryptic. Rhett ended with telling me that the author of the story controls the action, the players, and the outcome. And Scarlett said that I have to remember that there are always consequences and that some will be grave."

"Interesting," Stephano said. "We should let Clark Dark examine that part. He's a detective."

"Clementine knows that," Albinia reminded him. "She created all of us."

I had. Granted, I never knew I would actually meet them in the flesh, but I felt like I knew them on an even deeper level now. Strange, but true. Actually, *really* strange.

"Well," I said, peeking up at the duo. "Most of the stuff I didn't understand was basically common sense. It's the end that I believe is the most important."

"Course it is, ass dancer," an unfortunately familiar voice grunted, then coughed up an internal organ.

"Oh my God!" I shouted, looking around my office. "Did you guys hear that?"

"Umm... yep," Stephano said with a grin and wide eyes.

"I most certainly did," Albinia added with a giggle.

"Where is she?" I demanded, looking under my desk. "Is she a ghost?"

"Are you fucking brain damaged?" the rude woman bellowed.

"Are you a dick?" I shouted back, still searching for the owner of the voice.

After another gag-inducing cough, the nasty piece of work kept going. "You need an anatomy lesson, shit-for-brains," she announced. "I don't have a dick so I can't be a dick. Now, if you called me a bearded clam or a fur burger, that would be more anatomically correct. Try again."

"Absolutely not," I snapped. "Show yourself now. I am done with this pussyfooting around."

"Getting warmer, dingleberry," she said with a cackle.

"What the hell is happening?" I asked, glancing over at a wildly amused Stephano and a positively giddy Albinia. "Can you two see her?"

"We can," Stephano said. "Would you like some hints?"

I paused my frantic search and sighed dramatically. The vampire had my number. "Yessssss," I hissed. "I want to guess who the awful woman is. Do I know her?"

"You do," Albinia said. "Quite well."

"Really?" I asked, perplexed.

"Really," Stephano confirmed. "If this woman—so to speak—lived in a house it would be a scratch pad."

"Ohhhhhh, good one," Albinia squealed.

I didn't get it. What kind of house was a scratch pad? It made no sense.

"Is she fictional?" I asked. She had to be. She was freaking invisible.

Albinia shook her head. "She is not fictional."

"Another hint," I insisted.

"Very well," Stephano conceded. "I would guess that her favorite dessert is chocolate mouse."

"You mean mousse," I corrected him.

"No. I meant mouse," he assured me with a sly grin.

I narrowed my eyes. They were screwing with me. "Another hint."

Stephano walked over to the couch and sat down next to Thick Stella, who seemed bored out of her violent furry mind. At least she hadn't attacked anyone. "As you wish. I would think her favorite color is purrrrrrrrple."

"I have one!" Albinia said, bouncing on her toes in excitement. "I would surmise her favorite subject is hisssssssssstory."

"Nice," Stephano told a delighted Albinia.

My stomach tightened and my head spun. Dropping onto the love seat with a thud, I tried to think. Only one answer came to mind and it was virtually impossible. Wait. Talking to fictional characters that I'd created in my imagination was *virtually impossible*. My entire existence right now was implausible, outrageous and absurd.

"Pretty sure I've lost my mind," I muttered, staring at the very now-interested fat ball of fur who'd tried to maim me for years. "Ask me pertinent questions."

Stephano obliged immediately. "What do you think this woman likes to read?"

"Catalogs," I said, staring straight at my cat, who lifted her leg in challenge at me.

"Correct!" Stephano said with a wide grin. "What would happen if this particular woman were to enter a dog show and win?"

"It would be a cat-has-trophy," I shot back immediately.

"About time, butt muncher," she said with a hiss and a cough.

"Unbelievable," I shouted at my cat, whose lips hadn't

moved even a fraction of an inch when she'd just insulted me. "You can talk?"

"Clearly," Thick Stella grunted, then extended her kitty claws. "I've been yacking for years, asshole. You just never listened."

"Your lips don't move," I accused her, wondering if Albinia might be a ventriloquist and she and Stephano were punking me.

Thick Stella flopped onto her back and literally rolled her yellow eyes at me. "No shit, Sherlock. It would look a little weird for a cat to fucking talk."

"I think it's weirder for you to talk without your lips moving," I pointed out. "And your vocabulary is horrid."

"Thank you," she replied.

"That wasn't a compliment," I snapped, running my hands through my hair. God, how many of my innermost secrets had I told the fat pain in my ass over the years? She could destroy me. "Can other people hear you besides me?"

"I'm a person," Albinia reminded me, sounding a little hurt. "A wonderful person."

Shit.

"Yes, you are," I told her. "No disrespect intended." I couldn't believe I was having this conversation. "But I'm referring to people who ummm…"

"Didn't have starring roles in your book?" Stephano questioned, helping me out tremendously.

"Exactly," I told him with a grateful expression.

The vamp winked at me. I laughed. I'd been accused of attempted murder. I'd witnessed Rhett Butler and Scarlett O'Hara almost get it on in a graveyard. I'd seen Flip's, Ann's,

Sally's and Joy's boobs today and I'd chased them around the headstones trying to dress them. Why should the fact that my murderous cat could talk without moving her kitty lips throw me?

"As far as I know, no one nonfictional can hear me except you, cheese butt," Thick Stella said.

"Thank God for small favors," I muttered, staring at the profane dummy. "Now that we can… umm… chat, would you like to stop attacking me?"

Thick Stella stretched and burped. "Nope."

While everything around me was a whirlwind of change, some things would always stay the same.

My eyes narrowed at her. "I can withhold treats," I threatened.

"And I can shit in your bed," she replied.

"Cat drives a hard bargain," Stephano pointed out.

"And a rather odoriferous one," Albinia added.

"Fine," I said, giving up on negotiating with my idiot cat. "Is there a reason I can hear you now? Is it important?"

"Guess we'll just have to wait and see, sphincter head," Thick Stella replied.

I rolled my eyes. The cat had no clue. None of us seemed to have a clue. We were the blind leading the blind and we were all nuts.

"Par for the course," I said, then stood up and gave Albinia and Stephano quick hugs. "You guys take off for a bit. Seth is due any minute and I can't get busted talking to people he can't see. I'm already in enough trouble."

Albinia kissed the top of Thick Stella's head. The cat hocked up a hairball for her. Stephano reminded me that a quick shag with Seth might relieve some tension. While he might have a point, that wasn't on the table. There were still up to twenty days until my divorce from Darren was legally final, and I didn't want to jump from one man to the next.

Also, I had to clear my name and beat back the elusive darkness headed our way.

Bring it. At this point I had nothing and everything to lose. And unfortunately, I couldn't write my way out of this one.

CHAPTER FIVE

My stomach dropped to my toes and the welcoming smile froze on my lips. Seth looked like hell warmed over. He was a wrinkled mess and was wearing two different tennis shoes. For the best-looking man I'd ever seen, he wasn't doing so good at the moment.

"Oh my God. Am I going to jail?" I whispered.

"I'm sorry, what?" he asked distractedly as he walked into the house and paced my living room like a tiger in a cage.

"Jail," I repeated. "Am I going to the big house for a crime I didn't commit?"

"Did you hear something?" he asked, surprised.

I was wildly confused. Seth was my lawyer. He'd come over to go over new developments. He seemed more clueless than I was. This was bad on so many levels. "Umm... no. I was hoping you heard something," I said, pacing right behind him.

I'd put Thick Stella in the mudroom. I didn't want her calling me some nasty name and me returning the favor. Of course, she'd escaped and was sitting on the couch grooming her lady bits and listening to everything. Whatever. Maybe the obnoxious ball of fur would have something smart to say. Preferably, after Seth left.

Seth ran his hands through his hair, sat down on the couch and absently stroked my cat. I gave her a covert murderous look. If she so much as removed even an iota of Seth's skin, I would shave her bald.

"I'm sorry," Seth said. "Lots going on. My mind is all over the place."

Not exactly what a gal wanted to hear from her lawyer, but Seth was also my *friend*. I had no intention of turning our friendship into one with benefits. Seth had implied the previous day that he'd like us to be more than friends, but I would hazard a guess that the man had changed his mind.

I pressed my lips together and nodded. This was exactly how it should be. I was a walking shitshow. On top of that, I wasn't available for more. We were simply friends, and he was my lawyer for the love of everything ridiculous. Besides, clients who were barely divorced didn't date their lawyer who was representing them for attempted murder—even if I didn't commit the crime and was wildly attracted to him.

He rubbed his face. "I'm sorry," he said again. "I'm not fit company."

"Right. Of course," I said, thinking this was probably not a good time to talk. "Do you want to chat tomorrow?"

"No," he said quickly. "I need to talk to someone right now."

His worried expression made my stomach clench. I had a sinking feeling this wasn't about me or my case. This had the feeling of something entirely more personal.

I reached out and put my hand on his shoulder. "I'm here," I told him. "Talk to me."

"It's Cheeto," he said, sounding defeated.

"Where is she?" I yelled, then tamped it back. I sounded nuts. I *was* nuts, but I didn't need to broadcast it.

I felt light-headed and my knees turned to jelly. I sat down on the armchair as my mind raced over all the worst-case scenarios. Had Cheeto suffered a mental break because of seeing Darren in a bloody heap? Had she gotten hurt? Had Jinny Jingle gotten to Cheeto? I would rip the bitch to shreds.

No. That couldn't be right. None of that. There's no way Seth would be here if his daughter had been hurt, in the hospital, or kidnapped by a psycho with silicone knockers and overly enhanced lips.

"She's with my dad and mom," Seth answered, looking at me strangely.

Fair enough. I had used my outdoor voice. "Is she hurt? Sick? Upset about what she saw?"

Dumb question. She had to be traumatized by what she'd seen. I was freaking traumatized by it. It wasn't every day that you got to witness an attempted murder. Then see the culprit get nailed by a stun gun followed by an accusation by the jerkoff victim that was a flat-out lie.

I could kick my own ass a thousand times over for not returning Cheeto to the office before I'd approached Jinny beating the hell out of Darren. It had all happened so fast and I'd thought she was safe in my car. I had been wrong.

While Cheeto hadn't been physically harmed, she had clearly been emotionally scarred. And that was all my fault.

"I am so sorry," I choked out as I swiped at a tear rolling down my cheek. "She must be devastated."

Seth shook his head. "No, she's not. She's absolutely fine."

I squinted at him. "How is that possible?"

He shrugged. "I don't know. She told me that she's proud that she can save you. She's happier than she's been in a few years."

I blew out a long slow breath. I didn't want Cheeto to have anything to do with this. Having a seven-year-old little girl testify on my behalf wasn't in the plan. She barely spoke in public. Cheeto had already been through far too much in her young life with losing her mother.

"Look," I said, twisting my hands in my lap. "I don't want her to be involved at all. What I think we need is for Jinny Jingle to take a lie detector test or possibly Darren to take one."

Seth just stared at me. It was off-putting. Was that a bad idea? I wasn't a lawyer, but I did write mysteries and crimes into my novels. The lie detector seemed like a logical plan.

I got up and walked to one of my living room windows, staring out at nothing in particular. I couldn't ward off this sinking feeling that I was missing something terrible. Again, my stomach tightened to the point of pain. "Is Darren still alive?"

That would throw a terrible wrench into my future if my scummy ex-husband had bit it without retracting his statement first.

Seth stood up, crossed the room to me and pulled me into his arms. It felt all kinds of right.

"I'm an ass," he muttered. "You must be going through hell. Yes. Darren is alive. Jinny Jingle is nowhere to be found. She's technically on vacation from the TV station. We've been told by a source at the police station that she was out of town at the time of Darren's beating and that she has an alibi."

While hugging a friend was perfectly fine, my body wasn't reacting to his platonically. Mixed signals would not be helpful right now for either of us. "That's a lie," I said, disengaging myself from his arms.

Seth inhaled and nodded. "Agreed. It's a lie and I'm sorry…about the hug. You looked like you needed it, and I know I did."

I wanted to tell him it was fine. I wanted to tell him it was perfect. But I didn't. Anything I said would come off as encouragement, and while I did want Seth and everything that hug made me feel, it was not a good idea. Not now.

"No worries," I said politely, moving away so I didn't dive right back into his embrace. "What's the next step?"

Seth looked perplexed. "With us?"

I smiled. "Umm… no. In the case."

He had the grace to look embarrassed. Shoving his

hands into the pockets of his jeans, he glanced down at his mismatched shoes and chuckled. "Right. My bad. The tire iron has been sent off to a forensics lab to have the fingerprints evaluated."

"Didn't the rain wash the prints away?" I asked, thinking I might be well and truly screwed if Darren wouldn't come clean.

"Nope. Normally, a powder is used, but the rain makes that method moot. However, some elements in a latent print residue aren't water soluble. They'll remain on the weapon. They don't have the equipment for it here, so the tire iron was sent to a lab in Louisville to process."

"How long will that take?"

"A few days," he replied.

I nodded. Relief washed over me. Darren had far too many friends left on the force who might have been willing to *help* him out. Grabbing a sharp pencil and a yellow legal pad, I jotted down the information. It would be excellent in a book.

"What are you doing?" Seth asked.

I winced. "Writing that down to use in a book."

His brows shot up. "Is everything in your life fair game for your books?"

I eyed him. It was a loaded question. "Well, if you're a vampire, werewolf or demon, then yes. Otherwise, no."

"Good to know," he said. He walked back to the couch and sat down. "Can I change the subject?"

Tilting my head to the side, I considered his request. There clearly wasn't much new information on my future in prison right now, but I also didn't want to have to shoot him down if he wanted to discuss us...

He didn't want to discuss *us*. My absurdly oversized ego was embarrassing. He'd been worried about Cheeto, and once he'd told me she was fine, my writer brain had taken me down the "Is Darren dead?" rabbit hole.

"Absolutely," I told him. "Change away. You wanted to talk about Cheeto?"

He nodded, looking suddenly exhausted again. "Yes. I need to talk with someone who won't think I'm crazy. Although, there's a fine chance you'll kick me out of your house and fire me as your lawyer afterward." He popped his neck and closed his eyes briefly. "First, it would be helpful if I could tell you about my wife."

"Umm...sure," I said, feeling like I'd just been doused with a vat of ice water. Served me right. Confusing reality with my secret fantasies would not be helpful. I was looking at possible jail time. Being a friendly shoulder for my lawyer to lean on was in my best interest. It was pathetic to be jealous of a dead woman and former wife of a man who was nothing more than my friend. I really didn't like myself much right now. Owning the icky emotions I felt was not a good time. Pushing the petty feelings away, I focused on my lawyer and the father of the little girl I adored. "Shoot," I said, doing my best to sound neutral.

"Thank you," Seth said with so much relief in his voice, I felt bad for not wanting to hear about his wife. "Let me start at the beginning."

"It's a very good place to start," I said, quoting *The Sound of Music*. He didn't get it. His perplexed smile was a dead giveaway. I needed to save all my cheesy movie references for my agent, Cyd. That was her bag. "Sorry. Go ahead."

"I liked Lily a lot," he explained.

"Lily is... I mean, was your wife?" I asked, a little confused. *Like* was an awfully mild word for someone you were married to.

"Yes."

"Got it," I said, vowing to not ask questions. Hard but doable. I was a writer. I liked details.

"Lily and I didn't know each other well when we got pregnant," Seth admitted, looking down at the floor. "We were more casual acquaintances with benefits."

I nodded, a little sick to my stomach wondering if that was what he'd been suggesting we become. Reminder to me... pretty men were not on my to-do list. I'd married one and that had gone to hell in a handbasket. I wasn't about to get involved with another.

Seth sighed. "This doesn't paint a real good picture of me, but I want you to know."

Again, I nodded.

He went on. "It wasn't like we were kids," he explained. "We were consenting adults. Lily wanted to have the baby and I did the right thing and asked her to marry me. I don't regret it. Cheeto is the very best thing I've done in my life. While Lily and I weren't each other's great loves, we grew to respect and care deeply for each other. She adored our little girl as much as I do."

This wasn't what I'd expected and I wasn't sure how it made me feel.

"Is this strange for you?" Seth asked. "Because it's strange for me."

"Yes, strange, but strange isn't always bad," I told him.

"Right," he said, pressing the bridge of his nose. "This is a conversation I figured would come a lot later down the road, but there's a reason I'm telling you now."

"And the reason is Cheeto?"

"The reason is Cheeto," he confirmed. "When Cheeto was two, Lily was in a car accident. A bad one. She was hit by a drunk driver—broke her collarbone and both arms. The driver barely had a damn scratch on him. I thanked God repeatedly that nothing more serious had happened to Lily. Until something far more serious and strange happened. Lily changed after the accident. Her body healed, but her mind seemed to go."

My tummy tingled and my muscles tightened. Cheeto's woowoo juju was no accident. It was an inherited gift. I was pretty sure I could continue the story without Seth's input, but I kept my lips firmly closed.

He averted his gaze for a moment. "She began to believe she could do things that were impossible."

Lily didn't believe—she knew. The accident had been Lily's external disaster that brought on her woowoo juju. I was sure of it. "Not much in life is impossible," I said softly.

"Thinking you can fly?" Seth questioned with utter disbelief in his tone. "Believing you talk to animals? And that they answer you? She was in a constant state of hysteria. It terrified me and tore me apart. She was suffering and nothing I did helped."

I wasn't sure how to proceed. I was caught between a

rock and a really freaking hard place. "Did Lily have family? Parents? Siblings?"

"No, she was an only child and her parents had passed on before we met."

The picture was becoming tragically clear. Lily didn't understand her gift and had no one to guide her.

"It was as if the accident brought out a mental illness. I tried to get her to talk to someone. She didn't want to. She was jumpy and scared all the time." His voice was full of pain and raw emotion. "I was so angry with her. The shame I feel for that still haunts me. I didn't try hard enough and Lily paid the price."

My heart broke for Seth and for a woman I would never know. She wasn't crazy. She wasn't mentally ill. She was like me. And Cheeto was clearly like us, too.

Most importantly, there was nothing Seth could have done.

"What happened?" I asked.

"She took pills and killed herself," he said flatly. "I found her. Cheeto doesn't know that part. Although, I think she might. It's as if my child sees inside people."

"Cheeto is a very observant little girl."

He nodded. It was a jerky movement. "After Lily's death, Cheeto began to change."

"That would be normal," I told him. "She lost her mother."

"Her changes have been far more than *normal*," he said.

"Okay." I could put him out of his misery with the truth, but the truth could also land me in a straitjacket if he decided to have me committed for my own good.

"I took her to therapy," Seth said. "We went together. I needed to make sure she was okay."

I sat quietly and waited.

"One doctor diagnosed her as autistic. Another disagreed and labeled her with split personality disorder. Yet another doctor disagreed with both diagnoses and said she was depressed and needed to be medicated." His expression turned hard. "She was three. I wasn't going to medicate my baby. Six other doctors gave entirely different opinions. All I want to do is get her the help she needs, and I can't find anyone to give me an answer so I know how to get her treatment. My God, she didn't even speak to anyone but me until I moved us back to Kentucky."

I was unsure where all of this was leading. It was very clear to me that there was nothing wrong with Cheeto. But I worried Seth wouldn't be able to handle the truth.

"Tell me why you're sharing this with me, please."

Seth stared at me for a long moment. He looked like he was on the edge of losing it. "Cheeto says she has magic powers. She says that *you* have magic, and Flip… and Flip's friends. She believes this. And yes, I am very aware I sound insane. Clearly, my little girl is delusional. I don't know what to do. Maybe she does need medication."

"No!" I shouted. The word left my lips before I could stop it. Cheeto didn't need medication. She wasn't sick, she wasn't mentally ill.

Seth looked at me and waited for more.

I felt like I'd been busted for an unforgivable crime. I needed some assistance. Flip was here. Getting her to help me explain might be wise.

"Tell him, assface," Thick Stella grunted. "Cheeto needs allies. You're supposed to be the leader of the fucking idiots. Buck up and do your damned job."

My silence was deafening. My head spun with all the different ways this particular chapter could go. However, this wasn't fiction. I couldn't write a neat and clean ending where everyone would be happy. I also couldn't let Seth keep taking Cheeto to doctors who wouldn't be able to understand her in a million years. Thick Stella was an asshole, but she was correct.

Seth might leave here more confused than when he'd arrived, and he may take his daughter and get the hell out of Dodge, but according to the bible, the truth shall set you free. Or more possibly in my case, send a man running for his life and sanity.

"There is nothing wrong with Cheeto," I said carefully. "There was nothing wrong with Lily. There is nothing wrong with me or Flip. It all depends on how you define the word wrong."

Seth looked hopeful and wildly doubtful at the same time.

"You started it, douche rag. Finish it," Thick Stella advised in her lovingly disgusting way.

Inhaling deeply, I smiled at Seth. I didn't need the beautiful man as a lover, but I needed him as a friend. I needed his trust so that I could help his daughter. "Do you truly believe in God?"

"What does that have to do with anything?" he asked, squinting at me warily.

"Just answer me," I said.

He crossed his arms over his chest, leaned back on the couch and let his head fall back. "Yes. I believe in God."

"With no proof?" I questioned. "Without ever seeing him or her. You believe in God?"

Seth's head jerked up. "It's called faith," he replied, frustrated. "You can't look around at all the beauty in the world and not believe that some kind of higher power exists."

"Some don't believe in a higher power," I pointed out.

"That's their loss."

"So, you're willing to believe in things you can't truly see or understand? You're willing to have faith with no proof?"

"Clementine, where are you going with this?"

"Cheeto is seven," I said. "Magic can have many definitions to a child."

"You're fucking up, chicken shit," Thick Stella cut in.

I ignored her. Figuring it was better to ease Seth into the woowoo pool than to throw him in and watch him drown, I kept going... my way.

"Let her believe in magic," I said. "I believe in magic."

Seth sat silently and gazed off into the distance. "So, you think Lily was telling the *truth*? That if I'd had faith in her, she'd still be alive?" His voice was angry.

"I think everything is relative," I said, staying diplomatic.

"If it was this *magic* you speak of, why was it so terrifying? Why did it lead to Lily killing herself?" he demanded, trying to stay with me but having a damned difficult time.

I didn't blame him. It was still difficult for me to believe sometimes.

"I'm not sure I can answer that question," I told him, even though I probably could. "But maybe it would have been helpful if she'd had…" I stopped myself short of accusing him of anything. It wasn't his fault. He didn't know and didn't understand. Hell, when my woowoo first showed up, I had thought I was losing my mind. I was lucky I had Aunt Flip. Lily hadn't had anyone.

"It would have been helpful if I'd believed in magic?" he asked in a tight voice. "Faith in a higher being is one thing. Believing someone can fly is against the laws of physics. Playing games and encouraging mental instability is not the way I roll."

I wanted to put my head through a wall. Even if I told him, I couldn't prove a darn thing. He couldn't see my characters, not that any of them were here right now anyway. I couldn't knock down a tree or transport myself like Jess. I couldn't drink five beers and render myself invisible like Joy Parsley. I couldn't shift into a house cat like Ann Aramini—

Shit. But I could prove that magic existed. My fat furball could help me.

So much for us ever having a date somewhere down the line. I was about to freak the man out. "If I could prove that magic is real, will that ease your mind?"

Seth grimaced. "Clementine, please stop. This is absurd."

"Life is absurd," I shot back. "Faith and religion are absurd. People are absurd. Open your mind to me for five minutes and let me help you… and Cheeto."

"Are you about to use me and abuse me, dipshit?" Thick Stella inquired.

I nodded at her.

"Fine, but I want tuna. Real fucking tuna from a can…

and salmon cooked on the grill," the furry asshole bargained.

Again, I nodded.

"And I want belly scratches. Daily," she added.

Seth looked down for a moment and I flipped my cat off. She could have whatever she wanted to eat. There was no way I could afford to lose a finger by scratching her bulbous belly. I needed my fingers to write. There would be no tuna in a can or salmon if I didn't bring home a paycheck.

Thick Stella cackled and hocked up a hairball.

Lovely.

"Do you trust me?" I asked Seth.

Seth nodded curtly. He was trying. I had to give him that.

"Okay, I'm going to put my fingers in my ears and you are going to whisper a secret to my cat."

"Because?" he asked, gaping at me like I was nuts.

"Just do it. Make sure it's something I would never have any way of knowing," I instructed as I plugged my ears.

Seth shrugged and looked at my cat. Thick Stella eyed him. Cautiously, he leaned down and whispered in her ear. When he sat back up and looked at me expectantly, I removed my fingers.

"What did he say?" I asked the furry menace. "And remember, tuna in a can and salmon are riding on you not being an asshole."

"Said he's been in love with you since high school, jack-hole," Thick Stella announced.

If she was lying, she was dead. If I spoke that aloud and

she'd punked me, she had about ten seconds left in this world.

"What did I say?" Seth asked, watching me carefully.

"Well, clearly you lied to my cat," I said, feeling the heat crawl up my neck and land on my face. "I'm pretty sure she misunderstood."

"Didn't, asswad," Thick Stella hissed.

"Cake hole. Shut it," I snapped at my cat.

Seth looked confused and a bit alarmed. Hell, I was confused and alarmed. I was tempted to say I'd been lying. Problem was, I wasn't lying. And this wasn't about me. It was about him beginning to understand his daughter. My humiliation would be worth it if it helped Cheeto.

"Fine," I said, looking away from Seth. I didn't need to see him laugh. "Thick Stella, who is not long for this world if she is messing with me, told me you said you've been in love with me since high school."

Seth paled and gaped at me like he'd seen a ghost. "Oh my God," he muttered.

Holy crap. Had he really said that?

Immediately, he leaned down and whispered to my cat again. Whatever he was sharing was taking a while. "Tell me what I said," he demanded.

I glanced over at Thick Stella, who was now having a go at her bits. "He said he peeked in your pink journal at Jess's one time and found that you had written his name and yours with hearts around it on at least ten fucking pages. Which, by the way, is pathetic," she informed me.

"He said it was pathetic that I wrote our names in hearts

on ten pages?" I asked Thick Stella, horrified about so many things, I could barely function.

"Nope, I added the pathetic part and I stand by it," the cat said with a grunt of laughter.

"No," Seth shouted, backing up my asshole cat. "I didn't say it was pathetic. Made me feel great."

The man then went even paler. He was so ashen, I was pretty sure he was going to pass out. I was glad he was seated.

"Your cat's lips didn't move," he pointed out in a shaky voice.

"I know," I replied with a weak smile. "You really snooped in my pink journal in high school? That's kind of weird."

Seth blew out a long slow breath and stared at me like I had several heads. Then he laughed. It was a laugh that verged on a breakdown, but I totally understood. I let him have at it. At least he hadn't bolted. It took him about five minutes of laughter followed by at least ten of just staring at me before he pulled himself back together.

"Tell me something," he said, then sucked his lower lip into his mouth for a moment. "At the library when your aunt Flip said you were talking to yourself... were you?"

"No, I wasn't," I said, watching him with concern in case he lost his shit.

"Who were you talking to?"

I sighed. I was treading water in the deep end. "You're not going to freak?"

"Already past that, I think," he told me.

At least the color had come back to his face and he didn't look like he was going to faint.

"I can see and talk to the characters from my books," I admitted, waiting for him to laugh.

He didn't laugh. "Are you a witch?"

I laughed. "Umm… no—not as in fly-on-a-broom, wart-on-my-chin kind of witch. I have magic. It's passed down. I recognize the magic—or woowoo juju, as Aunt Flip calls it —in Cheeto. She got it from Lily. Lily didn't have people in her life to help her realize she wasn't crazy. I have Flip and a few others."

Seth was quiet for a long moment as he took in my words. The pain of knowing Lily had ended her life because she didn't comprehend what was happening to her was etched all over his face. My heart hurt so badly for both of them.

"So, there's more than one witch in town?" Seth asked, clearly trying to wrap his mind around the impossible news.

"Probably better to call them badass bitches instead of witches, but yes," I told him, feeling such profound relief that he seemed to believe me—relief for me and for Cheeto. "And we can help Cheeto. She will never be scared of her gifts."

Seth scrubbed his hands over his face. "What are my daughter's gifts?" he asked, kind of chuckling at himself for asking such a bizarre question.

"I don't know yet," I told him. "*She* might not even know yet. But we can help her figure it out."

"And I can help her too," he said.

I smiled. God, he was a wonderful human being. His love

for his daughter trumped whatever disbelief he might harbor. "You already do by loving her," I said. "And now you can help her even more by understanding her."

Seth stood up. "I think I'm going to go home now," he said.

"Okay. You sure you're not freaked out?"

"Oh, I'm definitely freaked out," he replied with a pained laugh. "However, I feel like an enormous weight has been lifted off me."

Again, amazing.

"It's a secret," I explained as I walked to the front door and opened it. "It's not something to share randomly."

"Not to worry," he said, patting Thick Stella on the head, then whispering something to her. "My lips are sealed."

I was dying to know what he'd said to my cat, but wasn't about to ask... well, not until he left.

"Can we talk tomorrow?" Seth asked, standing next to me at the door.

"Yep. Hopefully, there will be some news on the case."

Seth nodded and walked down the front porch steps to his SUV. "I didn't lie to your cat," he said as he got into his car. "All of it was true."

If I could have swallowed my tongue, I would have. The timing of all of this was whacked beyond belief. So instead, I waved. Speaking was not a smart move right now.

Closing the door, I pressed my forehead to the cool wood. "That was insane."

"Called that right, butt munch," Thick Stella shouted. "That hot piece of man just told me that he was going to marry you."

I shook my head and groaned. "I'm not all the way divorced yet," I told the fat bearer of terrifying news. "And I'm never getting married again."

"Good luck with that," she grunted, then puked.

"Thanks," I replied. "You want tuna now?"

"I sure as hell earned it," she replied, waddling past me to the kitchen.

She certainly did and then some. Life was getting more complicated by the minute.

CHAPTER SIX

"WE'RE GONNA NEED A BIGGER BOAT!" CYD SHOUTED INTO the phone.

Rubbing my eyes, I glanced over at the alarm clock and had half a mind to hang up on my agent. It was seven in the freaking morning. I'd been up most of the night fretting about everything I'd told Seth and what he'd told Thick Stella. My cat had been useless as far as someone to talk to. After finishing off four cans of tuna, she spent an hour in her litter box then passed out in exhaustion. I'd thought about waking up Aunt Flip but decided against it. We'd deal with whatever mess I'd created in the morning. I just didn't expect my morning to start at seven. Honestly, I wouldn't be surprised if Seth showed up shortly with men in white coats to take me away.

"Are you okay?" I asked, flopping back down in my bed. "Did someone die?"

"No! Nobody died," she shouted. "What movie did I just

quote? I know you know it."

God, she was loud. Putting my volume-impaired agent on speakerphone so I didn't go deaf, I grabbed my sleep mask and slapped it over my eyes. I made a mental note to call Cyd at four in the morning soon to pay her back.

"*Jaws*," I told her.

"That's right! And we're gonna need a bigger boat to hold all the money you're earning!"

"What are you yelling about?" I asked, still considering hanging up.

"Come on, you know," she said with a bellow of laughter.

"No, I really don't. And this better be good. I didn't go to bed until three."

"Why? You're done with the book. WAIT! Did you start a new book?"

"Nope," I told her. "Got a little situation going on at the moment that I have to take care of."

"I'd say so," Cyd remarked gleefully at a decibel that could attract stray dogs. "The marketing department wants to kiss your brilliant ass! *Everybody* is talking. You've really gone and stepped it up this time."

"What are you talking about?" I screeched as I jerked to a sitting position and yanked off my sleep mask. How many nose dives could my life take? Had the black and decker pecker wrecker called my publishing house and told them I'd been accused of freaking murder? "How much do they know?"

"All of it. It went viral on the internet, baby! When I first saw it, I said to myself, Houston, we have a fucking problem."

"That's not the line from *Apollo 13*. They didn't say fucking," I pointed out as I felt a massive headache exploding in my frontal lobe. How in the heck was there a video of Darren's almost murder?

Wait. If there was a video, I'd be exonerated. I had no clue who took a video and posted it. It certainly wasn't the Weather Hooker. Video proof would send her skanky ass to jail.

"Was it just the part where I shot the ho-bag with the stun gun or did it include her trying to beat Darren to death with the tire iron? Please, please, please tell me the tire iron part was in it."

There was dead silence on the other end of the line. I thought Cyd might have hung up on me. I was wrong. I was wrong about everything.

"Are you meshugenah?" Cyd bellowed, laughing. "Or is that the plot of the new book?"

"What?" I asked, confused.

"What do you mean, what?"

"I mean what as in what?" I told her.

"Aren't you the funny one," Cyd grunted, still chuckling. "I got another call coming in. Get a cup of coffee and call me back. We'll discuss. And congrats. That was genius. Your books are flying off the shelves."

She hung up on me.

Houston, I was pretty sure I had a new *fucking* problem. I just didn't know what it was yet.

The smell of burned toast and watery coffee was familiar and real. Aunt Flip, in a purple muumuu, rolling a joint at the breakfast bar, was a beautiful sight. My life was spiraling out of control. I needed some normal—not that seeing your aunt rolling a joint first thing in the morning was exactly normal, but it was my normal.

"There's some kind of video on the internet," I said, pouring a cup of crappy coffee and grabbing a piece of charred toast.

"Of what?" Flip asked, offering me the joint.

"No thanks," I told her. "And I don't know. Cyd called all excited. Said my books were selling like crazy because of some viral video. I thought it was of the Weather Hooker trying to kill Darren and me blasting her with your stun gun, but I don't think that's what it is."

"Woulda loved to have seen you shoot that tart," Flip commented, adding the joint to the pile on the counter. "Any word on where the murderin' hussy is?"

"Supposedly on vacation with an alibi," I told her with a groan of disgust. "But the good news is that the tire iron was sent to a lab in Louisville to get the fingerprints."

"What about the rain?" Flip questioned. "Been worried that it would wash them prints right off."

"I had the same thought. Apparently fingerprints leave a non-water-soluble residue," I explained.

"You gotta use that in a book," Flip said with a raised brow.

I grinned. We were definitely cut from the same cloth. "On it."

"Good girl," she said. "I got a question."

"Shoot," I said, biting into the toast and hoping I didn't chip a tooth. At the rate my life was careening towards the bottom, it wouldn't surprise me to end up toothless.

"What in the ever-lovin' hell did that cat eat? The litter box smells like rotten ass on fire," Flip announced.

I sniffed the air and gagged. She was correct. Without missing a beat, I stood up, picked up the rank plastic kitty potty and put it outside on the back porch.

"Tuna from a can," I said, seating myself at the counter and taking a sip of semi-caffeinated water. "Oh, and Thick Stella talks."

"Well, I'll be darned," Flip said with a giggle. "What did the little cutie say?"

I rolled my eyes at the terms little and cutie for my cat, but beauty was clearly in the eye of the beholder. Flip needed glasses. "She cusses like a sailor. The cat is rude and socially unacceptable."

"I can hear you, butt dancer," Thick Stella shouted from the living room. "Watch that trap or I'll take a dump in your shoes."

"Try it," I yelled back. "I will shave you bald so fast you won't know what hit you."

"Eat me," Thick Stella grunted.

"That's a possibility," I told her. It was definitely *not* a possibility, but she clearly responded well to threats.

"What'd the furry critter say?" Flip asked as she divided the joints into little individual baggies with flowers and bumblebees drawn on them.

"Said she was going to take a dump in my shoes." I shook my head and laughed. "How is this my life?"

"It's a darn good life, Clemmy," Aunt Flip said, tweaking my cheek and stealing what was left of my toast. "Every dark cloud has a silver lining, girlie. Sometimes you gotta look real hard to find it, but it's always there."

"Promise?" I asked, resting my chin on my hands and staring at the empty spot where my kitchen table used to be. I'd trashed the table after I'd caught Darren banging Jinny Jingle on top of it.

"Yeppers," she said. "I'm gonna deliver some flowers to a couple of friends in need this morning. You want anything from the grocery?"

In any other world, I'd be concerned that my aunt was about to make her pot rounds through town. However, in my warped world, I was proud of her. She didn't sell her *flowers*. Nope. One of her woowoo juju gifts was that she could detect illness in others. She sought out those who could use a little comfort from marijuana and made sure that they were well supplied. Heck, she was even helping out Nancy with her hot flashes.

"No, nothing from the grocery," I told her, then paused. "Do you consider yourself a witch?"

Flip thought for a moment. "Nah, I'm more of a healer who spreads good juju into the world. But being called a witch don't offend me. Why?"

I realized I hadn't gotten my aunt up to speed on some seriously important news. The viral video had thrown me off this morning. I needed to find out what it was all about, but part of me wanted to pretend Cyd had never called. There was only so much I could handle this morning.

"I told Seth about the woowoo juju," I said.

Aunt Flip almost choked on her toast. "Holy crap on a cracker. Did he hightail it out of here?"

I shook my head. "He wanted to talk to me about Cheeto. He was desperate. He's taken her to so many doctors I lost count. So… I told him."

"And he believed ya?"

"I proved it," I told her.

Flip pursed her lips and looked confused. "Not followin'. Your woowoo ain't real showy."

"Correct," I admitted. "I had a little help from a profane, hairball-puking butthole."

Flip slapped her skinny thigh and laughed. "Dang it, I miss all the good stuff. Was Seth okay with it?"

"He's freaked out, but he seemed so relieved to have an answer that he didn't pass out or have a breakdown."

Flip sat quietly for a bit and munched on her toast. "He's a good boy, that one," she mused aloud. "Cheeto will be okay havin' that much love in her corner. Makes me curious about her momma."

Sighing, I pressed my temples. "It's not a pretty story."

"Kinda figured that. Tell me, baby girl."

I did. Aunt Flip cried and I did too. It made me wonder how many others had suffered like Lily. It was so wrong and so very tragic.

"Breaks my heart," Flip said, giving me a tight hug. "I'm thinkin' part of our woowoo destiny in the future is to find the others and help them. Woowoo juju is a beautiful gift, but it could be a real scary thing without guidance."

"I agree. However, that's not on the plate right now. Plate's kind of full at the moment."

"Roger that," Flip said, slipping into her Birkenstocks and stuffing her contraband into her big purse. "Let me know about that video. Maybe with all that money comin' in you could buy yourself a new kitchen table. Or I could get you one as a surprise!"

I laughed. I had plenty of money to buy a table. "How about I buy it, but we pick it out together?"

"Sounds like a plan, Clemmy," she said, giving me a kiss and skipping out the front door. "I'll be back in a few hours."

"I'll be here," I said, dumping the awful coffee into the sink and making a stronger pot. Calling Cyd back required caffeine. Flip's coffee wasn't gonna cut it.

Sitting back down with a cup of coffee that could singe the hair off of my head and a pile of cold burned toast, I took a deep breath and prepared myself. For the life of me, I couldn't figure out what kind of video of me had gone viral on the internet.

"Just stay calm until calm isn't an option," I told myself as I dialed Cyd's number. "Thick Stella, could you come in here, please. I need some moral support."

The fact that I asked a cat who keep threatening to crap in my stuff and who had an obsession with calling me names that had the word ass or butt in them spoke volumes about my state of mind. I was losing it. But the choices were limited. It was either embrace the crazy or go crazy.

"That's gonna cost you six cans of tuna," Thick Stella grumbled as she waddled into the kitchen and hopped up on the counter.

My mouth fell open. With her girth, it was shocking that she could jump at all.

"What you lookin' at, hiney smacker?" Her tail twitched ominously.

"Umm... nothing," I replied, still trying to figure out the physics of what she'd just done. Although, my train of thought was ridiculous. I completely accepted that she could talk. If she could talk, which was scientifically impossible, of course she could jump even though her stomach practically dragged the ground when she walked.

I thought about suggesting a diet, but I had a feeling I'd find cat dumps all over the house. It was a subject I'd broach after the shitshow had blown over.

"I'm calling Cyd," I told her as the phone rang.

"Your agent?" she inquired.

"Yep." It didn't surprise me a bit that Thick Stella knew who Cyd was. She'd clearly been eavesdropping for years.

"Put her on speakerphone. That broad is fucking hilarious," she instructed.

I was taking directions from a smack-talking cat. Whatever. When in Loony Land, get on the bus and go along for the ride.

"Clementine!" Cyd shouted at a volume that made me wince and Thick Stella spew out a string of swear words. I was relieved that no one could hear my obscene cat but me.

"That's my name, don't wear it out," I said. "You need to explain the video to me, please."

"I can do better than that," Cyd bellowed. "I'll send you the link. It's called Naked Satanic Rituals in the Boneyard starring Psycho Romance Author, Clementine Roberts."

"I'm sorry, what?" I asked, squinting at the phone in horror.

"It's damned hilarious. Whoever posted it put *The Devil Went Down to Georgia* as the soundtrack," Cyd went on. "You got people thinking you raise the dead. Couldn't have come up with that one if I tried."

"I am so fucking confused," Thick Stella muttered.

"Join the club," I said.

"What's that?" Cyd questioned.

"Umm... nothing," I replied quickly. Note to self... do not talk to Thick Stella while talking to Cyd. "I'm still not clear on what you're talking about."

"You're not?" Cyd asked.

"No. Are you sure it was me?"

"Positive," she shouted. "You're in a graveyard with a bunch of topless old gals. All of you are running around the graves screaming and calling to the dead. You were killing it screaming at all the ladies. I couldn't have been prouder if I was your mother. It was the funniest damn thing I've seen in years. I think you need to write a necromancer novel to capitalize on your witchy status—maybe make it comedic. Would fly off the shelves."

I felt faint. I almost threw up in my mouth. Joy Parsley, Ann Aramini, Sally Dubay and Aunt Flip now had a porn video on the internet. Thankfully, Nancy and Jess and I hadn't been *boobs to the wind*. And apparently, we were calling up the dead. It wasn't all that off base, but still damning in so many ways.

"Shit," I hissed. "This is so, so, soooo bad."

"No!" Cyd assured me. "It's not bad. Your books are

selling like hotcakes. You got the world thinking you're into all that hoodoo hinky stuff. My guess is we're going to see copycat videos from other paranormal romance authors shortly. But you, my genius and favorite client, beat everyone to the punch. Congrats!"

"Gotta go," I said, hanging up the phone before screaming at the top of my lungs.

"What the hell did you idiots do yesterday?" Thick Stella inquired, hopping down off the counter and looking for her litter box.

"Oh my God," I ground out, pacing the kitchen and trying to figure out what the hell I was supposed to do now. That video needed to come down. My aunt was half naked for the love of everything scandalous. We lived in a small town. I already knew how life altering it could be to have something awful about you go up on the internet. It had made me furious, embarrassed and depressed. However, when someone messed with my people, I wanted to blow a freaking gasket. "Flip and the gals wanted to do a bonding conjure," I said, speaking a mile a minute. "They took off their tops and I chased them around the graveyard and tried to dress them. It was appalling, ridiculous, wonderful and fun. We FREAKING BONDED. They have sunburnt boobs. It was a beautiful experience and someone has destroyed it."

"My guess would be the piece of trash who fornicated with your sorry excuse of an ex-husband," Cassandra announced as she appeared in the kitchen and almost gave me a heart attack.

The gorgeous demon was dressed from head to toe in coral Chanel. Her vivid green eyes missed nothing. She was a terrifying person. I should know, I created her. However, I also not so secretly adored her. The impeccably turned-out grande dame was more bark than bite. I mean, she was still a demon and could incinerate her enemies with a flick of her perfectly manicured finger, but I was onto her.

"I need help," I choked out, grabbing my phone. "How do I remove a video from the internet?"

She sat down at the breakfast bar and crossed her long, shapely legs. "I have no idea," she admitted. "Do you mind if I smoke?" Her already arched brow was raised high. She knew full well she wasn't allowed to smoke in the house. She was trying to undermine me when I was in a state of panic. If you gave a demon like Cassandra an inch, she would take a mile and then some.

"Nope," I snapped, narrowing my eyes. "If you've come to screw with me, go back to wherever you live when you're not here. If you're here to help, then help me."

Cassandra shrugged and put her cigarette and solid gold lighter back into her Hermès Birkin bag. "You need to find the bitch. She's still after your house."

"I'm divorced," I reminded Cassandra.

"Not quite," she replied. "The ink on the paperwork isn't dry until the decree is stamped and signed by the judge. If you die, your spineless, under-endowed, soon-to-be ex-husband gets your home."

"Dammit, you're right," I said, wanting to go for a jog to release some energy. Problem was I didn't jog. "How would putting up a video on the internet kill me?"

Cassandra eyed the burned toast disdainfully and pushed it away. "It won't. However, look at the state you're in right now. You're a disaster. Disasters are sloppy. If the whore pushes enough of your buttons, she will have a fine chance of succeeding."

I took a deep breath. Then another. And yet another. Cassandra was correct. However, I still had a potential shitshow on my hands. The older members of the woowoo clan were boobs to the wind for the world to see.

"Okay," I said, holding onto the counter for dear life. "I get what you're saying. I think you're right."

"I'm always right," Cassandra cut in.

"And humble," I added with an eye roll.

"That too," she said with a smile that could charm the Devil himself. "I'd suggest gathering the strippers and making sure no one is caught with their pants down… or bras off, so to speak."

"Right." I grabbed my phone and sent a group text to the gals telling them to haul ass to my house ASAP. "What do I do when they get here?"

Cassandra rolled her eyes. "Do I have to tell you everything?"

"Right now? Yes," I growled. "I'm losing it. And if I have a panic attack that leads to my demise, I can't write the next book in your series. That means you get stuck in Heaven completely redeemed from all your heinous deeds. So start talking, lady."

Cassandra paled considerably. She had been wildly displeased that I'd redeemed her in *Exquisite*—wildly displeased being an understatement. Before the book had been finished, I'd threatened to kill her with a pack of pigs—

Flip's awful idea. However, that was off the table now since I'd planted her evil ass in Heaven.

"You're quite bitchy," Cassandra said with a smile of approval. "I now see where I get it from."

"Great," I said, running my hands through my wild curly hair and waiting for a suggestion that made sense. For the life of me, I couldn't think of one.

"Look," she said, checking her manicure. "No press is bad press. Just depends on how you spin it."

"How exactly do I spin women in their twilight years topless in a graveyard?" I demanded.

"You're the writer, Clementine. Figure it out," she said, standing up. "We'll be casing the area looking for the dreadful skank. If we find her, one of us will return immediately. Clark Dark has made the plan and divided us into teams, so at least it makes a modicum of sense."

I nodded and smiled. "Thank you. I really do love you."

Cassandra looked as if she had swallowed a lemon. "Don't say horrible things like that," she hissed. "For the love of everything evil, I've gone soft enough as it is."

I laughed. "Too bad, so sad. I do love you and you're going to have to get used to it."

The demon's eyes narrowed dangerously and she literally hissed at me. However, the sparkle in her bright green eyes gave her away. She was delighted with my admission.

And so was I.

All I had to do now was figure out how to spin the fact that senior citizens were sprinting through the cemetery boobs to the wind...

CHAPTER SEVEN

"Mandy?" I shouted in shock as I opened the door to my other BFF.

It was only nine and the day had already gone to hell several times.

Mandy, Jess and I had been besties since high school. I loved her like a sister. However, her timing sucked. The woowoos were on their way over, and Mandy knew nothing about woowoo juju.

"Bad time?" she asked, taken aback by the sheer volume of my voice.

"Umm... no. Of course not." I opened the door and scanned my driveway for the gals. No one was in sight. "So, what brings you here this morning?"

"We're supposed to go for breakfast," she said, looking at me strangely.

Where Jess was short and curvy, Mandy was tall like me.

She was a striking blonde with piercing and intelligent hazel eyes. She was smarter than hell. Mandy had recently gone back to work as a lawyer at Seth's dad's law firm after having triplets via IVF. Mr. Ted, the name we called him because we'd known him since we were kids and couldn't bring ourselves to call him Ted, was thrilled to have her back. He'd even created childcare and put a playground in the grassy area behind the office. The girls were now four and Mandy had lost herself a little bit. While she adored being a mom and had fought hard to become one, she missed working. She and her hubby David were total relationship goals. They supported each other completely, raised the girls 50/50 and still had great sex.

"Shit. We were supposed to go to breakfast?"

"Nope," she said with a laugh. "Just messing with you. I wanted to talk to you about Tiny Pecker."

"Oh my God," I whispered. "Is Darren dead?"

"Sadly, no," Mandy said with a huff of disgust. "However, we don't want him dead… yet. The bastard is sticking to his story that you tried to kill him."

"He's such an asshole," I ground out.

"I'll second that and raise you a dick and a son of a bitch."

"My fingerprints are not on the tire iron," I told her.

"Bingo," she said, walking into the kitchen and pouring a cup of coffee. "The results will be back soon and we can put this bullshit to bed." She took a sip and almost choked. "Holy crap, this is strong."

I grinned. "I'm making up for Flip's barely caffeinated water. Had a bad morning."

"Did Darren contact you? Because I will slap him with a restraining order so fast it will make his head spin," she said, going all badass.

I loved Mandy's badass. Combine her brains, badassery and loyalty and you had one hell of a good friend.

"No. Is he still in the hospital?" I asked.

"He is," she said, grabbing a banana and peeling it. "Supposed to go home later this week. The black and decker pecker wrecker roughed him up good."

I nodded. The scene would live in my nightmares for a while. Darren meant little to nothing to me anymore, but I certainly didn't want him dead. "Did he make a formal statement to the police?"

"He did. However, there were holes."

"Like that's a surprise?" I asked, pissed. "Explain."

She rolled her eyes and pulled out her notes. "He says you came at him from behind and attacked him."

"Why is that a hole?" I asked, pouring myself another cup of engine fuel.

"Because all of his injuries are from the front. Also, you're right-handed, correct?"

"I am."

"Awesome." Mandy's smile was victorious. "The most severe injuries are on the right side of his head and body."

I grabbed a notebook. I could already tell I wanted the info for a story. "And that means it's more likely he was beaten by someone who's left-handed," I finished as I jotted it all down.

"Double bingo," Mandy said with a raised brow. "And guess who just happens to be left-handed?"

"The Weather Hooker," I said.

"Triple bingo."

Tucking my pencil behind my ear, I stared at the paper. All of the intel was academically fascinating, but there were still issues. "Seth told me that she's on vacation and has an alibi."

Mandy rolled her neck and popped her knuckles. "The information that was given came from her nasty buddy. Said she flew to Florida. Problem is, there's no record of that. So, then the story became that she must have driven. However, her car is parked at her house. Swiss cheese doesn't have as many holes as the fiction that was spewed out."

"I am so sick of stupid," I said, twisting my hair in my fingers. "Are the cops looking for Jinny?"

"They are, but not with purpose," Mandy confirmed. "However, with Darren's statement, she's not a suspect right now."

"She will be when they get the prints."

"If she can be found," Mandy said, topping off her coffee.

Jinny Jingle was still in town. I was certain of it. The Weather Hooker had made the video. I'd bet my next book advance. "I think she's still around."

Mandy considered what I'd said, then nodded. "Chances are you're correct. I just can't believe that Darren is so whipped he'd lie like that."

I laughed. It was hollow. "She hates him. Hell, you should have heard what she said about him at the diner."

"I would have loved to," Mandy said.

I froze as a tingle of excitement shot through my body.

"Wait!" My hands shook as I pulled out my phone from my pocket. "I recorded it. You can hear it and how damned insane she is."

"Play it," Mandy instructed, all business. "It might come in very handy."

Finding the audio took no time at all. Preparing myself to hear her voice took a few seconds.

"You okay?" Mandy asked, concerned.

"More than," I replied and pushed play.

"That dress is so ugly, I'd hire you to haunt a damn house," Jinny's bitch friend said.

"She's so ugly, she didn't just get hit with the ugly stick, the old bitch got nailed with the whole tree," another gal pal added.

"So, now we've graduated to ugly jokes? Pathetic," I said.

"I wouldn't leave so fast if I were you," Jinny purred. *"You might regret it."*

"Or not," I said. *"You got Darren. You're not getting the house. We've already done the old jokes and the ugly jokes, not sure what you want to chat about."*

"I want what you have," she hissed.

"You already got it."

"Hardly," she said. *"Give Darren the house."*

"Nope."

"I need that house," she snarled. *"I know what's there. It belongs to me. If you don't give it up, I'll destroy you."*

"If you ever threaten me again, I'll wipe the ground with your ass in a court of law. You'll have no career left. I will leave you a broken woman."

"You are not getting the full picture," Jinny said in a cold voice.

"I got Darren, and I'll get the good-looking one you like now. I will make your life a living hell."

"Are you right in the head?" I asked. "What's the end game here?"

"Simple. To win," she said flatly. "I've waited too long. It could all be solved if you give me the house."

"Darren," I corrected her. "Not you."

"When he gets the house, I'll marry the loser. Bing bang boom. The house is mine."

"Why is the house so important?" I asked.

"Playing stupid is beneath you, Clementine," she said. "Give up the damn house or the fun will begin. And trust me. It won't be fun for you."

"Holy shit," Mandy said, her eyes wide. "She threatened your life. I need a copy of that."

Pulling out her phone, she recorded the conversation. I hated listening to it again, but it was necessary. Thick Stella growled the entire time it replayed.

"Weird," Mandy said, staring at my cat. "It's like the violent furball knows what's going on."

I gave Thick Stella a warning glance. "I think she can feel my tension," I said, trying to divert Mandy's accurate assumption.

"Animals are smart," she agreed with a laugh. "Sometimes I like them far better than humans."

I just smiled. Thick Stella was an asshole. I wasn't sure I liked her more than humans, but I did love her.

"I'm out of here," Mandy said, giving me a quick hug. "I want Mr. Ted to hear this, then we'll figure out if we're taking it to the police. Would you be willing to press charges?"

"Is the timing right?" I asked, mulling her question over.

"Good point." Mandy put her phone into her bag and pursed her lips. "We might hold onto this until we can use it at the most damning time possible. Has Darren heard this?"

"No," I said, plotting like a madwoman. "Do you think he should?"

Mandy's brow wrinkled in thought. "Can't hurt," she mused aloud. "However, you paying him a visit is a very bad plan."

"Obviously," I said with a sarcastic chuckle. "That would not look good."

Mandy's grin was positively evil. "Doesn't mean someone else can't pay him a visit."

"Who?" I asked.

"Let me think on it," she said, hustling out of the kitchen and heading for the front door. "I'll give you a call later if there are any developments."

"Who's representing me? You or Seth?"

Mandy paused at the door and eyed me. "Well, the two of us both have conflicts of interest in this case," she said with a raised brow. "You're my best friend and Seth has it bad for you."

"Umm…"

"Mandy rolled her eyes and grinned. "Umm… nothing," she said. "We're all on your team, but Mr. Ted will technically represent you… if you need to be represented. I think once the fingerprints come back, the charges will be dropped and Darren will be shit out of luck."

"From your mouth to God's ears," I muttered.

"Amen, sister," she said. "Talk soon."

I watched as she jogged to her car and drove away. Aunt Flip was right. It was a good life. The dark clouds were heavy in the sky, but Mandy was one of the beautiful silver linings.

CHAPTER EIGHT

Thankfully, I'd had time to take a shower and get cleaned up before the ladies arrived. I shouldn't have bothered. After a short internet search, I'd found the viral video Cyd had told me about. Watching it had made me feel icky, dirty and pissed off.

"Holy heck, I think my hooters look fantastic!" Ann Aramini announced as we all stood in front of the laptop in my office and watched the horrifying video again.

I almost choked on my own spit.

"Well, I'll be damned," Joy Parsley said, putting on her readers and getting closer to the screen. "My left boob is definitely bigger than the right. I'd always thought it was the other way around. Who knew?"

Sally Dubay giggled. "I'm relieved they didn't capture me flying and crashing into the crypt. That would have been hard to explain and just terrible."

Like their boobs on display to the world wasn't terrible enough?

"Word," Aunt Flip said, patting Sally's back. "I think my knockers are looking real nice for a gal of my advanced age."

"Yep," Ann said with a nod of approval. "Flip's beanbags are the firmest. Less bouncy than the rest of us."

"Agreed," Joy said, still peering at the screen of my laptop. "Gotta say, I'm a little surprised one of my girls didn't haul off and slap me in the face. I mean, my God, my bazooms look enormous." She was grinning with pride like the cat who'd swallowed the canary.

Nancy was slack-jawed in shock. Jess held a hand over her mouth in an attempt to hold back her laughter. I was gobsmacked.

"You guys aren't upset about this?" I choked out.

"Oh dear, no," Sally said with a giggle. "I spent five years at a nudist colony back in the day. The naked human body is a beautiful thing and nothing to be ashamed of."

"And on the plus side, I do believe this will help Ann Aramini get laid," Joy Parsley pointed out.

"Can I get a copy of the video?" Ann questioned. "I'd like to have it for the senior citizen dating website I'm joining—Oldies, But Still Got the Goodies. I think it'll appeal to younger men who don't need Viagra."

The gathering was not going the way I'd thought it would. It had taken a sharp right turn into Knock Me Over With A Feather Land. It wasn't looking like I was going to have to spin a thing. The narrative... *and nudity* seemed to be just fine with the nutbags.

"Umm... sure," I told Ann, still trying to take in the completely nonplussed reactions. "So, no one is mad? I was going to try to get it removed."

"Hell to the no!" Flip said with a cackle. "I always had a little dream about bein' in the movies."

"Me too!" Sally squealed with delight. "I didn't quite expect it to be soft porn, but I'll take what I can get."

"I agree," Ann Aramini said. "We're gonna be the most popular gals at the senior center."

I shook my head and grinned. They were crazy.

"Question is, who put it up?" Jess asked.

"Had to be Jinny Jingle," I said as Joy Parsley hit the button to replay the video.

"Oh dear," Nancy said, fanning herself with a napkin. "She's still around? Word on the street from a few of the dead folks I ran into at the hardware store is that she skipped town."

I nodded. The fact that Nancy chatted with the dead was still strange to me. However, I didn't know why at this point. Strange should've been my new middle name. "I believe she is. But the good news is my fingerprints will not be on the tire iron."

"Best news I've heard since the invention of Viagra," Ann Aramini grunted. "But even better news would be that the idiot, scum-suckin' dawg retracted his lie about you trying to kill him. That sum-bitch likes to talk with his tongue hangin' out of his shoe."

"Half the town thinks you did it," Joy Parsley announced. "Half thinks you didn't. But the kicker is the whole town thinks he deserved it. Just so you know, I'm gonna report all the ones who think you did it to the town council. Gonna make their lives a living hell."

I blew out a long, audible breath and my mind raced with ideas—all of them bad. "I'm not sure if I'm flattered or insulted by the gossip. But Ann Aramini, you're right. It would be a whole heck of a lot better if the jerk took back his statement before the fingerprints come back as not belonging to me. Gossip is a hard thing to snuff out."

"Clearly, Darren is hard to snuff out too," Sally said. "Honey Swartz, who works at the hospital, said he had a cracked skull, broken nose, crushed cheek and shattered collarbone. He had to get over a hundred and fifty stitches. Just terrible."

I sighed. Why I felt sympathy for a monster who had wrongly accused me of trying to kill him was beyond me.

Joy Parsley hit replay again. "Flip told me you told Seth about woowoo juju."

"Holy shit," Jess said with a gasp. "How did that go?"

"Weird and good."

My cat hocked up a hairball. "Went fucking awesome because of me. So awesome that I want some tuna in a can, butt sphincter," Thick Stella grumbled as she wove her way around my legs.

"No more tuna today," I told her, cleaning up the nasty, phlegmy mess. "Your litter box and my nose can't take it."

"I heard that!" Ann Aramini bellowed. "That cat has a foul mouth."

It shouldn't shock me that Ann could hear Thick Stella. She could shift into a house cat. A feat I'd still never seen and wasn't sure I wanted to.

Thick Stella purred and nudged Ann with her bulbous head. "Tell that ass skater to get me some tuna or I'll shit in her Grape Nuts."

"Harsh," Ann said with a raised brow.

"What'd she say?" Jess asked, looking down at my fat cat.

"That she'd poop in my cereal if I didn't get her tuna," I replied with an eye roll. "It's her go-to threat when she wants something."

"Okay, ewwww," Nancy said with a giggle. "Ohhhh, I almost brought a new friend with me. But she disappeared before I knew she was dead."

"Not following," I said, watching Joy Parsley play the video yet again. Her eyes were glued to her large knockers. "Why would you bring someone to a woowoo gathering?"

Nancy mopped her forehead and sat down on the couch. "Normally, I wouldn't think of doing something so risky, but I was certain she had woowoo too."

"Really?" Sally asked, clasping her hands together with joy. "How wonderful. If you see her again, please extend an invite."

"But she's dead," Jess pointed out logically.

"True that," Flip said, putting out snacks that consisted of catsup, tortilla chips and cream cheese. "But once a woowoo, always a woowoo. Dead or alive, we're a sorority that sticks together."

"Did you get her name?" Ann asked.

Nancy shook her head. "No, she didn't say a word. Just followed me around the hardware store."

"Interesting," Joy said, taking a photo of the screen with her phone of a scarily up-close shot of her large bazooms.

"If you see her again, let her know you see her magic. Might make her curious to meet the rest of us."

"Will do," Nancy promised.

"As a matter of fact," Flip said, pulling a container of pot brownies out of her big purse and handing the hot-flash-prone Nancy one, "I think we need to search harder for our kind once we beat back the darkness. Not good to be alone with the woowoo."

She shot me a glance and I shook my head. If Seth wanted to share Lily's sad journey with the girls, that was his decision. Not mine. At least, not right now. Seth was filled with enough guilt about her death. Especially now that he believed in magic.

"I love that idea," Sally gushed. "We could really create a Goodness Army then."

We had seven in our Goodness Army to fight the undefined darkness. My beloved werewolf detective, Clark Dark, had told me eight were needed. With Cheeto there was eight, but we'd all agreed she was far too young to be involved in something that could be dangerous. Searching for others like us was a smart move. It might also save women like Lily who had no support.

I nodded and gave Sally a kiss on the top of her gray head. "It's a plan. But we need to figure out what the darkness means."

Nancy raised her hand. Her mouth was full of pot brownie. "I have a thought," she said as she swallowed.

"Spit it out," Ann Aramini said.

"The brownie?" Nancy asked, confused. "I already swallowed it."

"Umm... no," I said with a laugh. "The idea."

Nancy slapped herself in the forehead and giggled. "Right. I think the darkness is a never-ending fight."

"Well, that certainly sucks," Jess said with a groan.

"Follow me here," Nancy said. "I don't mean it in a bad apocalyptic way. I just mean that it's something we'll have to constantly be on the lookout for. Just like goodness is all around us, so is the darkness. We wouldn't even know the extent of how beautiful life could be if it wasn't juxtaposed with the bad."

Her words were so profound I was stunned. Grabbing my notebook, I jotted her statement down. "Can I use that in a book?"

Nancy shuddered with delight. She was probably my biggest fan. "Yessssss! I'd be honored."

"Trust me," I said with a smile. "The honor is mine."

"Anyhoo," Nancy said, still preening that I loved her idea. "Just like a bunch of small acts of kindness can make insurmountable differences in the world, removing small acts of darkness can do the same. Our job isn't to fix the Universe. It's to keep the balance."

Now everyone was stunned to silence. I smiled at our woowoo version of Confucius. "Nancy, you're freaking brilliant."

"You can use that too," she said with a giggle.

"I will," I told her. "And I think you're right. The very ugly darkness right in front of our noses is Jinny Jingle. Somehow we need to stop her."

"We have to find her first," Jess pointed out. "And let me add, we have no clue what she is capable of now that she has the woowoo mixed with darkness. She could be deadly."

"We also don't know if she's found others who have dark woowoo," Joy Parsley added ominously. "She could be creating a Shitbag Army as we speak.

The thought was appalling, but not out of the realm of possibilities.

"Jinny Jingle is stupid," Flip pointed out. "Stupid is dangerous. If brains were leather, she wouldn't have enough to saddle a June bug."

"You got that right," Ann Aramini agreed. "That hussy could throw herself on the ground and miss."

I began to pace my office. All the points were accurate, but Jinny Jingle might not be as stupid as we thought. My to-do list kept growing. While my characters couldn't actually affect anyone in the real world with their powers, their knowledge could come in handy—especially Clark Dark's. The werewolf was savvy and smart, and he had dealt with foes just as evil as Jinny Jingle in his previous adventures.

"No one approaches Jinny alone," I instructed. "In fact, it would be better if we stuck together in pairs or trios if we're not all together."

"Roger that," Joy agreed. "Sally, you and Ann will stay with me. I got plenty of room. Clementine and Flip are already living together. Jess, can you and Nancy shack up for a few days?"

Jess looked a little terrified, but nodded.

Nancy bounced up and down on the couch. "My husband is on a fishing trip with his buddies for a week. I'm single and ready to mingle."

"Mmmkay," I said with a laugh, watching Jess's expression turn from terror to abject horror. "We're not going to party—so to speak. We're going to protect each other."

"Of course," Nancy said, shaking her head. "What about work? I have to go into the office. Can't afford to lose my job."

"I can join you and use Mandy's office," Jess volunteered, realizing she was stuck. "I'll tell her my internet is on the fritz. She'll be cool with that."

"Rest of us are retired and Clemmy works from home," Flip pointed out. "This is a good plan. I like it. Jumper would be proud."

"She would?" I asked, surprised and delighted.

Flip winked. "Damn proud, little girl."

I smiled. The tingle that shot through me was reassuring. The future wasn't as comforting, but we had a plan. It was seriously vague, but we were working with what we had.

"Let's make Jumper even prouder," Ann Aramini suggested, looking out the window.

"If you're considering another topless romp around the cemetery, I'm going to have to say no," I told her.

Ann grunted out a laugh. "Nope. We've got visitors, and I think Jumper would be mighty pleased if we helped them."

"Visitors?" Jess asked, peeking outside.

"Seth and Cheeto have arrived," Ann Aramini announced, rubbing her little hands together. "It's time to get to work, gals."

I felt a little shaky. Not only had I explained Cheeto to Seth, Seth had confessed his feelings for me. Granted, it was through my smack-talking cat, but I felt off center about it all.

Too bad, so sad. Pushing the thoughts away, I had to focus on the right now. There was far too much at stake to be a dummy. Seth and I would deal with *Seth and me* at a later date.

A date in the far, far future.

CHAPTER NINE

"Have you seen my bazooms on the internet?" Joy Parsley demanded of Seth as he and Cheeto walked through the front door. "They're famous."

He clearly was unsure how to answer. I didn't blame him. The question was heinous.

"Can't say I have," Seth answered, looking to me for help. Joy was flat-out terrifying.

"Not to worry," she assured him, pulling out her phone. "Got a picture of them right here."

"Nope and zip it," I said to Joy as Cheeto took a running jump into my open arms.

The little girl was sporting her *look*. It was beautiful just like she was. She looked like a doll. Her eyes were an unusual cornflower blue and her blonde curls were a tumbled and adorable mess. Her tiara was placed haphazardly on her head and her pink and blue sparkly tutu went tremendously with her daisy-covered, orange t-shirt, purple shorts and red cowboy boots.

"Did you miss me?" she asked, covering my face in kisses.

"So much," I told her, happily accepting her greeting.

Seth had been correct. She didn't seem to be affected by what she'd seen go down in the parking lot. My relief was visceral, but I was very aware she could be suppressing her emotions. We would have to keep a close eye on her.

"Daddy believes in magic," she whispered in my ear.

"I know," I whispered back.

"Alrightyroo!" Flip said, taking Cheeto from my arms and hugging her close. "I want some of that sugar too."

Cheeto obliged and Flip danced them around the room as her beautifully wrinkled face got covered in sloppy kisses.

"Wouldn't mind a little sugar over here," Sally Dubay said with a wide smile.

"You got it," Cheeto shouted as she wiggled out of Flip's arms and dashed over to Sally.

Seth watched his daughter with an expression of grateful awe on his face. The man looked as if he might cry. It was moving and heartbreaking at the same time.

"She's going to be okay," I told him softly as Cheeto made the rounds and laid some sugar on everyone, including Thick Stella.

"Thanks to you, Clementine," he said, looking down at me.

I shook my head. "Nope. Thanks to you," I insisted. "Not everyone would open their mind to the impossible."

Seth sucked in a breath through his teeth. Unfortunately, the move was sexy. I tried to glance away. I couldn't.

"If you love someone enough, anything is possible," he said, staring straight into my soul.

Reality to Clementine. Do not plunge into the shark-infested waters. Instead of speaking, I nodded. I was getting better at deflecting.

"We might wanna go outside," Ann Aramini said, holding a giggling Cheeto upside down by her feet. "It would suck if we blew up the house."

"What exactly are we going to do?" Seth asked, alarmed.

"Not a clue," Flip told him, grabbing his hand and pulling him towards the front door. "That's gonna be up to Cheeto."

"Shit," he muttered under his breath as he let Flip drag him outside.

Joy Parsley blocked my exit from the house. If she showed me the picture of her bazooms, I was going to let her have it. "You got five beers?" she asked.

I squinted at her. It wasn't even noon yet. "Why?"

"Need to tie one on to go invisible," she replied like I was a dummy.

"Right," I said with a shake of my head. "In the fridge. Help yourself."

"This is going to be out of control," Jess said, following me out of the house.

"Possibly," I agreed.

"Umm... I'm going to go with definitely," she said, pointing at an airborne Sally Dubay.

I winced. There were a lot of trees in my yard. Crossing

my fingers that she didn't nail one and have to go to the hospital, I held my breath and watched.

Sally came close to smashing into a branch on the huge oak, but miraculously she missed. My yard was normally peaceful and serene. Standing in the grass barefoot was poetry to my soul. The spring air smelled sweet and the butterflies danced on the array of colorful flowers. I wasn't sure what the birds, bees and butterflies made of the flying ninety-year-old woman invading their space, but I was kind of mystified.

Cheeto was mesmerized. Seth looked terrified. Nancy and Jess were amazed. Everyone else was used to it.

"Yay!" Cheeto squealed as Sally turned flips in the air.

Sally wore bright blue granny panties with white polka dots on them under her housedress. It was bizarrely and inappropriately adorable.

"Can I try?" Cheeto asked Seth.

Seth was at a total loss and very much out of his comfort zone. I was impressed he hadn't grabbed his daughter and hauled ass out of here. He was trying hard to make sense of what he was seeing. It wasn't every day that a ninety-year-old woman *literally* flew by.

"I don't know," Seth choked out. "Looks kind of dangerous."

Sally almost clipped a car as she dipped down to show off.

"Keep your idiot butt in the air," Ann Aramini bellowed. "We don't have time for you to concuss yourself today."

"Good plan," Sally yelled, zooming higher.

"Daddy, please, can I try?" Cheeto begged.

Seth shot me a glance filled with uncertainty. "Is that smart?" he asked me.

I didn't know. Looking to Flip, I raised my brows in question.

"Let the little one try," Flip said. "Best we know what she can do. That way we can help her control it. She might not even be able to fly."

"Pleeeeease, Daddy?" Cheeto asked with a huge grin on her face.

Seth inhaled deeply and blew it out slowly. He was doing great for only knowing about woowoo juju less than twenty-four hours. "Yes," he forced out with a weak smile. "You can try."

Cheeto screamed with excitement and kicked off her cowboy boots. Taking a running sprint, she launched her little body into the air and joined a delighted Sally Dubay.

"Holy heck on a sharp stick," Joy Parsley shouted as she downed her beer. "Look at her go!"

Sally and Cheeto soared through the air. It was beautiful and kind of scary. The backdrop of the bright blue sky dotted with puffy white clouds made me feel like I was watching a movie with incredible special effects. However, this wasn't a movie. It was very real. Twice Cheeto ran interference and kept Sally from slamming into my house.

"She's better at flying than Sally," Jess commented with a laugh and a shake of her head.

Seth turned in surprise at the sound of Jess's voice. Clearly, he hadn't realized she was here. The man had been a little distracted since he'd arrived. Seth had been best friends with Jess's brother during high school and I was pretty sure he still was.

"Oh my God, you're a witch too?" he asked, stunned while still keeping an eye on his flying daughter.

"A witch?" she asked with an evil little glint in her eye.

Seth held up his hands and laughed. "No, no. My apologies. I meant badass bitch."

"Much better," Jess said with a grin. "And yes, I am a badass bitch witch."

Seth clearly wanted to ask more questions, but was treading lightly.

Jess rolled her eyes. "I only found out recently. I thought I was going nuts for a few years," she explained.

Seth paled and pulled her in for a hug. "You're okay?" he asked, concerned. "For real?"

Jess glanced up at the man she considered another brother and gave him an odd look. "I'm good. I promise."

Jess clearly didn't understand Seth's unease, but I did.

Seth nodded and released her. "So, what do you do?" he asked.

Jess shrugged and laughed. "You really want to know?"

Seth paused a moment, then dove in headfirst. "Yes, I really want to know."

"I can knock down trees and stuff with my hands and I can transport short distances."

He closed his eyes and nodded. "I see."

"Actually, you don't," Jess said, punching him in the arm. "Do you want to?"

Seth waved at a thrilled Cheeto as she zipped by. "I don't know. Do I?"

"You do," I assured him. "It's incredibly cool. Cheeto, can you come down to the ground for a sec?"

"Do I have to?" she asked, hovering in the air.

"Yes," Seth said sternly. "If you're going to try new things you have to listen to the instructions."

"Okay, Daddy," Cheeto called out cheerfully as she lowered herself to the ground.

Sally's landing wasn't half as graceful. She landed with a thud and a scream in my vegetable garden.

"Mighta squished your broccoli plants," she yelled as she got to her feet.

"No worries," I told her, happy that the only thing that got *squished* was a vegetable. Sally was the cutest woman alive and she was a complete menace in the air.

"I'll get you some new plants," she promised as she joined back up with the group. "What's next?"

"I'm going to transport," Jess announced.

"I'm so dang excited for this," Flip said, clapping her hands. "Never seen ya do it."

"What does transport mean?" Cheeto asked, perched on Seth's shoulder.

Jess smiled at her. "It means I can move from one place to another without walking there."

"Like this?" Cheeto asked, disappearing from Seth's shoulder and ending up standing right next to Jess.

"Umm… yep," Jess said with huge eyes. "Just like that."

Seth sat down on the ground. My knees felt a little weak too, but I stayed on my feet. Cheeto was freaking powerful.

"Wanna do it together?" Cheeto asked Jess.

"Sure, hot stuff. How about we transport to the garden,"

Jess suggested, pointing to the white picket fence around my vegetable garden. It was about a hundred feet away.

"Yes!" Cheeto yelled, taking Jess's hand. "Ready."

"Set," Jess said.

"GO!" Cheeto shouted.

In the blink of an eye, they disappeared and landed safely right beside my garden.

"Shit," Seth muttered. "Hide and seek just went straight to hell."

I laughed. He had a point.

"We got a big one on the line," Ann Aramini muttered.

She was right. Cheeto's arsenal was large, and I had a feeling there was more.

"Get your bahookies over here," Flip told them. "I want to test a few theories."

"Safely," Seth said, trying to sound like he wasn't internally losing his shit.

"Always," Flip promised him. "Not a hair on that child's head will be harmed under my watch."

"Thank you," Seth said, slightly less tense.

He was being an incredibly good sport and very brave considering the impossible insanity he was watching.

"Cheeto, do you wanna know what I can do?" Flip asked.

Cheeto stared at Aunt Flip with a big smile on her face. "Yep."

"Well, one of the things isn't real showy," she said, squatting down in front of Cheeto. "I can tell if people are sick inside their bodies. And then I can help them if they are."

"That's beautiful," Cheeto said, touching Flip's cheek

with reverence. "Am I sick inside? Lots of doctors said I was."

I could literally feel Seth's body tense with fury, and I wasn't even beside him anymore.

"No, darlin," Flip said, looking straight at the child. "You are not one bit sick inside. I promise you that. Them doctors you saw just didn't understand you like I do."

"I'm special," Cheeto whispered. "My daddy says so."

"Your daddy is correct," Flip whispered right back. "Wanna see what else I can do?"

"Umm… is that a good plan?" I asked, a little worried that Cheeto seemed to be able to copy everyone's gifts. Flip started fires. We might want to wait on that one.

"It's a very good plan," Flip said. "If the baby has that in common with me, better we know and teach her how to use it."

"What exactly can you do, Flip?" Seth asked warily.

"Watch," she said with a wink. "It's handy on a campin' trip."

Flip had piled up some paper and twigs on the driveway and surrounded the pile with rocks. I had to hand it to her, she definitely made sure it was safe and contained.

"You think I can set that on fire?" she asked Cheeto with waggling eyebrows.

Cheeto clasped her hands together in excitement and bounced up and down. "I think you can do anything in the world, Flip. You are magic!"

Flip slapped her thighs and laughed with delight. "You got a real high opinion of me, child. I'm mighty flattered. Watch and learn."

Flip stared at the pile. Within seconds, the paper began to smoke and a fire followed immediately.

Seth gasped. Cheeto cheered. I still wondered if this was a good idea.

"Can I try?" she begged.

"Sure can," Flip said, leading her over to a second little fire pit that she'd created on my driveway. "Go for it."

Cheeto scrunched her little nose and stared at the pile of twigs and paper. After about three minutes of concentration, a few sparks popped. A thin plume of grayish-blue smoke wafted up, but there was no fire.

"You got the gift," Flip said, hugging the little girl. "Gonna take a while to hone it though. I need you to make me a promise."

"What's that?" Cheeto asked.

Flip went nose to nose with her. "You can never, ever, ever, ever, practice this unless I'm with you. No ifs, ands or buts about it. Clear?"

"Yes!" Cheeto said, kissing Flip's nose. "I promise."

"That's my little woowoo juju girl," Flip said with a giggle. "Let's keep goin'!"

Ann Aramini moved the flower pots on my front porch with her mind. Cheeto did the same. Ann thought she should hold off on shifting. Apparently, the first time she shifted it took her a week to go back to being human. Everyone agreed that getting a child stuck in an animal form was a bad plan. Seth was speechless and just kept nodding his head spastically.

Jess picked up the front end of her car. Cheeto one-upped her and lifted the front end of her father's SUV. Seth got up from the grass then as if he was going to bolt. Joy Parsley slapped him on the back and handed him a beer. He stared at it for a long moment, then popped the tab and took a healthy sip as he walked over and stood next to me for what came next.

Nancy explained that she could talk to people who had moved on. Cheeto was fascinated, but there were no dead hanging out in my yard to test if that was in Cheeto's bag of tricks. I told her about my characters and Thick Stella. She loved that I had a talking cat. However, my fat furball was napping somewhere so that was another untested theory at the moment. I was a little worried about Thick Stella's vocabulary around a child. I'd have a discussion with my profane feline before we figured out if Cheeto could hear her too.

And then it was Joy Parsley's turn. The old gal was buzzed and ready.

"Now this one is gonna have to wait until you're twenty-one," Joy told Cheeto tipsily.

"Why?" Cheeto asked.

"Cause you need beer, and I will whoop your cute little butt if I catch you drinking any booze before you're of legal age."

"Got it," Cheeto said with a giggle. "What are you gonna do?"

Joy Parsley grinned and took a wobbly bow. "I'm gonna render myself invisible."

"Is she nuts?" Seth muttered under his breath.

"Completely," I told him quietly. "But she can make herself invisible after a few brewskies."

He shook his head and laughed. "I'm glad we have to wait for Cheeto to try this one."

"Word," Aunt Flip agreed with him. "Don't need a seven-year-old disappearin' on ya."

"Do we need to stand back?" Nancy asked, concerned. "I don't wanna go invisible too. I have enough going on with menopause."

"Nah," Ann Aramini assured her. "Only Joy vanishes. However, if you stand behind her nosey, tattling butt, it will seem like you're invisible too."

"Really?" I asked, surprised.

"Yep," Joy said, taking one last sip and letting out a long, unladylike belch. "Flip, stand behind me."

"Roger that," Flip said, hustling over and situating herself behind Joy.

"Ready?" Joy bellowed, very much feeling her beers.

"Whenever you are," Jess said with a laugh.

It was all kinds of wild and unreal. I'd never seen her do it. Heck, part of me didn't believe she could do it.

I was wrong.

Joy blinked her eyes, and she was gone.

Seth gasped. Sally and Ann cheered. Jess laughed. Nancy squealed with delight, along with a very impressed Cheeto. I simply stood with my mouth agape as seriously terrible ideas raced through my brain.

"Aunt Flip," I called out. "Are you still behind Joy?"

"Now I'm not," Flip said, stepping into view.

"Go behind her again, please," I instructed.

Flip did and she disappeared before our eyes again.

"How are you finding her if you can't see her?" I asked, approaching them.

"For the love of stupid questions," Joy grunted. "I might be invisible, but I'm still here."

Far be it from me to forget how pleasant Joy Parsley was.

"Yessiree! I can feel her," Flip announced, peeking out from behind Joy.

I laughed. She looked like a floating head since the rest of her body was still obscured.

"I'm holdin' on to Joy, so I can find her," Flip explained.

I nodded and bit down on my lip. "How long can you stay invisible?"

"Couple of hours," Joy said. "Why?"

"Just getting the particulars," I replied cagily.

"Not buyin' it," Flip said, popping out from behind Joy. "What's brewin' in that mind of yours, Clemmy?"

"A plan," I replied, wondering if I had the guts to carry it out.

"A bad one?" Jess asked, coming up beside me.

"Probably," I admitted.

"I'm in," Nancy announced.

"I'm in too," Ann Aramini chimed in.

"I'm always up for a crappy plan," Sally Dubay assured everyone with a giggle.

Jess paused and gave me the side eye. "I'm in."

"I'm in all the way," Flip announced. "I always say if you can't run with the big dogs, you better stay under the porch. I'm runnin' with the big dogs now!"

"I'm in," Cheeto yelled. "Please let me be in too."

I turned to her and picked her up. "The best thing you

can do right now is take care of your daddy. He just learned about how special you are and how special the rest of our group is. I think he might need some tender loving care from his favorite girl."

Cheeto considered my suggestion, then grinned. "I can take very good care of my daddy! I'll tell him a story and then run my tiny little cars up and down his back like he likes. Is that a good idea?"

"It's an excellent idea," Seth said, giving me a grateful glance, then taking his little bundle of energy out of my arms. "How bad is your plan? Is it a night-in-the-pokey kind of plan?"

"Only if I get caught," I told him with a wince.

Seth closed his eyes and sighed loudly. "You have my number. Call me if you or any of the ladies need to be bailed out of jail. However, I'd like to put it out there, it wouldn't look real good for you to get arrested right now."

"Fine point. Well made," I told him. "I'll call you later. I promise. And it won't be from jail. Good?"

He chuckled. "Good as it can be, I suspect. Ladies, thank you for an illuminating and slightly traumatizing afternoon." He glanced at Cheeto, who was falling asleep on his shoulder. "There are not enough words to show you my gratitude. My child is my world. I'm forever in your debt."

He ended his speech staring straight at me. My heart thumped in my rib cage and I just smiled. There was a lot that I would love to say to Seth Walters, but it would have to wait.

Timing was everything. And this was a bad time.

"You *will* call me," he said with a raised brow.

"I will call you."

And I would. That part would be true. I just hoped the other thing I'd told him would hold true as well. It would be pretty damned embarrassing to call him from the police station.

•

CHAPTER TEN

CLARK DARK WAS HESITANT.

Mina was not. Although, the witch was rarely cautious. She was more of a throw it at the wall and see if it stuck kind of gal. Of course, if things didn't go her way, she usually incinerated the problem.

My two characters had shown up shortly after Seth and Cheeto had gone home. They had found no trace of Jinny Jingle. That was bad news. However, I had a crappy plan to try to get Darren to admit the truth. If he did, the police would have to search for her with intent. As of right now, she was only a person of interest.

I was very interested in where she was and what she was up to.

"I think it might work," Mina said with a shrug. "Long shot, but I've seen many long shots work in my time."

Mina was a badass with an attitude through and through. She was the witchy heroine from my Magic and

Madness series and she dressed to kill. Today she wore a fabulous black Prada minidress and combat boots. Mina's wild red hair was twisted into a messy knot and her eyes glowed a glittering gold. She was breathtaking.

"Not so sure," Clark said, nibbling on the end of a pen and rocking back and forth on his feet. My favorite werewolf detective was in his customary rumpled dark suit with a splotch of mustard on the lapel. "If Clementine is caught in the hospital room it spells disaster."

"What if I don't get caught? I'm going to hide myself behind Joy Parsley. No one will see me except Darren," I told him. "What if I can get him to come clean after he hears the recording of what his gal pal really thinks of him?"

"Risky," Clark replied, taking notes as usual. "He wouldn't turn her in after she tried to kill him. What makes you think hearing her speak disparagingly of him will change his mind?"

"Desperation on my part," I said with a weak laugh. "If I can get the jerk to tell the truth, the cops will be after the Weather Hooker. We can't find her now. She's the darkness we're searching for. Jinny Jingle is the one we have to stop."

Clark sighed and Mina perched on the edge of my desk.

Mina hissed in annoyance. "We can't find her. I sense that she's in town, but she's hiding herself well."

I groaned and glanced over at the woowoo gals, who were silently sitting on the couch in my office waiting to hear what my characters had to say, except for Joy Parsley. The five beers had done her in, and she had fallen asleep.

"Clark, you're the smartest detective in the world," I told him, wanting him to support my bad plan. "You've been in situations far more complicated and came out without a scratch on you. Your mind is a steel trap of brilliance. Granted, you're a werewolf and I'm not, but I'm at a loss as to how to move forward. I think if I just do something it'll lead us toward figuring out what to do next."

"Listen to your words, Clementine," Clark said kindly.

"What do you mean?" I asked, confused.

Mina laughed. "Do you recall the time I was surrounded by warlocks who wanted to use me as a blood sacrifice and rule the magical world?"

"Of course, I do," I said, getting frustrated. I didn't really have time to reminisce about the good old days. "Is there a point to the conversation?"

"Always," Mina replied. "How did I get out of it?

I sighed and went along for the ride. My people tended to be kind of cryptic. "You used your powers to plant thoughts in their heads that made them turn on each other. They annihilated each other. It was gnarly."

"Ohhhh, I loved that book," Nancy chimed in from the couch. She was the only one who could see and hear my characters like I could.

I nodded at my sweaty buddy. She probably knew my novels better than I did.

"I used the truth," Mina reminded me. "The thoughts I planted were all true."

"The truth is always stronger and stranger than fiction," I said absently.

Clark took my hand and squeezed it gently. "Do you remember when I had to take down the cartel of lion shifters who were trying to infiltrate the human government and expose the shifter world?"

I nodded and smiled. "I do."

"How did I solve the issue?"

I didn't recall. I'd written a lot of books. Looking over at Nancy, I silently asked her for help.

"I've got this," she assured me, winking at Clark Dark. "Clark revealed the duplicitous nature of the alpha lion shifters to their pride. He left unmistakable clues in the hands of the most bloodthirsty members. My God, when Sheena, the mate of the dastardly Manfred, found out that he had banged half the pride, she went nuts. I still have mini nightmares about her clawing his face and scarring him for life in the war room. Never underestimate a female lion shifter scorned."

Clark searched my eyes. It was very clear I still wasn't following the clues.

"To put it in simple terms, I revealed the weaknesses of the weak, and let the righteous course of nature take care of the problem. Sheena took her mate down in front of the tribe and metaphorically castrated him."

"Umm... she did that literally too, if I remember correctly," I said.

"Yesssss, she did," Nancy added with a shudder of delight. "And she handed him his balls on a silver platter. I loooooved that part."

Clark chuckled. "I enjoyed that as well."

I expelled a loud sigh. "All of that was brilliant. It was well thought out and planned perfectly. Manfred was awful and he got what he deserved and you saved the shifter world. But that was you. I'm just me."

"Was it me?" Clark asked, raising bushy brow.

Mina's laugh bounced through the room. Clark observed me with great interest.

I felt like I'd just gotten smacked in the face. "It was me," I whispered. "I wrote that."

Clark's smile was so wide it had to have hurt his cheeks. I wasn't a werewolf. I wasn't a witch. I wasn't a vampire or a demon. I was an author who created deadly situations and got my characters out of them. In my stories, the good guys and gals always won. It was never easy. Easy was boring and no fun to read.

"Revenge is not in my plans," Mina said, grinning. "I usually have great faith that assholes will screw themselves."

I sat down. "I wrote that."

"You did," she replied smoothly. "Your mind is a warped and wonderful place to live."

"You think I can write my way out of this?" I asked, feeling tingly and unsure.

Clark Dark shrugged. "The author of the story controls the action... the players... and the outcome. It's up to you."

I squinted at him in surprise. "Have you met Rhett Butler?"

"Can't say I've had the pleasure," Clark replied.

Mina approached me and put her hands on my shoulders. "But you must remember, there are always consequences—and some will be grave."

The words were identical to the warnings from Rhett Butler and Scarlett O'Hara. I didn't buy that they hadn't met, but I wasn't going to push. It wasn't important, but clearly the words were. Words had power.

"I'm going ahead with my shitty plan," I told Clark and Mina. "I'm not plotting this story. I'm pantsing it. I figure if I just keep plodding ahead, the plot with come together by the end." At least, I hoped so. Otherwise, I was screwed.

"That's what you always do," Mina pointed out. "And in the end, it always works out."

"Always is a very attractive and definitive word," I muttered, wondering if I needed to physically start writing a new story to streamline my thoughts.

Mina's observation about my process was spot on. I never quite knew where I was going, but I always ended up somewhere. My books didn't work out so well when they were carefully plotted. Hell, my life didn't work out well when it had been carefully plotted, either. My marriage had blown up in my face. Everything traditional and normal I'd tried to do didn't end well. I wasn't normal.

Normal was for other people.

I was nuts. I had woowoo juju. I talked to imaginary people and made my living by telling their stories. My cat talked using horrible profanity and tried to gouge me daily. I loved her anyway. I was in a sorority of women who could do impossible things and I was proud to be a member. It was time to embrace the crazy. For real. It was time to rejoice in the unknown and write my own future. It would not be traditional. Orthodox was not how I rolled. The silver linings were there, I just had to write myself a sunny day so the clouds would part and reveal them.

I had no freaking idea how to actually do that, but worry

and indecision would get me nowhere. I was a forty-two-year-old woman of action. Or I was a forty-two-year-old woman about to bite it. It was only slightly comforting that if I died, I could come back and hang out with Nancy.

"We wouldn't exist unless you created us," Clark Dark said. "Nothing we have done would have happened if it wasn't for your imagination."

"But now... right now," I said, as a dark thought crept in like an insidious sticking point. "I didn't write this conversation."

"True and false," Mina said. "The words we're exchanging right now are not ones you wrote for us. However, you gave us the gift of being fully fleshed-out people. We have the ability to create our own futures, now, and speak our own minds to a certain degree. But that can change on a dime with a stroke of your mighty pen, my friend."

The responsibility was enormous and a little terrifying. I adored the characters who had burst into my life. I loved each and every one of them. They were like violent and socially unacceptable children to me. Well, Clark wasn't socially unacceptable. He was the most delightful and sweet man, who could shift into a killer werewolf, that I knew.

My head was a jumbled mess of thoughts—both good and bizarre. All the threads of a masterpiece were right in front of me. I just wasn't quite sure how to weave them together yet.

"We are all parts of you," Clark said sagely. "And you are part of us."

"Am I nuts?" I was glad Joy was sleeping so she wouldn't be tempted to answer.

"In the best way possible," Mina assured me.

I took that in and smiled. "Can I ask you something?"

Mina raised a perfectly plucked brow and waited.

The question was absurd and I had no business asking, but my writer brain wouldn't let it go. "Are you and Stephano a *thing*?"

She rolled her eyes so hard they should have gotten stuck in the back of her head. "Unfortunately, I banged the stupid vampire," she admitted with a groan.

"Ohhh, how was it?" Nancy asked, leaning forward.

Again, Mina rolled her eyes, but the saucy grin on her lips didn't lie. "It was surprisingly excellent. He's a fool, but he knows what to do with it."

"Interesting," I replied with a giggle. "Would you like me to write a mash-up series where you and Stephano actually have a real story?"

Her expression was one of horrified intrigue. Stephano was an idiot—a gorgeous dummy. But he was also a really good guy—albeit pretty violent. However, Mina was no shrinking violet.

"I'll think about it," she said breezily. "I'm quite unsure if the dumbass deserves someone as fabulous as me."

"I'd read the shit out of that," Nancy chimed in. "I think it would be riveting if you had a vampire/witch baby."

Mina wrinkled her nose. "Two problems there. One, his swimmers don't function since he's technically dead. Two, I would be seriously annoyed to ruin my stunning figure."

Nancy's brow creased in thought. It was kind of terrifying, but also fascinating. "I see where you're going with that," she said. "But there's a chance that his swimmers could work once a year—maybe on All Hallows Eve. And you don't have to worry about your figure. As a witch, you have incredible metabolism. Clementine could make a point of giving you an even better figure after you give birth to little Nancy. You know, your bosom could be bigger and sexier due to breast feeding."

"Little Nancy?" I asked with a laugh.

Nancy blushed and giggled. "Just a suggestion."

"You've clearly put some thought into this," Mina said, staring at Nancy like she was an alien.

"Nope, just pulled it out of my menopausal ass," Nancy replied. "I'm a little screwy."

I shook my head and grinned. "Nancy, have you ever considered writing a book?"

"Oh God, yes," she said, mopping her sweaty face. "I've started about a hundred of them."

"Then you are going to finish one of them," I told her. "I'll be your critique partner. It's time for you to let your crazy rip, my friend."

Nancy's mouth formed a perfect O. "You think I can?"

"You won't know until you try," I pointed out. "The only way to fail is not to try."

"Bingo," Clark Dark said. "That goes for you as well. Try, Clementine. I take back my hesitation. Bad plans can sometimes have advantageous outcomes."

I would have preferred the word always to sometimes, but Clark wasn't one to lie. Ever.

"Flip, can you check the fridge?" I asked.

"Sure, Clemmy. What am I looking for?"

"Beer. We need five more beers for Joy and then we're gonna go for it," I told her, hoping I sounded a little more confident than I felt.

"Woohoo!" Flip yelled as she hustled to the kitchen. "We're gonna have us an adventure."

Clark was smiling. Mina was as well. Sally and Ann were bouncing with excitement. Nancy was sweating profusely and Jess gave me a thumbs up. Thankfully, Joy woke up and no one had to rock, paper, scissors to see who would have the pleasure of disturbing her drunken nap.

It was time to get the tattling biddy buzzed again.

Chapter one, here we come.

CHAPTER ELEVEN

We waited until dark. Showing up during visiting hours was risky. It would be tricky enough getting me into Darren's hospital room without anyone noticing me. It would be more difficult to conceal myself from visitors. Hence, the after-hours mission.

Sally Dubay had gotten Darren's room number from her friend Honey Swartz who worked at the hospital. Every single move we were making leaned on the side of unethical and illegal, but it was a huge relief to be in cahoots with such well-connected gals. And when it was countered against what Darren had done and what the Weather Hooker could potentially do, I felt no guilt whatsoever.

Ann Aramini had come up with the B story. She'd suggested that one of our older members feign chest pains so that there was a reason they could be in the vicinity. I put a fast and decisive kibosh on that plan. Just in case anything we did in jest came true, I told them we needed an illness that wasn't deadly. In the end, Ann had volunteered herself to go in for constipation. Turned out she *was* constipated and was out of her meds to aid with her crapping problem—her words, not mine. She was lactose intolerant and refused to stop eating cheese and ice cream. So instead, every so often she would get a little something to clean out the poop shoot. Again, her words, not mine.

Jess was the getaway driver. We took my car since it fit all of us. Nancy wanted to steal some scrubs and walk around freely disguised as a doctor. There were so many plot holes with that, I cringed. Main one being that she knew everyone in town and everyone knew she wasn't a doctor. Nancy agreed to stay in the car with Jess. However, she had wired me up with a microphone and a digital recorder. None of us wanted to ask where she'd gotten the items, except for Joy. Joy Parsley was the nosiest person I knew. But I had to admit, I was relieved to learn that Nancy had purchased the surveillance equipment to see if she could record the voices of the dead, and not something more nefarious like spying on her husband.

So far, it hadn't worked for her as far as recording ghosts was concerned.

However, Darren wasn't dead, so as long as I could get him to talk, I had a shot at the plan working.

Flip and Sally planned to go in with the constipated Ann Aramini. That was not out of the ordinary as it was common knowledge that the women were close-knit. The hospital wasn't large and from what we'd learned from

Honey Swartz, Darren's room wasn't far from the emergency waiting area where Ann, Sally and Flip would be.

"One more beer," Joy announced as we pulled into the hospital parking lot and found a spot not too far from and not too close to the entrance.

"Down it," Flip instructed. "Here's what I say we do. Joy goes invisible. Clemmy gets behind her. When we get inside, Ann, you make a huge fuss about your poop shoot and draw all the attention to you."

Ann Aramini leaned forward and cased the parking lot. There was no one around. "I'm gonna start yellin' that I have a big one coming," she whispered. "A real blow-it-out-of-your-ass, come-to-Jesus kind of stinker."

I wasn't sure why she was whispering. It was only us in the car, but I went with it.

"Ohhh, I like it," Sally said. "We can run you to a bathroom. I'm pretty sure there's one near Darren's room."

"How do you know that?" Jess asked her.

"Sally hits a lot of stuff when she flies," Joy answered for her. "We take her into the hospital regularly."

"Got it," Jess said, shaking her head.

"Not to worry, sweetie." Sally patted Jess's shoulder. "I have very good bone density."

"Clearly," I muttered. "So, Joy and I will follow you towards the bathroom for Ann to talk to Jesus and then slip into Darren's room unseen."

Flip nodded. "That's the plan."

"Actually, I do have to take a dump," Ann added.

"The truth is overrated," Jess pointed out with a laugh.

"Ain't that a fact," Flip said with a chuckle.

"What's the deal when we get into the room?" Joy asked, punctuating her question with a loud burb.

"I play the recording of the conversation with the Weather Hooker and try to talk some sense into the asshole," I told her.

Nancy compressed her lips.

"What?" I asked.

"He can ring the nurse's station," she said. "Or use his cellphone to call for a witness and you'll be caught red-handed, which means you might be calling Seth from jail."

Shit. She was right. I'd promised Seth I wouldn't land in the pokey. I hoped I could keep my promise.

"Not a problem," Joy said. "I can remove both items and he won't see who did it. What I'd really like to do is shove them up his ass, but that seems to veer just a little bit from the ultimate goal."

"Yes, really far from the goal," I said, hoping she didn't take the story into her own hands once we got into the room. A phone and a contraption to alert the nurses lodged in Darren's ass wasn't in this chapter. Maybe in the epilogue, but not before we'd gotten to the happily ever after. Joy's wish for Darren was funny and well-deserved, but counterproductive.

I inhaled deeply. This wasn't fiction. It was real. I was incredibly grateful for any and all input right now—the electronics up Darren's ass notwithstanding. Normally, I wrote my stories without any input except my own imagination. This particular story was going to play out a little differently. It had to. We were a team. I might be the de facto leader, but I was lost without my woowoo juju gals.

"We ready?" I asked, feeling excitement course through my body.

"You're the heroine in your own book," Nancy said, squeezing my hands. "Go kick some ass."

From Nancy's mouth to God's ears, or possibly Jesus's ears since Ann was about to have a chat with him.

～

"I'm dyin'," Ann Aramini yelled as she stumbled into the empty emergency room with a frantic Flip and Sally right behind her.

Joy and I were trying to keep up without revealing I was hiding behind her. Joy's footing was a little off due to all the beers, but so far so good.

"Haven't crapped in a week," Ann moaned as two nurses ran out from behind the desk to aid her.

"Do you normally have blockage?" one asked, settling Ann into a wheelchair.

"She's lactose intolerant," Sally said, wringing her hands.

Flip looked like she was about to cry. Her hands were flapping and she was as distressed as I'd ever seen her. The old broads were damn good actresses.

"Do either of you know what she's eaten today?" the other nurse questioned, taking Ann's temperature.

Ann was moaning like she was dying. It was a little much, but the nurses seemed to be buying it. Joy and I inched toward the swinging door that led to the hospital rooms. When Ann went through it, we had to be prepared to follow. Since Joy was a little drunk, I figured the closer we got the better.

Flip pulled out a hanky from her monster-sized purse and dabbed at her eyes. "Well, she ate some cheese."

The nurse tsked. "How much cheese?"

"Probably about a pound," Flip said. "Then we went for ice cream."

"And nachos with extra cheese… and cheese pizza," Sally added. "We just feel awful."

"Not their fault," Ann grunted, rocking back and forth in the wheelchair like she was gonna drop dead. "I know better. My gut can't take it. And my ass is in for an explosion."

The younger of the two nurses bit back a laugh and did her best to stay professional. I detected a slight golden glow around her. We were going to have to approach her and get to know her very soon. I was pretty sure she had woowoo juju.

"HOLY SHIT! Pun intended!" Ann bellowed, jumping out of the wheelchair and throwing her hands in the air. "I think I can do it."

"Do what?" the older nurse asked, trying to get Ann to sit back down.

"I think an assquake is comin'," she announced to the thankfully deserted lobby.

"Oh my God," Joy muttered, trying not to laugh.

I pinched her. It wouldn't be a smart move to get busted when we were so close.

"Need to bust a grumpie," Ann yelled, wild-eyed. "Need a crapper."

The older nurse pointed to a bathroom on the far side of the waiting area—not in the direction of the hallway that led to where we wanted to go.

"Can't code brown in a public potty," Ann grunted and jackknifed forward in phantom pain. "Need privacy to evacuate the poop shoot."

"I know!" Sally said, grabbing Ann's hand. "I was in the hospital two weeks ago. There's a private bathroom right through that door."

"I'm sorry, you can't use that bathroom," the younger nurse said.

"You want me to make a deposit in the lobby?" Ann shouted. "Because I'm about to release the chocolate hostage."

"Please?" Sally begged. "She's serious. She will crank an eight ball right here in the waiting room."

The nurses exchanged horrified glances and quickly opened the door to the hallway. Joy and I slipped through, immediately followed by a constipated Ann and her buddies who were trying not to laugh.

Nancy had turned the recording device on in the car. I was happy as heck that I'd just recorded the entire poopy conversation. Jess was going to laugh until she passed out after hearing it.

"I'm comin' Jesus," Ann yelled as she sprinted to the bathroom and slammed the door. Sally and Flip paced the hall and created a distraction for Joy and I to move to the target.

Thankfully, the doors to all the patient rooms were open. God, all the little moving pieces of committing a crime were complicated. Not that I was actually committing a crime per se. I was just going to visit a dick who had accused me of attempted murder. And I was pretty sure he wasn't expecting me.

Quickly leading Joy into the room, I almost screamed when the door seemed to magically close behind me.

It wasn't magic at all.

It was a person. The very person we'd been looking for...

Moving Joy to the corner so I'd be hidden, I waited and held my breath. If the Weather Hooker could sense Joy and I were in the room, the jig was up. I had no clue what I would do, but I'd figure it out if I had to. After a few minutes of Jinny pacing erratically, I was pretty sure we were safe. Her only focus was the man in the bed who she'd tried to kill.

If Jinny Jingle had come to finish Darren off, I'd tackle her to the ground and hold her there until the cops showed up. Of course, that could backfire in about a thousand ways, but it was what my gut told me to do.

There was a chance both of them would try to pin it on me, but when the tire iron prints came back the bitch was screwed.

Darren looked like hell warmed over ten times and Jinny wasn't looking much better. Her bottle-blonde hair was tangled, and twigs and leaves were embedded in her 'do. She must have been hiding in the woods. She even smelled a little gamey.

"Oh, Honey Buns," Jinny gushed to a very wary Darren. "I am so sorry for hurting you. Can you ever forgive me?"

"Why?" Darren asked, sounding weak, whipped and pathetic. "Why did you do it? I love you. I've given you everything I have."

"I didn't mean to," she said as big fake crocodile tears rolled down her cheeks. "I was just so disappointed I'm not getting the house I had my heart set on. Surely you can understand, Snookie Pie."

Darren seemed torn and confused. I was shocked and appalled. He'd never been the sharpest tool in the shed, but he'd only been semi-spineless and ignorant when we'd been married. Now? Now he was an imbecile being led by his dick.

"Are you really sorry, Noodle Doodle?" he asked in a whiny tone.

"I am," Jinny promised, crossing her evil black heart. "I would never hurt my sexy hunk of man meat."

Her definition of *hurt* and mine were quite different. She'd almost killed Darren. If I hadn't stepped in, she would have. If that was a love pat, I'd hate to see what she thought real damage looked like.

"We're still getting married?" Darren asked, using a baby-talk voice that made me want to puke in my mouth.

"If you can get me the house, I am all yours," Jinny told him, rubbing her overly enhanced body against his.

"Baby Cakes," Darren said, grabbing one of her silicone boobs. "The divorce is done. The bitch got the house."

Jinny flashed her knockers at the weak piece of crap and giggled. "Not quite," she purred as she reached under the sheets and ran her hands over his tiny junk. "The judge has to stamp and sign the paperwork for it to be legally over. We have time."

Darren shook his head in confusion. However, he was getting a hand job. He had so few brain cells to start with, his puny erection redirected the ones he had left.

"Time to do what?" he choked out as Jinny's hand began to move faster.

"If she just happens to die, you'll get the house since you're still technically married," she said.

Darren had the decency to pale. "Umm… you want me to kill Clementine?"

It took everything I had to stay behind Joy. The only thing that kept me from stepping out and revealing myself was the fact I was pretty sure I would attack. While I could destroy people with words, I wasn't so sure I could do it with brute force. The Weather Hooker was half my age and she might be able to kick my ass now that she had magic. That would not end well for me. The buttercream icing on the shit pile of a cake was that I was recording all of this.

"Not necessarily *you*, sexy," she said, increasing her efforts to the point I was sure Darren's eyes were going to roll back into his head. "You have friends… who might be able to make it look like an accident. Don't you?"

"I don't know," Darren hissed, moving his hips and clearly getting close.

Jinny stopped. She left the repulsive imbecile hanging.

"If you want me, you will kill her," she snarled. "I trusted you. I loved you. When I make a promise, I keep it. I wish I could say the same for you."

Darren writhed in the bed. His blue balls were clearly getting the best of him. "I'll do it," he choked out. "I'll get you the house. I promise."

Jinny Jingle's giggle was shrill and would visit me in my nightmares. She was the basest human being I'd ever come across. Getting rid of her would be hard. I was hoping the law would help me out. Her incarceration would be a fine start to ending her reign of terror over me.

But first she had to get caught. The audio of this little meetup was going to be the cornerstone of her downfall.

I hoped.

Jinny gave Darren a passionate kiss, but refused to give the asshole relief. Walking over to the window she'd clearly entered through, she gave Darren what she assumed was a sultry gaze. She looked more constipated than Ann Aramini.

"I'll come back when she's dead. Make it happen this week." She flashed her black lace panties at him. "I can't wait to be together."

"Neither can I, baby," Darren whimpered. "I'll get you whatever your heart desires."

Pathetic.

"Promise?" she asked, crawling out of the window.

"Promise," he called out, sounding every bit the desperate loser that he was.

I knew for sure that hearing the conversation from the diner would have done nothing. Clark Dark was right about that. However, I'd struck gold.

Darren wasn't torn. Darren felt no guilt that he'd agreed

to kill me. If it wasn't for my aversion to spending the rest of my life in the pokey, I'd have strangled him right then.

The entire scenario before me felt like I was watching someone else's story. I wasn't. This was my life and it was a horror novel. Dispassionately, I watched as Darren picked up his cellphone and made a call.

"Are you in the area?" he asked.

I didn't hear the reply, but it was clear the answer was yes.

"Need you to come over here now and bring Brady and Kinter. I'm calling in favors," he said coldly.

My stomach clenched. Joy's body trembled with rage.

That son of a bitch had just called his cop buddies and was going to ask them to kill me. How was this my life? The silver linings were getting damned harder to see.

"We're staying," Joy said so softly I almost missed what she'd said.

Squeezing her back, I let her know I heard her and agreed. I prayed the recorder would get all of it. It wasn't the old school cassette kind. It was fancy and digital. Fingers crossed that it would get all the incriminating evidence we needed.

Hatred didn't even begin to describe what I felt for the man lying in the hospital bed. It was increasingly clear that I'd never known the asshole I'd been married to for so many years.

I smiled. Payback was going to be a bitch. Like a ten-to-twenty-year-stint-in-an-orange-jumpsuit bitch if I had anything to do with it. Clearly, he had some heavy stuff on his cop buddies if he thought they would murder me. Which meant Darren had been harboring illegal secrets.

He was a dirty cop, a filthy human being, and not nearly good enough for me. He never had been.

The plot kept twisting and the ending was not at hand. Whatever. I was excellent with a twist.

Bring on the bad guys. I was ready to rumble.

CHAPTER TWELVE

It was midnight. We'd gotten out safely and undetected from the hospital after Darren's cop buddies had stopped by. Only one of them had wanted nothing to do with Darren's murderous plan and left the moment my deceitful ex laid it out. The other two stayed. However, the plot had twisted majorly in my direction. There was a piece of news that almost made me shout with glee. Thankfully, I hadn't.

Joy literally shook with rage the entire time, but I now had enough evidence to bring down the head honchos of the police department along with my shitty ex-husband.

No one said a single word on the drive home. I was sure the expression on my face terrified everyone. Joy was scary on a good day. In the car, her fury was palpable. It took me a half hour of pacing the front yard under the light of the moon to cool off enough to talk.

"I called Seth," Jess said as I reentered my house and found everyone sitting silently in the living room.

"Why?" I asked, running my hands through my hair.

"Because Joy told us some of what went down," she replied.

"You listened?" I asked, closing my eyes and wishing all of this was a dream.

"Nope," Flip said. "We're waitin' for you, Clemmy. But I agreed with bringin' Seth in. Can't call the cops, most of 'em are dirty from the sound of it."

I nodded and flopped down on the love seat next to Jess. She immediately began to give me a tickly on my arm. My bestie knew how to calm me down.

"Joy, tell me the stuff you have on Lewis, Brady and Kinter again, please," I requested, leaning on Jess so my body didn't crumble and fall apart. I felt like I'd been mowed down by a truck.

"Lewis wears lacy panties," she ground out. Joy was still flipping furious. "Brady has a secret second family two towns over. Kinter eats dog kibble."

I sighed. "That's not going to do us any good."

"Don't need that crap anyway," Joy grunted, punching a pillow. "We got all we need on the tapes."

When the doorbell rang, I didn't have the energy to answer it. "Flip, can you let him in?"

"Sure thing, baby girl," she said, hustling over to the door.

Seth walked into the house with a grim look on his handsome face. He seemed stressed and agitated. Wait until he heard the recordings. He was going to lose it.

"Mandy's with me," he said tersely.

Mandy followed him into the living room and took in the occupants with a pale face and a confused and befuddled expression.

Seth held up his hands. "Mandy saw Cheeto fly," he said flatly. "Cheeto doesn't quite understand that her woowoo is a secret. Before I could make her understand it was classified information, Cheeto outed everyone."

I jumped to my feet and paled far more than my BFF. "Oh my God."

"Do you have alcohol?" Mandy asked in a hoarse voice. "I need alcohol."

"You want weed instead?" Flip asked, pulling out a tin of pot brownies.

"After the alcohol," Mandy told her with a weak smile.

"Roger that," Flip said, taking Mandy's hand and leading her to the couch. "Ann Aramini, get this gal a wine cooler."

"On it," Ann said, jogging to the kitchen.

It took two hours and four wine coolers to get Mandy somewhat up to speed about the magical world that existed around her and right under her nose. She took it far better than I'd expected.

"Wait," Mandy said, biting into a brownie. "You can fly like Cheeto?"

Sally giggled and nodded. "Actually, Cheeto is better in the air than I am. I tend to crash a lot."

"Understatement," Ann Aramini said with an affectionate pat on Sally's back.

"And you're a cat?" Mandy asked Ann with doubt written all over her face.

"Yep." Ann nodded. "And I can move shit with my mind. Wanna see?"

Mandy shrugged and laughed. It was only slightly hysterical. I was really proud of her.

"Sure. Why not?" she said.

Ann proceeded to rearrange all the lamps and candles in my living room with her mind. I couldn't believe it, but it actually looked better. When she offered to put everything back, I declined.

"Do you need to see anything else, dude?" I asked her with an apologetic smile.

"Think that's all I can take," she said. "But I might want to see more in the future."

"Deal," Jess said, handing Mandy another wine cooler. "You know, it might be a good thing that Mandy is here and that we don't have to hide anything."

Jess was right. Mandy was a shark in the courtroom. She struck fear into anyone who tried to out-argue her. She was freaking brilliant.

"Why's that?" Mandy asked.

"Because we have explosive proof that Darren hired some dirty coppers to kill my Clemmy," Flip announced.

Seth's eyes narrowed to slits and a few choice words that Thick Stella would have approved of left his lips. Mandy's eyes were even scarier. I was so happy to be on their good side.

"Word of mouth?" Mandy asked, putting down her wine cooler and pulling a pad of paper and a pen from her purse.

Seth pulled a small notebook from his pocket and gratefully accepted an extra pen from Mandy.

"Audio proof," I said.

"Hot damn," Mandy said. "Let's hear it."

"Wait," Seth said, eyeing me. "How did you get this proof?"

I hesitated for Mandy's sake, but she seemed okay with the crazy. Plus, there was no time to be careful. "Joy drank five beers and went invisible. I hid behind her and snuck into Darren's room. My plan was to play the conversation between me and the Weather Hooker to try to get him to realize she hated him and to make him retract his accusation."

"Did you play the conversation?" Mandy questioned.

"Never got the chance," I said.

"Nope," Joy grunted, rubbing her temples, obviously hungover from all the beers she'd downed today. "Got something way better."

"We were there too," Ann added. "I played like I was constipated."

"You actually were constipated," Sally reminded her.

"Still am," Ann admitted. "I was hopin' to drop the kids off at the lake when I was holed up in the bathroom, but no such luck."

"Real sorry about that," Flip said.

"Yeah, well, shit happens… or it doesn't," Ann said, cackling with laughter.

I smiled. I couldn't help myself. The people in the room were my silver lining despite the very dark clouds hanging over my head.

"Does that actually pertain to the matter at hand?" Seth asked with a wince.

"Nope," Ann assured him. "Just wanted you to get the full picture."

Seth chuckled. "Got it. Thank you."

Ann gave him a thumbs up. "Welcome. Such nice manners that boy has," she commented.

All the old gals nodded and smiled at Seth. The absurdity was laughable. The rest of what was going on... not as much.

"We have that part on audio as well," I said with a grin as Ann gasped, then started laughing again. "We'll save it for another time and get right to the incriminating sections."

"Smart," Nancy said, playing with the equipment and fast forwarding through the shitshow... pun very much intended.

Everyone listened in silence as Jinny and Darren had their conversation. It was unfortunately clear that he was receiving sexual favors. It wasn't pleasant to hear it again, but to get to the good stuff sometimes you had to trudge through the mud.

"She solicited your murder," Mandy ground out.

"And Darren agreed," Seth added, icily furious.

"We're taking them down," Mandy snapped, taking copious notes.

"To Hell," Seth muttered, making his own notes.

"Just wait, it gets better," Joy said, texting away on her phone a mile a minute.

I pressed pause and glanced over at Joy. "What are you doing?"

She raised a brow and huffed. "I know it won't make any difference in the big picture, but I'm letting the town council and the newspaper know that Lewis wears women's underpants, Brady practices polygamy and Kinter eats dog food. I'm just gettin' the ball rollin' for the big stuff comin'."

"I like it!" Sally announced with a giggle. "Serves them right to have their dirty laundry aired."

"It's about to get a whole lot dirtier," I said, pressing play.

Everyone sat back and listened. It was not a pretty story.

"I'm calling in my favors," Darren said coldly.

"You think so?" Lewis asked with a condescending laugh.

"I know so," Darren hissed.

"Yep, well, it's lookin' like the prints on the tire iron don't belong to your ex-wife," Lewis drawled. "Can you explain that, boy?"

"That's excellent news," Mandy interjected.

"Yep," I agreed. "Hold tight. The really bad stuff is coming up."

Darren sputtered. "It all happened so fast. Maybe it wasn't her. I think it might have been a man. Yes," he said, waffling. "It was a man. A large man. Never saw him before."

"So, the statement you made against Clementine Roberts was false?" Kinter asked coolly.

"I was in shock," Darren snapped. "I must have been confused. I was almost killed."

Brady cleared his throat. "You made the statement twenty-four hours after it happened."

"So what?" Darren yelled. "I have a concussion. Look at me. I came close to death. What do you expect?"

"I expect that we're gonna have to find Jinny Jingle and bring her in for questioning," Lewis said.

"She has an alibi," Darren quickly and viciously corrected him.

"She is my fiancée. I would think I would know if my fiancée tried to kill me. Don't you dare go after her."

"You tellin' me how to do my job, boy?" Lewis asked.

"Watch your tone," Darren warned. "Let me make this very clear. I made a mistake. It was a large man who attacked me. Not Jinny Jingle and not my ex-wife. I am calling the shots right now, boy. I'd suggest you behave accordingly."

"Call them," Lewis said, coldly. "While you might have something on me. I have plenty on you."

Darren laughed. It was unhinged. "Lewis, your wife cheated on you. You set up her lover and got the man falsely charged for murder by tampering with evidence. He's serving life. A murderer is running free and an innocent man is doing his time. Not a real good look."

"Fuck you," Lewis hissed. "You can't prove that."

"Are you sure?" Darren asked.

Lewis was silent.

"Brady," Darren went on smugly. "Besides having a secret family, you were the ringleader of the Ponzi scheme that bankrupted the town council and the school district. You set up senile old Jimmy Bunson to take the fall. Old geezer is doing ten years. He's gonna die in jail for your sins."

Brady swore under his breath.

Darren laughed. "Kinter, I got nothing on you except that you're now an accessory to the crimes of your brothers in blue. If you don't go forward with this knowledge, you may as well have committed the crimes. So, unless you want that outed, I'd suggest you play ball."

"Screw you, you loser," Kinter growled. "I heard nothing. I'm out of here. Fuck you and the fucked-up horse you rode in on."

The door slammed and now there were three.

"What do you want?" Lewis ground out.

"I need you to create an accident," Darren said emotionlessly.

"What kind?" Brady asked.

"A deadly one. Clementine Roberts needs to die in an accident within five days. If she doesn't, I'll go to the head of the force, the news, the FBI and the papers. If she does happen to befall a tragedy, all is forgotten."

There was silence.

"Do we have a deal, boys?" Darren asked.

There was more silence.

"Answer me," Darren snapped. "It would be such a shame for you to spend the rest of your days in prison."

"Deal," Lewis grunted.

"Deal," Brady snapped. "But I want some kind of guarantee that this is the only favor you're gonna call in."

"Guess you're just gonna have to trust me on that," Darren said. "Five days. Clementine Roberts dies within five days."

I hit the off switch and looked around the room. Everyone was shocked. What we'd just listened to was the plot of a bad made-for-TV movie. This kind of stuff didn't happen in real life... except it did. The kicker was that it was my life.

One by one, my characters arrived. First came Albinia and Clark Dark. Albinia was dressed to the nines in an over the top hot pink Regency gown and looked as if she'd been crying. Clark was very solemn. Mina and Stephano showed up together. Surprisingly, they held hands and walked quietly to the corner to watch the action unfold.

However, the most shocking was that Cassandra and her

stepdaughter Sasha arrived together. There was no love lost between the two demons. They were arch enemies in the series. Sasha was stunning as usual—long raven-back hair and a body that defied gravity. Both women wore Stella McCartney and looked as if they'd walked off the pages of a magazine. Sasha was my demon heroine in the Exotic series. She'd been furious that Cassandra had been redeemed in the latest installment—even threatened to leave the series over it. But now? Now they were getting along. That was almost more alarming than knowing Darren had blackmailed people into killing me. Something was afoot.

I'd deal with that shortly.

"I need a copy of that," Seth said. "Two hard copies. One to put in the safe at the office and one back up. I also need you to send me one via secure email. CC Mandy and my father as well. Can you do that, Nancy?"

"I can and I will," she replied.

"Excellent. Thank you. Clementine, I don't want you to leave the house. I'm hiring a security crew out of Louisville to protect you until this is over," Seth said in a voice that dared me to fight him.

I had no intention of putting up a fight. I was happy to have armed men and women who weren't on the local police force all over my property. "Thank you," I said.

"Welcome," he replied. "Mandy, you want to go after this? We have to move very quickly."

"On it," Mandy said, writing on her pad like a madwoman. "I'm going over their heads and taking it straight to the Kentucky Attorney General's office first thing tomorrow morning. I'm also reaching out to the FBI."

"Ohhh, I had relations with the Attorney General's pappy back in the day," Sally overshared. "If he gives you any trouble, I'll call his pappy. We're still friends on Facebook."

"Ooookay," Mandy said with a laugh. "Thank you."

"No worries," Sally told her with a sweet smile. "He was my partner at the nudist colony. Such a lovely man."

That caused about a minute and thirty seconds of silence. And then we moved on. Because we had to.

Flip raised her hand. "Are we allowed to know what we actually know?"

A shot of fear ripped through me. I'd written enough mysteries into my paranormal romances to know the answer to that one. "No," I said firmly. "Until they're behind bars, none of you know anything. Clear?"

"Roger that," Ann Aramini said. "In fact, I think we're all gonna stay right here until this shit blows over."

"Ummm…" I said, wrapping my brain around all the woowoo juju gals camping out in my house.

"Yeppers," Flip said. "We're gonna need the Goodness Army together. No telling what kind of bender the Weather Hooker is gonna go on when Darren gets busted."

Mandy stopped writing. "If Darren is out of the picture, he can't get the house. Therefore, she can't get the house."

"Until the decree is stamped and signed by the judge, it's not technically legal," I reminded everyone.

"Who's the judge?" Flip asked.

"Parker," Seth replied.

"Scooby Parker?" Flip asked with a hopeful grin.

Seth winced at the unfortunate name and nodded his head.

"Not a problem," Flip said with a whoop of joy. "He's one of my customers. Old geezer has glaucoma. Goes through my weed like a kid in a candy shop. I'll have a word with Scooby in the morning and get his ass moving on them papers."

Mandy's mouth was wide open. Seth ran his hands through his hair and looked up at the ceiling with a pained grin on his face.

"That's a little more info than we need, Flip," he said. "But I will gladly accept your offer to get the old geezer's ass moving."

"Happy to do my part," Flip said with a laugh.

"Another question," Mandy said. "What's a Goodness Army?"

"I'll take this one," Nancy said with a smile. "It's a group of woowoo juju practitioners who fight back the darkness."

Mandy scratched her head and nodded. "What's the darkness?"

"Right now, it's Jinny Jingle," I said.

"Yep," Joy grunted in disgust. "The black and decker pecker wrecker got her some woowoo. If you ask me, she doesn't have the juju to go with it, but she's a dangerous piece of trash."

Seth squinted at Joy in unhappy surprise. "I'm sorry, what? Jinny Jingle has woowoo juju?"

"She does," Sally said, fidgeting with her dress. "Got it when Clementine shot her with the stun gun. It was her external disaster. Darn tootin' shame."

"I understood very little of that," Seth said. "But are you telling me there are bad witches?"

"We prefer badass bitches, but yes," Jess explained.

"All children have the woowoo," Ann went on explaining. "For most it disappears naturally as they age. For some, like this nutty crew, it stays with us till the day we bite the big one. However, there are some who remember the woowoo and that they lost it."

"Yep," Flip said, walking around and handing out brownies. "And they're the dangerous ones. They'll do anything to get it back… and I mean anything."

"Got it," Mandy said, glancing over at me. "Why does she want the house so badly if she already has the magic back?"

I realized I hadn't considered that. "Not sure. Originally, it was because it's on a ley line."

"Ley lines can be very powerful for our kind," Sally said, biting into her brownie. "Helps us refuel so to speak."

I passed on the brownie. Being high right now wasn't on the agenda. I needed to talk to my characters when I got done with this conversation. "Are we more powerful on the ley line?"

"Good question, Clemmy," Flip said. "Ain't sure, but I'm gonna go with a yes. I always feel stronger in this house."

"Ditto," Joy added. "There's something magical here."

"And does Tiny Pecker know about the woowoo juju?" Mandy asked.

"He doesn't," I told her. "He's clueless."

"In more ways than one," Ann said.

Seth stood up and began to pace the room. His fists clenched at his sides and he swore under his breath. "I would love to kill him. He's an asshole who never deserved you." He let out a frustrated growl. "He should've spent every day figuring out how to make you the happiest woman alive. Instead, he—" He turned and met my gaze. "He never deserved you," he repeated.

I don't know if it was his tirade against Darren, his desire to see me happy, or just that he looked so flippin' hot when he was angry on my behalf, but I strolled over to him and I kissed him. I wasn't sure who was surprised more, me or him, but Seth accepted the invitation. He took me into his arms, his warm lips caressing mine in an insistent kiss that curled my toes. My lips tingled as the passion between us threatened to explode.

The entire room applauded—even my characters. The outburst was as effective as someone throwing a bucket of cold water on me.

"Umm… okay," I said, a little mortified and at the same time wanting so much more.

"Sorry," Seth said. His dazed expression was anything but sorry.

"Don't be." I put a little distance between us. "Totally my bad."

"Look," he said with a grin that made me laugh. "I understand that the timing sucks. But you know how I feel. I'll respect whatever boundaries you want to throw up, but I'm also okay anytime you want to cross those boundaries."

I nodded and touched my still tingling lips. "I know I'm the one who crossed the line, and that's not fair to you." Especially when he'd already said he was in love with me. Well, he'd confessed it to Thick Stella, anyhow. Still, my libido might be ready for more, but I wasn't sure the rest of me was. "Please don't get frustrated with me, but it's going to take me a little more time," I warned him. "I just can't jump into something new before the ink's dry on my divorce papers." I stepped toward him and put my hand on his cheek as I met his gaze. "But when I'm ready," I said softly and with complete sincerity, "it's going to be you." Staring up at him, I was fairly certain it always had been. "I hope you can wait."

Seth gave me a reassuring smile and nodded. "I've been waiting since high school. What's a little more time?" He placed his hand over mine and squeezed. "And speaking of time, it's two in the morning. We all have a big day tomorrow. I say we call it a night."

"I second that," Joy said, standing up. "I've got one mother humper of a headache."

"I'll show you gals to the guest rooms," Flip volunteered. "We're gonna have a slumber party!"

Jess elbowed me as she followed after the woowoo gals and Mandy—who I was pretty sure wasn't sleeping over—as they headed out of the living room to give Seth and me a moment alone.

"It's about time," my BFF said out the side of her mouth. "You've been hot for that man since forever. Don't blow it."

"Oh my God," I said on a nervous laugh as she exited the room.

"Hot for me since forever, huh?" Seth asked with a grin.

I closed my eyes and sighed dramatically. "I guess you're not the only one who's been carrying around a torch since our teens."

Seth glanced around. "I'm really not sorry you kissed me, Clementine. I've been dying to do that for a long time. And I really hope that I don't have to wait another quarter of a century for it to happen again."

A giggle escaped me and I tried to dial back the giddiness. "Seth, not going to lie, that was the best kiss I've ever had. But I still need to go slow. I'm into this... Into you, but I'm also into finding out who I am on my own."

He nodded and took my hands in his. "I get it. I don't love it, but I get it. I'm a patient man, and I'll go as slow as you need."

God his lips were so sexy that I wanted to kiss him again. But I didn't. Because while my body and lips were like yes, yes, yes, my brain was a total party-pooper. "Thank you," I told him.

"Welcome," he replied. "However, my lips are available twenty-four-seven if you want to stick your toe over the line again." He waved his hand with a slight flourish. "Just putting it out there."

"Good to know," I said with another embarrassingly girly giggle.

He turned to leave, and my eyes dropped straight to his perfect jeans-covered butt.

"You're looking at my ass," he said without turning around.

"Possibly," I admitted.

"Like what you see?"

I nodded my head and laughed. "It's okay."

"Not half as good as yours," he shot back as he walked out the front door and into the night.

I was in so much trouble. But, frankly, Seth Walters was exactly the kind of trouble I wanted to be in.

CHAPTER THIRTEEN

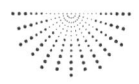

"The answer is no," I said firmly as my stomach roiled. I kept my voice down so I wouldn't wake up the woowoo juju gals.

Clark Dark smiled at me in such a loving and fatherly way, it made my eyes tear up. This felt more like a terrifying and tragic ending rather than a ridiculous and silly middle-of-the-night meeting with my characters.

I'd been correct about Albinia's tear-stained face. She'd been crying. She was still crying. I had no clue what the consequences of what my characters were suggesting might be, but my gut told me they wouldn't be good.

Cassandra pulled out a cigarette and eyed me expectantly. I waved my hand at her and rolled my eyes. "Go ahead," I said, giving up. Right now, I didn't care if she smoked. Hell, I thought about asking her for one, and I'd never smoked in my life.

Stephano plucked the cigarette from Cassandra's fingers

and broke it in half. She flipped him off, pulled another out of her Prada clutch and fired it up.

"I think Clark Dark is correct," Stephano said. "You have to do it, Clementine. There are too many unknowns. If the darkness wins, our fates are sealed. If you die, we die with you. If we can help you, no matter the outcome, we live on through you. It seems fairly simple to me."

"Is the world ending?" I asked, feeling a little hysterical.

Sasha stood up and peeked out of the window into the dark night. "As far as I can tell, no," she said. "What makes you ask?"

Picking apart the brownie that I'd refused to eat, I sighed. "Stephano sounded like an adult who makes sense. That's just all kinds of wrong. There wasn't one reference to a female body part. I don't like it."

Mina threw her head back and laughed. "It is a bit bizarre that there wasn't mention of a sweaty shag."

"Or a juicy bottom," Sasha added with a grin.

"Or bouncing knockers," Albinia chimed in with a small smile as she swiped at a tear.

Stephano took a bow. A very naughty smirk pulled at his full lips. "While I appreciate the hero worship of my newly found maturity and mastery of the English language, this chatter about bottoms, shagging and bouncing melons is giving me a raging boner."

"Oh my God," Cassandra said, lighting up a second cigarette. "You are socially unacceptable, vampire."

"Thank you," Stephano replied gallantly.

"And brain damaged," she added with a huff and a smile she couldn't hide.

"Again, thank you," he said, winking at her. "But back to the matter at hand, which is truly an erection deflator. I think there is no choice."

"There's always a choice," I pointed out. "No story has to have only one ending. There are always millions of roads that can be taken. I never know how a book will end until I get there."

"That's the point," Sasha said, removing the lit cigarette from Cassandra's lips and taking a drag. She blew out a thin tendril of bluish-gray smoke, then coughed. "Think about that."

I squinted at her in surprise. "You don't smoke."

"Obviously," she said with another cough, handing the lit cig back to Cassandra. "Today I do."

Thick Stella waddled in and rudely examined our guests. Flopping down on the floor in the middle of the living room, she extended her back leg and had a go at her privates.

Stephano sighed dramatically. "I so wish you'd given me more flexibility."

"What?" I asked, nudging my cat with my foot. She was disgusting. "Why?"

"If I were a contortionist, I could blow myself," he replied as if that was a normal thing to say. "It would have saved me from banging quite a few unsavory women. Although, I'm so talented with fornication, I completely understand why my sexual prowess was so appealing to the readers. I helped you sell millions of books with my active rod."

There was the vampire I knew.

"I completely regret banging you," Mina snapped. "You're a horse's ass."

Stephano placed his hand over his non-beating heart and dropped to one knee. "My gorgeous witch, never have I shagged a woman as beautifully bendable as you. The way your legs go over your head is truly astounding. You have ruined me for all others. You are the sole cause of the party in my pants. My trouser snake is yours to command from this day forth."

Mina laughed. Clark's chin dropped to his chest, and he groaned. Sasha and Albinia applauded the profane verbal love letter while Cassandra simply rolled her eyes and continued to chain smoke.

"That was a lot," I said, shaking my head.

"Thank you," Stephano replied. "I wanted to be clear."

"You were," I told him. "Abundantly."

The vampire nodded with satisfaction. "Mina, and Mina alone, is the cause of the angle in my dangle. And you can use that in a book if you want."

Pressing my lips together so I didn't scream with laughter, I simply nodded at the idiot. I wouldn't be using that line in a book. Ever.

"Ass sweater," Thick Stella grunted, taking a pause from her *bath*. "Two things. Firstly, since you put the litter box outside, and my backside is too large to fit through the fucking cat door, I took a shit in your closet. I just wanted to put that out there. It's your fault, not mine."

I closed my eyes. Rehoming Thick Stella sounded like a good plan. However, I *had* forgotten to bring the darn litter box back inside. "The second thing?" I asked, hoping it wasn't another shit report.

"You need to open your ears, butt canoe," she said, flopping onto her back and displaying her goodies to all. "If you bite it, I don't get tuna. If I don't get tuna, I'll crap all over the damn house. However, if I don't have food in my belly, I will poop runny butt bombs and that is much more difficult to clean up than a nice firm BM."

"That didn't make sense," I told her. "If I'm dead, I won't have to clean up your butt bombs."

Thick Stella rolled her eyes and hissed at me. "You're missing the point, douche sphincter," she informed me. "All shit references aside, if you're pushing up daisies, we're all screwed."

"While I would use entirely different language, the cat has a point," Clark said, shooting Thick Stella an amused glance. "Please let us do this for you. We wouldn't exist without your wild and wonderful imagination. The very least we can do is ensure that your imagination isn't wiped off the face of the earth. It might not work. And it will not necessarily be all of us who can aid you."

I stared at the werewolf. "But if I do this, won't I wipe *you* off the face of the earth?"

Clark didn't have an answer. None of them did. All of the ironies were too hard to bear. When they'd shown up, I thought I was crazy—that I'd gone and lost my mind. I could see, could talk to, and could touch imaginary people —characters born of my imagination. Impossible?

No. Not impossible.

In the short time they'd been physically with me, I'd grown to love them even more than I had when I'd first written them down on paper. Creating a character was like having a baby—something I would never do in my *real* life. I'd missed that boat this go-round. Hence, these people were my children—my beautiful, naughty, fully fleshed-out, violent and socially unacceptable, in Stephano's case, children. Clark wanted to put me into a *Sophie's Choice* sort of situation.

I didn't think I could do it.

Albinia's sniffles drew me out of my chaotic thoughts and back into my strange reality.

"Why are you crying, Albinia?" I asked.

She was an emotional gal, but I'd never seen her so upset—not even when Horace had cheated on her with the costermonger.

She dabbed at her eyes with her hot pink hanky, then blew her nose. "I'm going by Allhoohoohaha now," she said through her sniffles.

I couldn't keep track of all the name changes, but she was trying to find herself. I understood that completely and would call her whatever she wanted me to call her.

"My bad. Why are you crying, Allhoohoohaha?"

"Because I have no barking irons to defend you," she sobbed. "I am just an incomparable who can't even get yonked. I am quite dicked in the knob and feel desperately mawkish. While I am on my courses at the moment and might be a tad more emotional than usual, my amiable manner is much too hard to display. I am a failure. I am sorry."

I had no clue what she'd just said. "Stephano, can you help me out here?"

"Of course," he replied. "Allhoohoohaha is devastated that she has no pistols to defend you from the darkness. She's embarrassed that she's a high-falootin' gal who can't seem to bag a man to marry. Allhoohoohaha feels silly and sickened by her shitty taste in men and the fact that she believes she's useless to you. Also, she's on the rag right now and is probably more emotional than usual, so she's finding it hard to keep her chin up."

I walked over to Allhoohoohaha and kissed her tear-stained cheek. "You don't need to get married. Ever. You are a strong woman, and you can stand on your own two feet. You are very valuable to me. You understood Rhett Butler and Scarlett O'Hara. I would be lost without you."

"Really?" Albinia squeaked out, clasping my hand in hers.

"Really," I promised.

"May I make a request?" she inquired.

"You may."

Her smile was radiant. I heard birds chirping.

"I saw a commercial about cotton sticks. I was wondering if you had any and wouldn't mind sharing?"

I glanced over at Stephano. He shrugged. He had no clue what she was talking about.

"Tampons," Sasha said with a giggle. "Allhoohoohaha wants to try out a tampon."

"Wow…" I said with a laugh. "Just… umm… wow. And yes. I will share my cotton sticks with you."

"Excellent," she sang with her first real smile of the

evening. "I watched a video about cotton stick insertion. Looked quite fun."

My brows shot up and I was momentarily speechless. Only Albinia would think putting a tampon in was *fun*.

"Great," I said since it was the first thing that came to mind. "I'll give you a box of tampons once I convince all of you people that I can't take a part of you."

My characters had come up with a wild plan that included me basically dissecting them to juice myself with their powers. It seemed selfish and, even worse, dangerous. For them. Hell, maybe for me. This was brand-new territory, which meant it might not work at all. Or maybe the act would erase my characters altogether. The thought of them disappearing hit me like a gut punch.

"I can't take a part of you," I said again.

"We're part of you already," Sasha pointed out. "Without you there is no us."

"Right," I said, getting frustrated. "I get that. But if you give me your powers, do you cease to be?"

"We will never cease to be," Cassandra said archly, putting out her cigarette in my favorite candle. "We are forever immortalized on the pages of your novels."

Ignoring her destruction of my stuff, I began to pace. "That was a non-answer. You know exactly what I meant. And I'd also like to point out that I'm human. I'm not a vampire, werewolf or demon. What makes you think taking on your powers will even work?"

Clark stepped in front on me and stopped my random circling of the room. "You're being far too literal. It's clearly not an option to turn you into an immortal creature."

Well, that was a relief. I was just getting used to my magic. Becoming a freaking demon wasn't on my bucket list. "Not following."

Clark led me to the couch, sat down and patted the spot next to him. I sat down and rested my head on his shoulder. He truly was one of the sweetest men I knew.

"The author of the story controls the action... the players... and the outcome," Clark reminded me.

My head jerk up and I stared at him. "Are you saying I should write myself into a story to absorb some of your powers?"

"Bingo, jackass," Thick Stella grunted as she waddled out of the room—probably to take a dump on my bed. "My work here is fucking done."

My mind raced with possibilities and the disastrous ways it could blow up in my face.

Clark raised a bushy brow, then winked at me. "Talk it out."

"Okay," I said, hopping back up and circling the room again. "What if I get stuck in my book?"

"That can only happen if you write it that way," Mina said. "Plus, you're human."

She made a good point.

"What if you guys get stuck in the book?" I asked, trying to figure out all the ways this could go terribly awry.

No one said a word. That didn't bode well.

"Answers please," I said, halting my pacing and eyeing them with suspicion.

Cassandra lit yet another cigarette. My house was going to stink, but it was what it was. "Fine. Whomever you take from will be stuck—so to speak—in the story. Happy now?"

"No," I snapped. "I'm not happy. I feel like I'd be killing you. Can any of you understand what I'm talking about?"

"I can," Stephano said with a sad smile. "Clementine, you must remember we are not truly real."

"But you are," I insisted. "If you're not then I'm insane. I am NOT insane."

"You are not insane," Clark assured me. "What Stephano means is that we don't exist in anyone's world except yours."

"Wrong," I said. "Nancy can see you. Thick Stella can see you, and I would bet Cheeto can see you too."

"Fine point," he conceded, unsure what else to say.

Mina handed me a yellow legal pad. Sasha handed me an extra-sharp pencil. I thought about crying, but it wouldn't help the situation.

"If the darkness wins, the magic will die," Sasha said softly. "All of it. We are the least of your worries, Clementine. You created us for many reasons. But in my dark demon heart, I believe you created us for this very moment."

I couldn't hold back the tears. "So, I created you to destroy you?" I choked out.

"Those are very black and white terms," Stephano said, touching my cheek lovingly. "The imagination is filled with unimaginable color—your imagination especially."

I started at the blank page in front of me. The thought of harm coming to Aunt Flip, Jess, Mandy and the woowoo juju gals was unacceptable. The thought of harm coming to Seth and Cheeto was debilitating. Would taking power from some of my beloved characters help me protect the people I loved? All of it was confounding. I loved the people I created as much as I loved the real flesh-and-blood people.

"Wait. What if I just borrow the power?" I asked as a feeling of hope bloomed in my chest.

"More specific," Sasha said. "Be more specific."

"What I mean is, what if I took a little of Mina's thought-planting skills, a bit of Stephano's strength, a tad of Clark's brilliant mind for solving crimes, a little Sasha's badassery."

"A lot of my bitchiness," Cassandra chimed in.

"Right," I said with a giggle. "Bitchiness always comes in handy. But the point is, what if I didn't take it permanently? What if I gave it back to you after I take down Jinny Jingle and the darkness? Would that work? Could you come back to me?"

Curious glances were exchanged. Everyone looked intrigued, but not one person looked confident that the plan would work.

Shit. Where in the heck were my silver linings?

"It might," Clark said. "I'm sorry that I can't give you a more definitive answer."

Albinia crumpled to the floor and began to have a tantrum. "I am useless," she cried out, hyperventilating.

"What are you talking about?" I asked, worried she was going to faint.

"I have no power to give you. I am not a vampire or a werewolf or a demon. I am nothing."

"Oh, for the love of the Devil," Cassandra hissed, striding over to Albinia and yanking her to her feet. "Snap out of it or I'll give you something to cry about. You are not nothing. You will stay with Clementine and talk her off of the ledge when she needs it. Or more possibly you will send her over it."

"Ohhhh," Albinia said, wiping her nose with the skirt of her gown. "You mean I will take care of Clementine in your absence?"

"Something like that," Cassandra said with an impressive eye roll as she walked back to her chair and lit up another cigarette.

"Umm... that was nice," I told the demon, who shot me a glare that would have withered a normal person.

I was not normal.

"It wasn't nice," she snapped. "The boohooing was giving me a headache. It was an entirely selfish move on my part and if anyone contradicts me, I will kill them."

No one said a word. However, all were smiling. Cassandra flipped everyone off and lit another cigarette. She was now smoking two at the same time—one in her left hand and one in her right. She played it off like she'd meant to do it.

She was a sweetie in a prickly shell.

"Shall we begin?" Clark asked kindly. "Time is of the essence."

"Now?" I asked, feeling my chest grow tight and my eyes fill up.

"Now," Clark confirmed.

I nodded and let my tears fall freely. I was about to lose some of my most precious friends. However, I was determined I would bring them back home to me. Just as I had given them life, they were returning the favor.

As the pencil connected to the paper, I knew there was

no turning back. The gift they were giving me was priceless and I would cherish it always.

"I love all of you," I whispered as I began to write. "I love you more than I love myself."

"We are you," Stephano said. "Please love yourself just as much. You are so very worth it, Clementine."

His words hit me hard and I smiled. "I'll try. I promise."

As the pencil raced across the page, Stephano and Mina were the first to shimmer and disappear. They held tightly to each other and smiled at me as they waved goodbye. My tears blurred my vision and droplets landed on the yellow paper. Cassandra and Sasha were the next to sparkle and leave. There was a bright pop of blood-red glitter as they vanished. It made me smile. They were demons after all. It was fitting for them to exit with a bang.

Clark stood next to me and waited his turn.

"I feel like I'm Dorothy in *The Wizard of Oz* and you're the Scarecrow," I whispered to Clark as I looked up from the story I was weaving.

Clark chuckled and rocked back and forth on his feet. An action I knew so well. "Good analogy. I do recall the Scarecrow, Lion and Tin Man were waiting for Dorothy when she got home to Kansas."

"But they were different," I said with fear and sadness in my voice.

Clark kissed the top of my head. "All things change, my dear. Not all change is bad."

I nodded jerkily. Albinia sat by my side with her slim hand on my back.

Putting the pencil back to the paper, I continued. Clark

faded away with an expression of pride and love on his wrinkled face. It was a beautifully sad sight and I tucked it away in my heart.

"They're gone," I whispered.

"I know," Albinia said. "Do you feel different?"

I glanced over at her. Did I? I couldn't tell. "I don't know."

Her smile was lovely. She took my hand and pulled me to my feet. "Sleep. You must sleep now, Clementine. The sun will rise soon, and the darkness draws near."

I nodded and followed her as she led me to my bedroom. Thick Stella was passed out on my bed. I shut my closet door. I'd deal with her mess in the morning. I didn't have an ounce of energy left.

"Will you stay?" I asked, Albinia.

"I will," she replied, settling herself in the chair.

"You can sleep in the bed with Thick Stella and me if you want," I offered. "It's huge."

"Is that proper?" Albinia asked, somewhat alarmed.

I laughed. She was nutty. "We're just going to sleep. I like men and you do too."

"Well, yes then!" she said as she crawled up on the bed and gave Thick Stella a kiss. "It will be okay, Clementine."

"Define okay," I whispered as my eyes grew heavy.

"Only you can do that," she said. "And I believe you will."

I fell asleep with the faces of my characters dancing in my mind. My dreams were out of control. I lived every second of the words I'd written. I'd placed all of us on a beautiful secret island in the middle of the aquamarine Caribbean Ocean. I added a portal to Hell just in case the demons needed to pop down for some reason. There were five-star chefs and miles of silky white sand. I was a little worried about Stephano since he was a vamp, but he was over ninety. In the Good to the Last Bloody Drop series, my vamps quit crisping in the sun at the age of seventy-five. He was safe. I also included an endless supply of bottled blood, so Stephano didn't drain the staff. That would have sucked... pun sadly intended.

Cassandra had been thrilled with the posh accommodations I'd created and had immediately made reservations for a massage, a mani-pedi and a facial. She'd also flirted mercilessly with the handsome demon cabana boys I'd written in to occupy her time and keep her out of trouble. She could be a deadly handful with too much free time.

Stephano and Mina had adjourned to their opulent suite right after they'd wrapped their arms around me and released some of their magic. Sasha was bummed that Damien wasn't with her. I solved that in a hot second and wrote her demon hero into the tale. Damien was slightly confused at what the heck was happening, but he'd get with the program quickly. He was hot, smart and easygoing for a demon.

Clark was going to try Jet Skiing and snorkeling. He was as excited as I'd ever seen him. He was also seriously hairy. I didn't recall writing him such a hairy back, but I could solve that prickly issue at another time. He seemed quite proud of his manly body-hair rug. Who was I to judge? I loved him no matter how much fur he was sporting.

Each had hugged me.

Each had shared their powers with me.

I didn't grow fangs or fur. My heart still beat, and I was fairly confident I hadn't damned myself to Hell. Only time would tell on that one. The shocker was that I could read their minds. That was one of Cassandra's powers I'd completely forgotten about. It was alarming. Knowing what people were thinking was not all it was cracked up to be.

I knew I wrote them into a happy place on purpose. If they weren't with me, I wanted them to have joy and fun. That was the easy part. Missing them was going to be the hard part.

Eventually, when this was all over, I would bring them back to me.

I had to.

CHAPTER FOURTEEN

"Holy Shee-ot, what happened to you, Clemmy?" Flip asked as I stumbled sleepily into the kitchen the next morning.

After a night of tossing and turning through character-driven dreams, I'd gotten maybe two hours of restful sleep total. I woke up to a death glare from Thick Stella, who was standing on my chest. The cat had to weigh twenty-five pounds. We were definitely going to discuss a diet in the near future. She'd informed me she was about to crap on my head. That didn't really work for me. I'd ended up cleaning out her litter box and bringing it back inside before anyone was up. Unfortunately, I couldn't go back to sleep. Albinia was a bed hog and she snored. Who knew? Instead of indulging in much-needed rest, I'd taken a long hot shower and dried my hair. If I didn't feel great, it was at least good to look presentable.

"Rough night," I muttered, pouring myself a cup of watery caffeine. "Where is everyone?"

"Doing Jazzercise in the backyard," she told me, putting a plate of burned toast and a bottle of catsup in front of me. "Joy Parsley is leading it. It's a hot mess. She don't know her ass from her elbow. I'm thinkin' they're all gonna end up in traction." Flip shook her head and giggled. "Go on now, eat. Can't have you wastin' away."

"Do we have butter?" I asked, gingerly pushing the catsup away. There was only so much gross I could take. I'd already dealt with the litter box and removed the stinky dump from my closet. Catsup on toast didn't cut it this morning.

"Whoopsiedoodle," Flip said with a laugh, replacing the catsup with butter. "Had it out for the gals. They put catsup on everything. Oh, and I called Scooby Parker. He's gonna sign and stamp them divorce papers today."

I nodded and stared at the toast.

"You want eggs instead of toast, Clemmy?" Flip asked, concern in her voice. "I can whip you up some eggs in a jiffy."

"No... no thanks," I said. "All my people are gone except Albinia."

"What do you mean?" She sat down next to me at the breakfast bar and rubbed my back. "Did y'all have a fight?"

I shook my head and forced a smile. It was sad and pathetic. "No. They gave me some of their power so I could fight the darkness."

"That sounds real dang nice of 'em," Flip said.

"I had to write them into a story along with myself so I could take some of their power."

Flip sat quietly and mulled over what I'd shared. "Was it fun?"

I glanced over at her, confused.

"To be in a book?" she clarified. "Must have been kinda wild."

"Actually, it was," I told her. "I put them on a beautiful secret island with everything they could possibly want. Sunny skies, clear blue water, white sand and a resort to beat all resorts ever built."

"Sign me up," Flip said with a laugh. "If they got some good dirt on that island, I could live and grow my weed in paradise!"

The thought hit me like a ton of bricks. Could I actually do that? No, that was absurd. I'd only visited the island with my characters in my dream. I mean, it was exactly as I'd written it, but I wasn't really there. My body was grounded in reality and my mind was living in a fantasy.

Right?

Did it matter? My people were safe. That was the important part. I had no clue if I'd actually absorbed any of their powers. I didn't feel all that different.

"What new fancy-schmancy tricks do you have?" Flip asked, putting the breakfast dishes into the dishwasher.

"Not a clue," I told her.

"Well then, why don't we go on outside and figure it out?"

"As long as we don't have to Jazzercise, I'm in," I agreed, shoving the last of my charred toast into my mouth.

"You're gonna have to take that up with Joy Parsley," she said as she hustled out the back door in her lime-green and baby-pink muumuu. "That old coot is darn hard to say no to."

Flip was correct. In Joy's Universe, it was Joy's way or the highway. Grabbing the butter knife to put in the dishwasher, I stared at it. The silverware was a wedding gift from one of Darren's friends. I couldn't remember who. I'd wiped most of the reminders of the asshole out of my house, but I'd forgotten about the silverware. I didn't want it anymore. I didn't want any trace of him anywhere in my life.

My hands trembled as I held the knife. It was still beyond my wildest imagination that he could so callously blackmail dirty cops into committing my murder... and I had a wild imagination.

Pretending the knife was Darren's neck I tried to snap it.

"Holy shit," I gasped out, dropping the broken knife to the floor and staring at my hands like they belonged to someone else. "Did I really do that?"

Quickly opening the silverware drawer, I methodically bent and broke every single piece. It was a waste considering I should give it to charity, but my anger kept building. Not to mention the shock of what I was doing kicked my adrenaline into high gear.

"Clementine," Jess said, popping her head into the kitchen from the back porch. "If I have to do Jazzercise with Joy Parsley, you do too... Oh my God. What the hell?"

Jess glanced down at the broken stainless steel on the

floor and the bent serving spoon in my hand. I gave her a weak smile. "Whoops."

"Did you do that?" she asked.

"I did."

Jess's brow wrinkled in thought. "Is this new?"

I nodded mutely.

"Alrighty then, let's take this shitshow outside. It's gonna be way more fun than watching Joy try to touch her toes."

"You think?" I asked with a laugh that verged on hysterical.

She pushed me out into the bright morning sunshine. "Trust me, dude. I know."

∼

"SEE IF SHE CAN RIP THE BUMPER OFF THE CAR," ANN ARAMINI yelled, pointing to a little blue Honda.

"Heck to the no," Joy Parsley grunted, limping over. The Jazzercise had clearly maimed her. "Just paid the dang thing off. If you want Clementine to rip off a bumper, it's gonna be your bumper."

"How about I don't rip off any bumpers," I suggested.

We'd spent the last hour and a half testing my strength. It was massive. It seemed to be the only *gift* that had shown up so far. My guess was that I'd get the power when I needed it. Or, at least, that's what I was banking on.

"Sweetie," Sally Dubay called out. "I need a few trees taken down in my yard. Do you think you and Jess could take care of that for me?"

I glanced over at Jess and giggled. She gave me a thumbs

up. "Yep, I think we can make that happen. It'll have to be in the middle of the night, so we don't get busted."

"Thank you," Sally said as she launched herself into the air and flew in circles around the group.

"So, all the characters are gone?" Nancy asked with a sad sigh.

"Except for Albinia," I told her, spying my Regency heroine coming out of the house wearing some of my sweatpants with her own corset and lace-up boots. The look was all kinds of wrong, but she still pulled it off.

"I did it!" she called out from the porch. "I have inserted the cotton stick. I'm afraid I might have masturbated while I put the cotton stick up my nether regions, but a good time was certainly had."

Nancy stifled a laugh. I didn't bother. Albinia was a nutty delight.

"Is she referring to tampons?" Nancy asked.

"Umm... yes," I said.

"Thank God," Nancy said with relief. "At first I didn't know what the heck she was talking about."

"Join the club."

Albinia made herself comfortable on a rocking chair and hummed happily as I destroyed a few more objects.

"Gotta take a crap. Gotta take a crap. Don't wanna miss anything. Ohhhhhhh, I gotta go," Ann said.

"Then go," I said, picking up the pieces of my industrial steel flagpole that I'd torn apart.

"Go where?" Flip asked, confused.

"To the bathroom," I replied.

"Already done my business today," Flip said.

I shook my head. "Not you. Ann."

Ann gave me a perplexed look. "Why would I need to go to the bathroom?"

I returned her perplexed look. "Because you just said you have to take a crap about three times, but you didn't want to miss anything."

Everyone went silent. Sally fell out of the air and landed in a heap at my feet. At least she landed on the soft grass and not on the asphalt driveway.

Ann's eyes narrowed. "I didn't say that out loud."

"You didn't?"

"No siree, I did not," Ann insisted. "Did you just read my mind?"

Double and triple crap. "I really hope not," I said. "Think something else."

Ann's brow creased and she stared right at me. I didn't hear a thing.

"Nope. Nothing," I told her.

"That's cause I was whisperin' my thought," she informed me smugly. "Try this one."

Again, I stared at her and waited. This time she didn't whisper.

"I'm thinking about goin' to a swinger's meetin' for seniors. Figure now that my knockers are famous on the internet, my jugs are gonna be in high demand. Maybe I'll get me an offer to do a centerfold in National Geographic. That would sure burn Joy's buns. Her hooters might be bigger, but mine are less lopsided."

I blanched. "Dear God, please stop," I choked out on a laugh. "I heard you and all of that is a terrible idea."

Ann Aramini slapped her leg and cackled. "Okay gals, if

you don't want Clementine to know what you're thinkin' make sure you whisper think. If you wanna talk to her without using your mouth, just shout in your head."

"Or not," I said, pressing the bridge of my nose. This gift was going to suck.

"What am I thinkin'?" Flip demanded, slapping her hands on her tiny hips.

I glanced over at her. She was grinning from ear to ear.

"Jumper is so proud of you and so am I. You are my sunshine, little girl. And I believe in you with my whole dang heart. You're gonna WIN! I feel it in my old bones."

Crossing the yard, I wrapped my arms around one of my favorite people in the world and hugged her close. "You're my sunshine too," I whispered in her ear. "I love you to the moon and back."

"Love you more, girlie," she said, kissing my nose.

"Excuse me," Albinia called out. "Clementine, your talking box is making noise."

"You mean my phone?" I asked.

"Possibly," she said, holding it in her hand. "Is this a phone?"

"It is," I said, taking it from her and checking the screen. It was Mandy. "Mandy?"

"Get down to the police station," she said.

"Now?" I asked, putting her on speakerphone so everyone could hear.

"Now," she said.

"Is that safe?" I asked.

"Beyond," she assured me. "We need you to make a statement."

"Coming," I said, looking down at my yoga pants, sparkly flip-flops and Tweety Bird t-shirt. "I'll be there in ten."

"Grab your purses, gals," Flip yelled. "We're headin' on down to the pokey."

"Not exactly," I said, following Flip and the gang into the house.

"Close enough," Ann Aramini grunted. "I'll meet you down there. Need to take a dump."

"I'll wait with Ann," Sally Dubay said, then pulled me to a stop. She stared at me like I had something on my face.

Before I could check, I realized what she was doing.

"Ann drives like a drunk blind woman. I'll hang out till she passes a nice BM then drive us over. Sound good?" The tiny ninety-year-old woman was grinning from ear to ear. "Did it work? I was shoutin' in my head like my rear end was on fire."

"Yes," I said with a laugh. "That worked and good plan."

I grabbed my purse and hightailed it to my car. An awful thought consumed me. It kind of seemed like everything was heading towards a nice clean ending with a happily ever after for the good guys. What if I'd sent my characters away for no reason at all?

And what if I couldn't get them back?

Inhaling deeply, I focused on what was happening right in front of me. Jess, Nancy, Joy Parsley and Aunt Flip were in my car. I had to drive to the police station and give a statement. Hopefully, Darren and his buddies were getting measured for orange jumpsuits.

"Ready?" Flip asked as she put on her seat belt.

"Nope. But that's not gonna stop me," I said, starting the engine and backing out of the driveway.

"That's my girl," Flip said, rolling down the window and sticking her head out. "It's gonna be a real good day. I can feel it in my bones."

I hoped her bones didn't lie. We needed a really good day.

CHAPTER FIFTEEN

From the way it was looking, I was going to be the only one in our group allowed in. Mandy had texted me the news, and that Seth would meet me and walk me in. I'd quickly let her know where we'd parked. Downtown was hopping. It was more crowded than it was on National Hollerin' Day or the Tomato Fight Festival. Small towns had bizarre customs. We were no exception.

This morning, however, the entire street was filled with State Patrol cars and black sedans with tinted windows. It was as if we'd walked on to a movie set where the government had moved in to take down the Mafia. Townsfolk wandered as close as they could get to try to see what was going on. The rumor mill was on fire and about to explode.

"This is some crazy stuff," Flip said as she and the gals gathered with me around the car. "You gonna be okay in there alone?"

"Yep," I said. "As long as no one tries to kill me, I should be good."

"Don't you even joke like that, little missy," Joy Parsley said, whacking me in the back of the head like I was a twelve-year-old child who'd just sassed her. "Words have power, young lady. Use 'em wisely."

The smack was less jarring than the last part of her statement. The pearls of wisdom from my little tribe kept on coming. Joy was correct. Words had power.

"Clementine," Seth called out as he approached me with two men wearing black suits and sunglasses flanking him on either side. "Let's get you inside before the news crews start showing up."

"News crews?" Joy asked, perking up considerably. "National?"

"Probably," Seth said as the two black-suited gentlemen stared straight ahead with no expressions on their faces whatsoever.

"Well butter my butt and call me a biscuit," Sally squealed as she and Ann hustled over and joined the group. "This is a big shindig. So exciting. Reminds me of the Washboard Music Festival crowd."

"Ann Aramini," Flip said, eyeing her. "Everything come out okay?"

"You can kiss my go-to-hell, but yep, the poop shoot is squeaky clean," Ann announced, looking around in surprise. "What in tarnation is happenin'?"

"Pretty sure Hell is raining down on a douchebag," Nancy said, glancing over at Seth. "You want me over in the office?"

Seth nodded curtly. "That would be helpful. Cheeto is there with my mom. If you could relieve her, I'd be grateful. There's a chance that the FBI might want to talk to Cheeto. I'll let you know if she needs to come over."

"Roger that and on it," Nancy said, heading down the street towards the law office.

"I'll join Nancy," Jess said, giving my hand a quick squeeze. "You've got this, dude."

I felt some relief. Last time Nancy had watched Cheeto, the child had ended up outside in the rain and had witnessed some stuff it would have been better if she hadn't seen. I adored Nancy, but Jess was solid and no bullshit.

"You think the news crews know about our knockers?" Ann Aramini asked.

The silent FBI guys exchanged confused covert glances. They had no clue what they were in for. This was the South, where people wore their crazy like a badge. Flip, Joy, Sally and Ann had about ten badges apiece.

"If they don't, they sure will shortly," Joy Parsley said, pulling out her phone. "Figured out how to watch the video on my phone. It's better on a computer 'cause you can see our hooters clearer, but they'll get the idea."

"You know," Sally Dubay said, fluffing her sparse gray hair, "we might be able to get a reality show out of this."

"You think we should cash in on our bazooms?" Joy asked, clearly very interested in the appalling angle.

"Why not?" Ann Aramini grunted. "World's already seen our boobs. We may as well make a little dough to supplement Social Security."

"True that," Flip added with a laugh.

"Should I even ask what they're talking about?" Seth questioned with a grimace.

"No. The answer is, no, you should not," I replied.

"No worries," Joy said. "My grandson taught me how to hex on a phone. I'll hex our hooters on over to you."

"Text," I corrected her.

Joy Parsley rolled her eyes. "Hex. Text. No difference as far as I can see. You just hit a dang button and pictures magically appear."

"I got a dick pic once," Ann announced loudly, much to the horrified amusement of the men in black. "Saved it."

"Of course, you did," I said with a groan.

One of the men in black spoke into a headset. "Yes, sir. On it. They're ready for you now," he said, addressing Seth and me.

I nodded and swallowed back my fear. I felt a little underdressed, but I'd had no freaking clue the entire Kentucky police force would be here including some FBI guys.

"I look bad," I whispered to Seth as we made our way to the entrance of the station.

"You could wear a burlap sack and still be beautiful," he whispered back. "My dad and Mandy are inside. We're working as a team to represent you."

"I'm in trouble?" I asked, shocked.

"Not even close," he assured with a smile that calmed me. "We're here in case you want to file a report."

"Do I?"

"Up to you, Clementine," he replied. "That is one hundred percent your call."

"Do I have to decide right now?" I asked, needing to understand what I was walking into.

"No, ma'am," one of the FBI agents escorting us inside said. "All we need you to do is identify the men you saw when you were in the hospital room and make a statement."

My eyes grew huge. I peeked over at Seth. He looked straight ahead. Crap. I didn't know the story. I couldn't exactly tell them that Joy had tied one on, went invisible and I hid behind her. That wouldn't fly.

"Can I go to the bathroom first?" I asked, texting Mandy to meet me there.

The taller of the two agents checked his watch. "Yes, ma'am."

"Thank you," I said, crossing the lobby and hoping Mandy had beat me in.

She had.

Pressing my finger to my lips, I stared at her hard. Cassandra had given me the ability to read people's minds. Mina had given me the ability to plant thoughts. I wondered if I could write in a little twist and use Mina's gift to have a conversation. I was about to find out.

"Can you hear me?" I shouted in my mind.

Mandy gasped, then grinned. She nodded.

Bingo.

"Think really loud and I can hear you," I told her. *"We don't know if the station is bugged. Can't take any risks. There could be more dirty cops than we know of."*

"THE ENTIRE FORCE IS UNDER INVESTIGATION," she bellowed inside my head.

When you told Mandy to do something, she gave it her all.

"You don't have to think that loud. Tamp it back just a little. You're gonna cause my head to explode."

"Roger that." She gave me a thumbs up.

"Tell me what you've told them as far as how and why I was in the hospital room?"

"Didn't I tell you that already? On the phone?" she asked, looking like I'd just sucker punched her.

"Umm... nope."

I didn't need to sucker punch her. She slapped herself in the forehead so hard, I was sure she'd have a headache soon. *"My bad. You were going to visit Darren to see if he was doing okay. You saw Jinny Jingle and hid in the bathroom with the door cracked. You were concerned that she'd come back to finish the job and wanted to stay and help... like you did the first freaking time she attacked him. When you realized what was going down, you recorded it."*

"Got it. Makes sense. Did you come up with it?"

"Nope, Seth did."

God, I was a lucky person to have so many amazing people in my corner. *"How did I get out of there without Darren seeing me?"*

"Well, since Joy Parsley was wasted and invisible, you walked out hidden behind her."

My eyes widened and my mouth fell open.

"Gotcha!" Mandy said with a laugh. *"You waited until Darren was asleep because you were in fear for your life at that point."*

I punched her arm. *"Oh my God, you suck so hard,"* I told her.

"Correct, my husband will corroborate that statement." She waggled her brows. *"You ready?"*

"I just have to identify them?"

Mandy nodded. *"And make a statement. I'd like to see you press charges against the Weather Hooker, Tiny Pecker and the two assholes who agreed to kill you, but that's up to you. The feds will go after all of them regardless, but you have every right to file a report."*

"What about Kinter? The cop who left the room?"

She smiled. It was vicious. *"The dog-food eater turned on them. He's singing for his supper. This whole department is in a shitload of trouble."*

"Wow," I said, shaking my head.

"And then some."

∼

THE LIGHTING WAS HARSH. FLUORESCENT BULBS HUNG FROM the ceiling. The floor was a dull gray littered with scuff marks and dirt. They stood in a line against a pristine white wall—well, Darren sat. He was still severely battered and bruised. On the white wall were vertical black lines with height measurements. There were six men. Three I didn't know. And three who would haunt my dreams for a long time. Each held a square, white piece of paper with a thick black number printed on it. They couldn't see me. I knew that, so I took my time to study the man I'd spent too many years to count with. What the hell had happened to him? When had he become a spawn of the Devil?

"Ma'am, can you identify the men you observed last night?" the man in black asked politely.

"I can," I said. "Can I ask a question?"

"Yes, ma'am. I don't know that I'll be able to answer it, but you're welcome to ask."

"Are they aware it was me?" I asked. "That I made the recording and turned them in?"

The FBI agent turned his back on me for a moment and spoke quietly into his headset. When he turned around, he removed his sunglasses, and looked at me with kind eyes.

"No, ma'am. They are not aware who turned them in. We didn't know who else might be involved. In the interest of your safety and the safety of your loved ones, you have not been identified as of yet."

I nodded. That answer wasn't working for me. Although, it might be a blessing in disguise. I wanted to see the bastard's face when he realized it had been me. I crossed my fingers and silently thanked Mina for her gift. I was about to use it.

"The men I saw last night who made plans to kill me are number 2, number 5 and number 6," I said flatly.

"Are you sure, ma'am? Would you like to take more time?"

"Nope. I'm sure. I've never been more sure about anything in my entire life, but thank you."

The agent spoke into his headset. Another agent who was in the lineup room received his message. I watched as the suspects were led away. I wasn't all that familiar with the police station anymore. It had been remodeled since Darren had been a cop fifteen years ago.

"Where will they go now?" I asked.

"They'll be questioned further then booked, ma'am."

"They can't get out, can they?" I asked, a little concerned about revenge. It wouldn't take long for word to spread that I'd turned them in.

"Not a chance," he ground out through clenched teeth.

Again, I nodded. The man in black was very polite and very passionate about his job. "Can I make my statement and leave?"

"Yes, ma'am. Follow me, please."

My heart raced and I felt light-headed. There was no outline to this chapter. I was winging it like I always did. Somehow it always worked out. I had no clue if this particular chapter would make it into the book or if it would end up in what I affectionately referred to as my shit folder. It didn't matter. I never threw anything I wrote away. Sometimes the shit turned into brilliance with a little love and care and some massive rewriting. Or in this case, a little magic.

This was my chance. Probably my only chance.

"Take me to the room where Darren Bell is being held," I thought as hard as I could. *"You want to take me to the room where Darren Bell is being held. You want to have your gun out and trained on him in case he comes at me."*

The FBI agent pressed his temples and shook his head. He seemed confused.

"Take me to the holding room where the suspect Darren Bell is. You need to take me there now. It's the most important thing you

will ever do. Need to move quick. Need to move now," I told him silently.

"Come this way, ma'am," the man in black said, drawing his gun and moving me fast and efficiently. "Eyes down. Stay with me."

I didn't say a word. I was afraid to break the spell.

The man in black held up his FBI badge to the local precinct cop at the closed door of the room the scummiest man in the world was in. I didn't recognize the officer, which meant he wouldn't recognize me.

"Here to question the perp," he told the uniformed man.

"Let us in," I said staring at the unsure cop at the door. *"You want to let us in and close the door behind us. You don't want to tell anyone that we're inside. This is the most important thing you will ever do. You won't remember any of this after we leave."*

The cop seemed perplexed, but he did as he was told without question.

Staring at the kind FBI agent, I dove in once again. *"You will never repeat anything you hear in this room. If you try, no words will leave your lips. This is forever our secret. When I'm ready to leave, I will let you know."*

The agent simply nodded and entered the room.

The FBI guy's gun was trained on Darren as he stood by my side. The look on Darren's face was priceless. It went from shock to fury to fear to woe is me. He was so easy to read. I stood silently and waited for my moment. It would come. I always let the bad guy monologue first. It was so very satisfying.

"Oh my God, Clementine. Thank God you're alright. I

was so worried," Darren cried out. He was cuffed to his chair, so he couldn't approach. That was good. With Stephano's strength, I wasn't sure I could stop myself from breaking him in two if he touched me with his despicable hands. If he thought he was bruised and broken now, he wouldn't know the meaning of the words if I went at him.

However, I was better than Darren. I was better than Jinny Jingle. In the immortal words of Cassandra Le Pierre, "I love sarcasm. It's like punching people in the face with words." I was going to punch the son of a bitch with words. Words he could replay over and over in his jail cell for a very long time.

"Were you worried?" I asked, doing my best to sound vapid and innocent. "Were you really?"

"I was, baby. You have to believe me. I was set up," he said, sounding desperate. "You have to believe me. I still love you. It's Jinny who wants you dead. Not me. Your death would kill me."

"Interesting," I said, opening up a black metal folding chair and sitting down across the room. His words about the Weather Hooker rang true. She did want me dead. The bitch was completely unstable. She might decide to finish what she'd started when she found out she wasn't getting the house of her dreams. Even so, I knew the rest of what he was saying was complete bullshit. "You have a strange way of showing it."

Darren shook his head and tried to force himself to cry. It was so freaking weird, even the man in black chuckled under his breath. "I was in shock. I was concussed, baby. I think I just saw you there after I was attacked and thought it was you. I am so sorry. I take it all back. You have to know I would never do that to you."

"I know, Darren," I said with a smile that didn't come close to reaching my eyes.

He didn't notice. He just saw the smile and thought he'd gained ground. Darren Bell was stupid. I didn't do stupid. Not anymore.

"Thank you, baby," he said, giving me a look that he'd given me a thousand times over the years. In the beginning of our relationship, I'd found it cute. Now? Now, it was repulsive. "I need you to back me up. I need you to tell these idiots that I didn't do this crap. It's ludicrous. I wouldn't harm a hair on your head, baby."

I sucked in an audible breath through my teeth. "My name is Clementine," I corrected him. "Not baby."

He laughed. It was thin and tinny. And his pornstache was gross. "Sorry, old habits die hard. You've been my baby for so long, I can't stop calling you that."

It was lovely how easily the word die rolled off of his tongue.

"You should try. Did you happen to hear the recordings?"

His eyes rounded for a brief moment and a flicker of fear shot through them. "Did you?"

I shrugged. "Not today," I told him.

The relief on his face was laughable. I wanted to slap the smile right off.

"It's all fake," he told me. "It's clearly been spliced together by some fucking asshole. You're going to laugh when you hear it. It's utterly ridiculous."

"Wow," I said. "That's just awful. Why did they arrest you if the audio is fake?"

"Excellent question," Darren said, gaining confidence. "What I need you to do is get the judge to set bail. Vouch for my character. If you could loan me the bail money, I'd pay you back within the month."

"You want me to go to the judge and tell him what kind of guy you really are?" I asked.

"Yes, baby. That would be great. I'd owe you big time."

"That is so sweet, Darren," I said. "Can I ask you a question?"

"Anything you want, baby," he said. "You're my baby. My baby can ask her man anything she wants."

"We're divorced," I reminded him.

"It's not legal yet," he said, giving me puppy dog eyes. "We can get it reversed. What's your question, baby?"

"Was it before or after the fingerprints came back as not mine that you retracted your statement?"

He looked confused. He pulled it back together quickly and chuckled condescendingly. "Before, baby. Way before."

"Lie," I said with a smile.

He stopped chuckling.

"How long were you aware that Lewis tampered with evidence and sent an innocent man to prison for murder?"

His eyes narrowed.

"Do I need to repeat the question… baby?"

"I heard you," Darren ground out.

"Awesome. And Brady? His wife is going to shit when she hears about his second family. Not to mention that letting poor old Jimmy Bunson take the fall was just awful."

Darren paled. This was not going well for him.

"Where did you hear that?" he asked, trying to laugh it off. He failed.

"Can't remember," I said. "But what I need to know is if you're sorry for that. I can't tell the judge what a great guy you are if I don't know that you're sorry."

Again, the man in black chuckled.

Again, Darren was wildly confused.

"Umm... yeah, I'm really sorry I didn't turn those crooked cops in. Really sorry," he said, trying to gauge me.

He couldn't. He'd never been able to keep up with me, and he certainly wasn't going to now.

"Okay," I said. "How about this? I'll go tell the judge that Jinny Jingle tried to kill you. I stopped her. Her prints are all over the tire iron, by the way."

That wasn't a lie. It was the truth. It simply hadn't been proven thus far because they hadn't hauled her skanky ass down to the station to match her prints yet.

Darren began to turn red. It started at his neck and rose to his face quickly. It wasn't even. It was mottled and made him look diseased.

"She's also going to be charged with soliciting murder. Bummer for her," I said.

His blotchy face turned ashen beneath the red spots. It was a bad look.

"Is this all because I dumped you? You're an over-the-hill, jealous bitch," he snarled. "What do you want? Revenge?"

I laughed. It felt fantastic. "Hell to the no. You did me a

favor. Divorcing you was the smartest move I've ever made. Thank you for that."

"Jinny is innocent—she was just joking around," he hissed as spittle flew from his lying lips and dripped from his mustache. "The people you want are Lewis and Brady. Not me. And not my Jinny."

"Wrong," I said, crossing my legs and brushing imaginary lint off of Tweety Bird. "It was me, *baby*. I was in your hospital room last night. I was the one who recorded you and *your Jinny* planning my death. Sadly, I was the one who had to listen while you got a hand job. But I've got to hand it to Jinny—pun intended—it's so itty bitty, I was impressed she could find it."

The man in black chuckled again. I liked the man in black.

"Anyhoo, I was the one who recorded you blackmailing the scum to kill me. It was me, baby. It was all me. And just so you know, your Jinny doesn't want you, she wants my house. You were just a means to an end. Sorry for your luck, asshole."

"You fucking bitch!" he roared, trying to pull free from his cuffs. His face was a mask of hatred and fury. It was also filled with terror. "You've ruined me."

"Oh, don't be silly. You didn't need me to ruin you. You did a really good job of that all by yourself. Good luck in the big house. From what I hear, cops aren't real popular."

"You will regret this, bitch," he shouted, sounding crazed as he realized he was truly screwed.

"Actually, I won't," I said, standing up and nodding to my

new buddy. "The only thing I regret is not kicking your sorry, pathetic ass to the curb sooner."

"You'll never do better than me," he ground out, still trying to free himself.

"Darren. Look at me," I instructed coldly.

His eyes rose to mine. His expression was wary.

"Alone is preferable to you. A horse's ass is preferable to you. My vibrator is preferable to you. It's also much larger than you. But… most things are larger than you. The day of our divorce, I wished you well. I take that back. I wish you nothing. Absolutely nothing."

"Go to Hell," he shouted.

I smiled and winked. "Trust me. My Hell will be a whole lot more fun than yours."

Nodding to the nice man in black, we left the room. I was getting closer to "the end". The words "the end" were the sexiest words in an author's vocabulary. I just wasn't quite there yet.

The darkness was still on the loose. With the cops and the feds after Jinny Jingle, there was a good chance they'd solve my biggest problem for me. But the Weather Hooker was desperate and stupid.

It was a deadly combination.

CHAPTER SIXTEEN

"You okay?" Seth asked, putting his arm around my shoulders as we walked out of the station.

"Define okay," I said with a small grimace.

Mr. Ted, Mandy and Seth had been by my side as I made my statement. There was now a manhunt going on for Jinny Jingle. I passed her bitchy buddies who were brought in for questioning as we left the building. I'd made eye contact with one. She was no longer on her high horse. The young woman looked terrified. Talk shit. Get hit. They were all about to get hit hard. I felt no pity. None.

I wasn't sure how involved the Weather Hooker's friends were or how much they knew, but they didn't have woowoo juju. There was no golden glow laced with darkness around either of them. That was a profound relief. If Jinny had gathered an army, she'd be more difficult to stop. Main problem right now was that I wasn't sure what stopping her meant. Ending her life wasn't on the table. While my characters dispatched the bad guys in grisly ways in my books, this was real life. Killing Jinny Jingle to beat back the darkness would end with me in an orange jumpsuit and a room near my ex-husband.

"Took you a long time to ID the suspects," Mandy commented as we made our way through the throngs of people and reporters.

We walked right through without being stopped. Word had clearly not gotten out yet.

"The man in black wanted me to take my time." I'd tell her everything later. Seth would be privy as well. Mr. Ted knew nothing about woowoo juju and it wasn't a good time to let him in on the secret.

"I was very proud of you, Clementine," Mr. Ted said. "You handled yourself beautifully."

I smiled. Seth's father was a lovely and intelligent man. He'd represented me in my divorce with kindness, compassion and shark-like focus.

"Thank you," I said as we approached the law office. "I can't thank you enough."

"Not necessary," Mr. Ted said with a fatherly smile as he gave his son a quick hug. "I'm going home for about an hour to check on your mom. She was worried. I'll be back in the office afterwards."

"Take the day, Dad," Seth said, running his hands through his hair. "Mandy and I can cover your appointments."

"Roger that," Mandy said. "My calendar is free. I can handle your clients, Mr. Ted... I mean, Ted."

None of us, not even Mandy who worked with Mr. Ted,

could call him Ted comfortably. It was like calling a high school teacher by his or her first name. It just felt wrong.

Mr. Ted chuckled. "As the senior-most member of our firm, I'm giving everyone the rest of the day off. We've earned it. I'll make a few phone calls and postpone the meetings on my agenda. Sound like a plan?"

"Sounds like a plan," Seth agreed.

I could feel the tension in Seth's body. It matched mine. While Darren and his killer buddies were in custody, Jinny Jingle was not. Part of the danger had been contained. Part was still on the loose. And the part on the loose was more dangerous than Darren, Lewis and Brady put together.

"Shall I have Nancy make the calls?" Mandy asked. "She's at the office with Cheeto."

Mr. Ted shook his head. "No, I'll do it. Let Nancy know she's free to take the day off as well."

"Will do," Mandy said. "A day off sounds heavenly."

We watched and waved as Mr. Ted drove away.

"I have a lot to tell you guys," I said.

"Office," Seth replied, scanning the street. "More private."

"Agreed," Mandy said, following Seth's lead and glancing around cautiously.

My stress level rose as I looked up and down the street. Jinny Jingle was out there somewhere and none of us were safe until she was behind bars.

"She wouldn't dare show her face around here right now," Mandy said.

I inhaled deeply and exhaled slowly. "Stupid people do

desperate things," I said. "Never underestimate stupid. If she knows Darren got busted, there's no telling what she'll do."

"I texted Flip and the gals to meet us at the office. I also cancelled the extra security for your property," Seth said.

I squeezed his hand. "That's perfect. Since they have Lewis and Brady, I don't think we need it. We'll have to use magic on the Weather Hooker if she comes at us. I'm glad we won't have to hold back because people are around."

Seth nodded. "I still think it's a good plan for you and the ladies to stay together at your place," he added. "Until she's apprehended."

"Which will hopefully be soon," Mandy said.

"From your mouth to God's ears." I chuckled. "Not sure how long I can take living with Joy Parsley."

Mandy winced. "I overheard someone at the station gossiping. Are you aware there's a viral video of Joy Parsley's naked boobs?"

I laughed. The feeling was freeing and wonderful. I couldn't believe with everything that had happened and was still ongoing that I could still smile. "Yep, I'm aware. She's exceedingly proud of her bazooms. And so are the rest of the gang."

Mandy squinted at me and gasped. "Are you saying there are more naked boobs than just Joy's?"

"Yep. You want proof?" I asked, raising a brow.

Mandy pressed her temples and giggled. "Do I?"

"You do," I assured her. "What do you say we go in and get on the internet for a few minutes before we leave for the afternoon."

Seth groaned. "Not sure I can handle this."

I elbowed him. "You just have to watch it. I had to live it."

"Fair enough," he replied with an exaggerated shudder. "Your wish is my command, Clementine. Always."

His gaze was intense. It made me tingle all over. Yes, the timing was off, but I was beginning not to care. Tomorrow wasn't guaranteed. Today, I would start living. My new chapter would include getting to know myself and Seth at the same time. It was slightly convoluted, but my stories tended to work out in the end. I'd take this chapter one page at a time.

Seth's words were loaded. He knew it and I knew it. I liked the sound of them. Words did indeed have power, and Seth wielded them well.

"It's time to see something that you can never unsee," I said. "Prepare yourselves."

∽

THE OFFICE WAS EERILY QUIET. NOT A PERSON WAS TO BE found… until we found them.

"Oh my God," Mandy shouted, turning on the lights in her office.

Flip, Ann Aramini, Joy Parsley, Sally Dubay, Jess and Nancy were all tied up with duct tape over their mouths. Jess was bleeding from her hairline and Nancy's left eye was swollen shut. The older women were in better shape. There was no sign of Cheeto.

I thought I was going to puke. An intense sensation like that of rabid mice skittering up my spine made me shiver.

My blood pressure dropped to zero, and I moved with speed I hadn't been aware I possessed.

"Where's Cheeto?" Seth bellowed, turning and sprinting out of Mandy's office to search the area.

Fury and fear threatened to overwhelm me. "Untie them," I barked at Mandy, whose feet seemed to be glued to the floor. "NOW."

Flip's bindings were partially burned. She'd clearly tried to set a fire to release herself. She'd only succeeded in singeing her arms. Carefully peeling the duct tape from her mouth so I didn't rip away the skin, I led her to a chair, then went to work on Jess. Mandy had finally gotten with the program and was freeing the others.

"Talk. Now," I said tersely as I assessed the wound on Jess's head. It would need stitches, but the bleeding had slowed.

"Jinny Jingle," Jess ground out as I removed the tape from her lips. "Has Cheeto."

"We couldn't stop her," Flip lamented. "She has some evil and powerful woowoo juju."

"Was she alone?" I demanded, making sure Sally, Ann and Joy weren't hurt.

"Alone," Sally choked out, crying. "Has the strength of an army. Controls the wind, blew us all into a pile and tied us up before we knew what was happenin'."

That was not good news.

"How long?" I ground out.

Seth barreled back into the room looking like he was going to implode. "I can't find Cheeto. She's not here!" He turned and put his fist through the wall.

This wasn't a paranormal romance novel. It wasn't fiction at all. Seth wasn't immortal and he didn't heal immediately. He'd probably just broken his hand. I understood the impulse, but we didn't have time to go to the emergency room.

"Calm," I snapped at Seth. "Ease up. Focus."

He nodded jerkily and cradled his hand close to his body. "Cheeto is gone," he whispered brokenly. "I can't find her."

"Jinny Jingle took her," I told him.

He swore and punched the wall again. If he kept it up, he would need hand surgery when this was all over.

Nancy was sweating so heavily, it looked like she'd taken a dip in a pool. She might be a hot mess, but she wasn't letting that hinder her. My friend was sopping wet, but she was as cool as a cucumber. "Ten minutes ago," she said, gingerly touching her swollen eye. "Left out of the back door. Cheeto wasn't tied up or harmed when Jinny took her."

"Where?" I demanded, helping Ann Aramini to her feet. "Do you know where she took her?"

"Did she make any demands?" Mandy questioned, handing Jess a wad of tissue to help stem the bleeding.

"No," Jess replied, nodding her thanks to Mandy. "Told us to tell you to come and find her."

"She ain't right," Flip said weakly. "Jinny, I mean. Her eyes were messed up and she was filthy."

"Call the feds," I instructed Mandy. "Tell them Jinny Jingle kidnapped a child." I glanced over at Seth, and I could see all the rage and terror bubbling below the surface. "Tell them she took Cheeto."

Seth unlocked his phone screen and handed it to Mandy. "I have current photos on there if they want them."

Mandy nodded and took his phone. "On it."

I slipped my hand into Seth's. His fingers were ice cold, and I couldn't imagine all the awful things running through his mind. Actually, I probably could. Jinny Jingle was evil, and there was no telling just how far someone evil would go to get what they wanted. "We are going to find her," I told him. "I swear. She's going to be all right." I prayed it wasn't a lie.

He nodded, the muscle in his jaw twitching. "She's going to pay for this."

"And then some," I said. I remembered Jinny's disheveled state when she'd been at the hospital and turned to Mandy. "Tell the feds to search the woods around town. I think that's where she's been hiding out. Her hair had twigs and leaves in it last night."

"Pine needles?" Nancy asked.

I shook my head. "Not that I saw. Mostly leaves."

"Probably not the park then. It's full of pines," Nancy shouted. "Try the reserve and the zoo. More oak and maple there."

Mandy nodded and relayed the information. Then she held out the phone to Seth. "They need some personal details about Cheeto that I don't know."

I let go of his hand as he took the phone from her.

Joy limped across the room and picked up a teddy bear. "Cheeto was playing with this before the monster bitch took her," she said. "Has to have her scent on it. Do the feds have search dogs?"

Mandy snatched the bear out of Joy's hands. "Brilliant. I'm running this over to the station. Seth, let them know I'm coming."

He gave Mandy a tight-lipped attempt at a smile and a jerky thumbs up.

"We need to search. We have to find her," Sally said, wringing her hands. "It's time to use the woowoo. I'm gonna fly around town and look for the beautiful baby."

"I'm shifting. I can search in the woods faster that way. Watch out," Ann yelled as a pop of golden light blinded me momentarily.

Ann was gone. A fat orange Tabby sat in the exact spot Ann had been standing in only seconds ago.

"Holy shit," Jess said. "I didn't think she could actually do that."

"Never underestimate the woowoo," Joy grunted, glancing around wildly. "Is there any beer here? I need five."

"Doubtful," I replied, thinking it probably wasn't a good plan for Joy to be drunk. "Joy, did you get a copy of the audio?"

I figured she did. She was nosy and liked having ammunition on everyone.

She blanched. "Umm... yes. I recorded it on my phone when we listened to it last night."

"Normally, I'd be pissed. Right now, I'm thrilled that you're a sneaky busybody," I said, pressing my temples and trying to streamline my thoughts. "Send it out."

"What do you mean?" she asked, pulling her phone from her pocket.

"Send it to the most gossipy people in town," I ordered. "Make sure you send a message saying Jinny Jingle kidnapped Cheeto."

"You sure about that, Clemmy?" Flip asked.

"Positive," I replied, looking for any clues the Weather Hooker might have left behind. Clark Dark always cased the room where the crime had happened. I wasn't Clark Dark, but I possessed some of his smarts. "We need more than just the cops and the feds searching for Cheeto and the bitch. If the town gets wind, the search team just increased by a couple hundred."

"On it," Joy said, texting like a madwoman.

"I'm sorry, what?" Nancy asked with her back turned to us. "I can't understand you. Please slow down."

"I think she's concussed," Flip said as Ann meowed loudly. Flip pointed to Nancy, who was conversing with the wall. "She got clocked in the face real hard when she tried to save Cheeto. That Weather Hussy has some scary strength. I'm surprised Jinny Jingle didn't crush poor Nancy's eye socket. The sound was just dang awful."

I watched Nancy. She wasn't concussed at all. I almost shouted with excitement, but I sucked it back with effort. If I screamed, I might scare away whoever was here. Nancy was talking to the dead. Maybe the dead could help us.

Walking over to Nancy slowly so I didn't mess with her train of thought or the dead person she was talking to, I cautiously touched her shoulder.

"Is someone there?"

"The woman from the hardware store—the one with the woowoo," she said, trying to stay calm. "I can't understand her. She's too upset."

"Ask her if she saw what happened."

Nancy turned to me. "She can understand you. You can talk directly to her. I'll tell you what she says if I can make it out."

I nodded. Every bit of what was happening was insane. I was about to talk to a dead woman. Nancy was going to interpret. Sally was preparing herself to fly over the town in search of Cheeto, which would end in the emergency room... for Sally. Not to mention, anyone who spotted her was going to need therapy. Ann was a freaking house cat and the rest of us were certifiable. I'd never been so happy to be crazy in my life. All of our crazy was going to save Cheeto. It had to.

Seth, Joy, Flip, Sally, Jess and Ann—in cat form—watched silently and waited. I could hear Seth's labored breathing. He was off the phone now, and the inaction was killing him. I understood, but action without direction could be our downfall. There was no time to rewrite this chapter. Each word and movement would be set in stone forever.

"Hi, my name is Clementine," I said, looking to the spot Nancy was focused on. "I'm like you. I have magic."

"She's listening," Nancy whispered. "She's calmer. Keep talking."

"We need to know if you saw what happened," I went on, trying to keep my eyes at a level that might feel like I was looking at her.

"She did," Nancy said.

My heart rate increased. It really did take an army—a Goodness Army. The dead woman made our army complete. We needed eight. Before we had seven. With our new invisible recruit, we had our perfect number.

"Okay." I needed to choose my words carefully. "Do you know where they went?"

Nancy squeaked. "She says she can't explain it, but she can show us. She says we have to hurry."

How in the heck were we supposed to follow a ghost? Didn't matter. We'd figure it out.

"Ask her if she can be transported in a car? Can she stay with us if we move?"

"She can hear you," Nancy reminded me. "And she thinks she can."

"We need to leave," Seth ground out. "Tell her that. Please. And tell her thank you."

"Yes," I added. "Thank you. Do you have a name? Something we can call you?"

"She's freaking out again," Nancy said, backing away.

"It's okay," I said quickly, holding my hands up. "We don't need to know your name. We're just grateful for your help."

"Not the issue," Nancy relayed. "I got her name. She wants us to hurry."

"Car," I instructed, scooping the cat version of Ann Aramini into my arms. "Let our new friend sit in the front seat. Nancy, you'll drive since you can hear her. The rest of us will sit in the back."

"You heard my girl," Flip yelled. "Move your asses!"

"Should I fly above the vehicle?" Sally asked. "I might be able to see more."

"While the idea has merit, let's keep you in the car for now. We don't need to freak the town out until it's necessary," I told her.

"I like that," Sally said, hustling out of the office as fast as her ninety-year-old legs would carry her.

"Text went out," Joy said, gathering up everyone's purses and heading out the door. "Shit's gonna hit the fan now."

"Mandy texted," Seth said, barely holding on. "The feds have dogs. The search is on. I'm going to follow in my car. I need to be in control of something right now or I'm going to lose it."

I understood. I wanted to drive as well, but I couldn't hear the navigator.

"Not a problem," I told him, touching his face. "Just don't lose us. I have no clue where we're headed."

"I don't plan to lose anyone I love," Seth said, kissing my lips hard and quick. "Not today. Not ever."

CHAPTER SEVENTEEN

The ride was quiet and tense as we drove out of town. Ann got car sick and puked up a hairball. Seth was tailing us entirely too close, but I couldn't blame him. The only one speaking was Nancy and it was a one-sided conversation.

"Left or right?" Nancy asked as she stopped at a red light.

We turned left. The same way I turned when I headed home from town.

"Clementine, she's asking if you love Cheeto?"

It was an odd question, but it was very easy to answer. "I do," I told the empty front passenger seat. "She weaseled her way into my heart from the first moment I met her. She's the most amazing little girl in the world."

"She likes that," Nancy told me. "She wants to know if you love Seth."

I was a little taken aback, but there was no way I wasn't going to answer the woman. She was the key to finding Cheeto. Maybe she was nosy like Joy. I had no clue how old she was or when she'd died. I knew nothing about her, not even her name.

The truth was far easier to remember than lies. I'd stick with that. "Umm… yes," I said, feeling Flip's happiness even though I wasn't looking at her. "It's new. I'm recently divorced." I pulled on my hair. I felt ridiculous but kept talking. "I still need to figure out me without a man to lean on, but… yes. I'm in love with Seth Walters."

Jess giggled. The sound was strange considering the circumstances, but the joy behind it was comforting.

"Since high school," Jess added.

I sighed and let my head rest on the leather of the seat. "It was a crush in high school. Didn't turn into more until recently."

"She wants to make sure you know Cheeto is part of the package. If you marry Seth, you marry Cheeto as well," Nancy said.

The interrogation was getting awfully personal, but maybe the woman had been some kind of counselor in life. Or possibly had been in the situation herself. Or she was Joy Parsley times ten. Whatever. It was easy to pacify her concern with the truth. "I love Cheeto as much as I love Seth," I promised. "In fact, I fell in love with Cheeto first."

"She likes that," Nancy told me. "Gals, keep your eyes open. Lots of woods around. Lily's voice is fading in the car. Don't know how much longer I'll be able to hear her."

My blood suddenly felt icy. My breath came out in short, uneven spurts. Was this a bizarre coincidence or fate? Had I just been grilled by Cheeto's mother? Seth's wife? "What did you say her name was?"

"You okay, Clemmy? You look like you just saw a ghost," Flip said, then slapped her forehead. "No offense meant, new friend."

My mind raced and I tried to go over everything I'd just revealed. Shit. I couldn't think straight. Was this woman really leading us to Cheeto or was this a trap? Was she furious that I might take her place?

"Tell me her name," I demanded, staring at the empty seat. "Please."

"Lily," Nancy said, concerned. "Is that a problem?"

"Ask *her*," I said, feeling wildly out of control.

Nancy glanced quickly at the passenger seat, then back at the road. "Doesn't look like it. She's smiling."

"Are you Cheeto's mother?" I asked. "Seth's wife?"

The car went silent.

"Oh my God," Jess muttered under her breath.

Nancy's brow wrinkled in concentration. She was listening to the dead woman speak.

"She is," Nancy confirmed, as shocked as the rest of us. "She comes in peace and love. She says she needs to watch over Cheeto until she knows she'll be okay. She wants to thank you for recognizing Cheeto's gift and for loving both her daughter and Seth."

"She ain't here for revenge?" Flip asked, putting her small hand on my shoulder.

"I'll rip that ghost a new butt if she's messin' with us," Joy warned. "Woowoo or no woowoo."

Ann Aramini hissed like we'd poured water on her.

"Back off," Nancy yelled, mopping her face while keeping one hand on the wheel. "She says she's here for her daughter. Period. If she's got issues with other stuff, we'll get into that later. Right now, we're a team. Our goal is Cheeto. End of story. Woowoo juju gals have to unite."

"Nancy's got some big balls," Joy Parsley commented with approval.

"Menopause gives you a little extra testosterone," Sally chimed in. "I grew a dang mustache when I went through it."

"Well, I'll be damned," Jess said as Nancy cut the engine at the end of the long driveway.

I should have known. If I'd thought about it, I would have. There was so much going on I had missed an obvious plot point. Clark Dark would be disappointed in me. I was disappointed in me.

Jinny Jingle had gone to her dream house to stake her claim.

My house.

Leaning forward and putting my hand where I guessed Lily's shoulder was, I let it rip. "I love your daughter. I will fight for her and am willing to die for her. Jinny Jingle cannot win. I swear to you, I will go at her with everything in my arsenal. You and Seth need to talk. I will back off. You have my word. Yes, I love him. Yes, I know what happened to you. Your story breaks my heart to pieces, and I wish I had known you when you were alive." I had no clue how she was reacting, but if I were in her shoes, I'd want to know. There was a chance I wouldn't have another opportunity to say it. "Just know that I respect you for loving and protecting your daughter. I can never replace you. I don't want to. But if you're good with it, eventually, I would love to carry on your torch."

"She said yes and godspeed," Nancy announced. "She's pointing to the house."

"Out of the car," I ordered. "It's time."

∼

I really needed to trim my bushes. However, the overgrown foliage was a blessing this afternoon. Seth had parked behind us at the end of the drive, just out of sight of the house. Didn't want to announce our arrival just in case it forced Jinny Jingle's hand. We all hid behind an unruly hedgerow as we formulated a plan.

I looked at the empty space on the left of Nancy. "Lily, can you enter the house and report back?"

"She can," Nancy said.

"Wait. Who?" Seth asked, paling.

"It's Lily," I told him. "She wants to help."

"My Lily?" he asked, confused and alarmed.

His use of the word "my" stabbed a little at my heart. That was ridiculous. She *had* been his Lily. She had been his wife. She was Cheeto's mother. Dead or alive, she would be a part of both Cheeto and Seth until the end of time.

"Yes," I said. "You can talk to her later. Right now, we focus on getting Cheeto safely away from Jinny."

He nodded and pressed his lips together. I was fully aware of his feelings of guilt and sadness over Lily's death. I didn't have time to think about that now. What the future held was anyone's guess. If we didn't concentrate on the now, the future would be moot.

"Joy, Flip, Sally and Ann will go around back and enter through the kitchen," I instructed as we hid in the bushes and made plans. "Stay quiet and look for Thick Stella. She's violent and could be an excellent ally."

"Roger that," Flip said.

Ann meowed. I glanced down at her.

"Is it smart for Ann to stay in cat form?" I asked.

"Yep," Joy grunted and shook her head. "If you think Thick Stella is violent, you're gonna change your mind when you see Ann Aramini in action."

"Seriously?" Jess asked, scratching Ann's furry head. "She's so sweet and cute."

"Remember when we had to go into lockdown 'cause that serial killer from Cincinnati was on the loose in our area?" Sally Dubay whispered.

"I do," Nancy said. "He got mauled by a wild animal."

"Named Ann Aramini," Flip informed us.

"You're shitting me," I said, gaping at the cat.

"We shit you not," Sally Dubay said. "Ann doesn't like serial killers."

"Understatement," Jess muttered, backing away from Ann a bit.

"Got it," I said with a wince. "Not sure we want the Weather Hooker mauled in my house. The goal is Cheeto's safety first. If the skank gets away, so be it. We'll go after her once we have Cheeto."

"Where do you want me?" Jess asked.

"Jess, you take the side door near my office. Can you rip the bumper off my car as a weapon just in case?"

"Of course," she replied.

"Great. Thanks. Nancy, you stay with me. I need to know if Lily has intel and you're the only one who can hear her."

"Affirmative," Nancy said. "Which door are we using?"

"The front door. It's my damn house."

"You go, gurl," Jess said.

"And me?" Seth asked, ready for action. "Which door?"

I looked at him. He was such a beautiful and good man. My feelings for him were enormous and real—more real than any I'd had to date. But thinking about the future when the present could explode was an exercise that could end tragically.

He wasn't going to like what I was about to say, but that wasn't my worry.

"Seth, you have no magic. You can't come in," I said, holding my hand up as he tried to interrupt me. "I need you to call the feds. Tell them you have a lead on Cheeto. Have them come here. That gives us about fifteen to twenty minutes to rescue Cheeto and go at Jinny with woowoo juju. Then they can clean up whatever's left of her."

"She's my daughter, Clementine. I can't just sit out here and do nothing."

"You're not doing nothing," I told him gently. "But Jinny's magic is strong. You saw what she did to a handful of women who also have magic, and she did it with very little effort." I met his angry gaze. "Please. I can't worry what she might do to you. Not if I want to rescue Cheeto."

"She needs me," he said. "She's my life, Clementine. I love her and I can't lose her."

I nodded. "I love her too, Seth." I caressed his cheek. I didn't blame him for being freaked out. Hell, I was freaked out. Losing Cheeto wasn't an option. "And I promise, if you can just trust me, I'll get her back. For you. For both of us."

Seth swore, then finally nodded his agreement. "I'll go." His gaze turned hard. "And if Jinny Jingle gets in your way…"

"She's gonna wish she'd never been born," I told him.

Seth took my hand and gave it a squeeze, then eased himself out of the bushes. He made his way back up the driveway staying hidden in the trees. I let out a slow sigh of relief. One person I loved safe and out of the way. Now, I just had to rescue the other.

"She's in the living room," Nancy whispered, looking at the invisible Lily. "Cheeto is tied up and laying on the couch. It doesn't look like she's hurt. No bruises or blood."

I swallowed back my scream of rage. I couldn't even imagine what Lily was feeling. "Where is the bitch?"

Nancy waited a moment then answered. "On the couch, next to Cheeto."

"Is she armed?" Jess asked.

"No," Nancy said.

"She's armed," Joy said with a grimace of disgust. "She's armed with woowoo juju."

"So are we," I reminded her. "And I have extra bells and whistles from my characters." Speaking of… "Nancy, ask Lily if she saw a woman wearing sweatpants, a corset and lace-up boots, please?"

Nancy looked toward the empty space where Lily must've been and nodded twice then turned back to me. "Yes. She says that Albinia is in the room with Cheeto and the horrible woman."

"Can the Weather Hooker see Albinia?" I questioned. "Are there others in the house? More than just Jinny?"

Nancy shook her head. "Lily doesn't know. She's going back in to check."

I shook my head. We didn't have time to wait for an answer. "The feds are probably on their way." Jinny wasn't going to go down without a fight, and I didn't want Cheeto getting caught in the middle of a shootout where real bullets were involved. "We have to move."

"Is there a more concrete plan once we get inside?" Sally asked.

"Nope," I said. "We write it as we live it. On three, everyone move. One. Two. Three."

CHAPTER EIGHTEEN

"Welcome to my home," Jinny Jingle snarled as I entered with Nancy by my side.

I scanned the room quickly to see if she had backup. She was alone. Albinia sat on the couch next to the bound and gagged Cheeto. Cheeto was fully aware that my character was with her. Her small hand was wrapped tightly around Albinia's. It was also clear Jinny had no clue Albinia existed.

The relief I felt that Cheeto hadn't been alone was profound. I knew Albinia couldn't save Cheeto, but she was a loving presence. It was up to me to save the little princess.

"Not your house," I said coldly.

"We can solve that with a signature," Jinny shot back with crazed eyes and a giggle that made my stomach turn.

"You're in a shitload of trouble, Jinny," I said calmly wondering how much physical strength I had from Stephano and how long it would last. If I punched her hard enough, maybe I could knock her out and get Cheeto out of here. Problem was her proximity to Cheeto, and I wasn't sure what exactly she could do.

"No, I'm not," she countered. "You're going to have to take the fall, bitch, or I'll kill the little girl."

Holding my composure and not attacking her was the hardest thing I'd ever done. I spotted Flip, Sally and Joy out of the corner of my eye. They were crouched low in the kitchen. Thick Stella and Ann were silently making their way into the room. Jess was out of Jinny's sight line and pressed against the wall of my office with the bumper of my car in her hands.

"How about a trade?" I asked, wondering if she would take the bait. If I could get all of us out of here in one piece, I'd consider it a win. The house was a house. Screw it. "The house for the child."

Jinny looked down at the frightened Cheeto and made a pouty face. "I don't think so. I'm going to need to keep her for a little while to ensure I don't have to go to jail."

"That's not how it works," I told her. "The police are an entirely different story. Kidnapping is not going to end well for you."

"I'm babysitting, you old stupid cow," she screamed, flicking her fingers and tossing a ball of flame at me.

Shit. This was far worse than just the wind. I narrowly ducked getting fried to a crisp. My armchair wasn't as lucky. It was on fire. If she kept this up, I wouldn't have a house to trade.

Thick Stella lost her shit. Ann was right behind her. Before I could shape the next plot point, all freaking hell broke loose.

"Charge!" Joy Parsley shouted as my fat asshole cat launched herself at the Weather Hooker. The explosion of fire and my cat's flaming body flying through the air made me see red. Literally. Thick Stella hit the far wall with a sickening thud and landed crumpled on the ground.

Jess sprinted in and nailed Jinny so hard with the bumper, I was pretty sure she'd killed her. Shockingly, Jinny was back on her feet almost immediately. The fortuitous part was that Nancy had snatched Cheeto and was making a run for it.

"Fuck NO," Jinny bellowed, shooting a fireball at the front door Nancy was headed for.

Nancy went flying back but took the brunt of the fall when she went down. Cheeto landed safely on top of her. As the room filled with smoke, Joy Parsley disappeared and began pelting Jinny from all sides. She'd clearly chugged the rest of my beer when they'd entered through the kitchen. Sally flew above and hurled lamps and candles at the unhinged nightmare. Flip had crawled across the room on her hands and knees aided by Ann Aramini. They got to Nancy and Cheeto and led them into my office. My hope was they'd crawl out of the window and get the hell out.

Every time I got close enough to take a swing at Jinny Jingle, she hit me with fire. I'd even gotten nailed accidentally by a flying candle that Joy had thrown.

Glancing around wildly and looking for an opening, I almost started crying as I spotted Flip, Nancy and Cheeto escape the house. The scene in front of me was scarier than anything I'd ever imagined. It was as if I'd walked into an epic battle from one of my books. So far woowoo juju had been tame. My gal's gifts were ones that were not destructive. They made the world a more beautiful place.

What Jinny had was the beauty of woowoo juju mixed with the ugly depths of darkness. It was horrifying. I was glad that Nancy had made it out with Cheeto and Flip. Losing Flip would've been worse than death itself. And I knew that Nancy could interpret and help Seth deal with his guilt over Lily. Seth and Cheeto could go on with a happy and healthy life, even if I wasn't part of the picture.

"Incoming," Sally shouted as she fell out of the air.

Jinny had waved her deadly hands. A vicious wind ripped through the room and fanned the flames. My living room was an inferno.

"Out," I yelled to Sally. "Get out. Joy, you too. Get out!"

"Not a chance," Joy bellowed over the crackling fire that was now licking up the walls and eating my curtains.

"You want to leave," I yelled in my mind. *"Sally and Joy, you will leave this house NOW. This is the most important thing you will do in your life. LEAVE."*

"That don't work on me," Joy shouted with a grunt as she nailed Jinny with a side table. "You can't woowoo a juju!"

So much for trying to plant thoughts in Jinny's head.

Jinny barely noticed the table that had just splintered over her head. She was after me. Even with eight of us in our Goodness Army, she was winning. My heart sunk into my stomach as the truth crushed me. Jinny Jingle's dark magic was unstoppable.

Ann Aramini appeared out of the smoke—a hissing, growling ball of furious fur. Her tail twitched and she was pissed. Her scratching and clawing of the Weather Hooker bought me a few precious seconds to think, to plan, to try and come up with a different ending.

"The author of the story controls the action... the players... and the outcome," Albinia insisted frantically as she shoved a yellow legal pad and pencil into my hands. "Write the ending, Clementine. You are the only one who can!"

"She's human," I ground out. "She's not fictional."

Albinia wrung her hands and began to cry. "Is magic fiction?"

"No. Magic is real."

She nodded. "Did you enter the world you wrote for the others?"

"I did."

Albinia shook me by the shoulders. "Your human body stayed here. Your magical spirit left. Fiction became reality. The author of the story controls the action... the players... and the outcome," she repeated forcefully. "You are the author."

"But the consequences," I said, feeling terrified. "The consequences could be grave."

"Or *you* and your friends could end up in a grave if you don't take the risk," Albinia said so calmly it was startling. "The choice is yours, Clementine."

Without another second of hesitation, I put the pencil to the paper and began to weave a tale. Joy and Sally ran interference as if they knew what was happening. Maybe they did. Albinia did her best to help. She tried over and over to tackle the evil monster, but she fought in vain. She wrapped her body around Jinny Jingle's, but Jinny had no clue.

My fingers and my words opened up the bowels of Hell.

The blazing blood-red fire eclipsed the raging inferno in my house. The deadliest of demons came to the beck and call of my prose. I greeted them with words and offered them a sacrifice.

Their sharp bloody teeth gnashed with rabid excitement as my sharp pencil flew across the paper. Describing Jinny in explicit detail, I delivered her into their scabbed and mutilated arms. The shrieks of delight made my body shiver in horror. I'd never written anything so dark and evil. But the beast in my home deserved no less.

As the story grew darker, Jinny began to stumble and choke. I watched in horrified fascination as she grew weaker and weaker. Albinia still held fast to her neck. My pencil had ceased to move, but the story had taken on a life of its own.

Joy and Sally detected an opening and tackled Jinny to the ground. I heard sirens in the background and watched as Jinny Jingle's spirit left her body. The sense of satisfaction was profound.

My body trembled violently as I squeezed my eyes shut and waited for the grave consequences.

Only...they didn't come.

I opened my eyes and glanced around. Where were the grave consequences? The fire had mostly abated when Jinny slipped away. My house was destroyed, but I didn't care. Cheeto was safe. And no one had died...

Oh my God. That was wrong.

"Thick Stella," I choked out, getting down on my hands and knees so I could crawl underneath the smoke and find her body. There was no way she was going to be left in here alone. She was an asshole, but she had been my asshole and I'd loved her.

"What a fucking shitshow," Thick Stella growled as I started to cry.

"You aren't dead," I said, tears falling freely.

"No shit, Sherlock," she snapped. "Got nine fucking lives. Think I might have used up about six. Did you get the bitch?"

"I did," I told her. "Need to check on Joy, Sally, Ann and Albinia. Stay here."

"You owe me tuna," she grumbled as I carefully made my way across the destroyed room. "Twenty fucking cans."

What I'd expected to see and what I saw didn't compute. It was wrong. It wasn't what I'd written—not even close.

"No," I cried out, dropping to the ground and checking for heartbeats. Ann was no longer a cat. Joy was no longer invisible. Sally wasn't able to fly and Albinia was gone. "Heartbeat. Heartbeat," I said frantically. "Please be alive. Please."

Ann's pulse was steady and normal. Sally's and Joy's were equally as strong. Sadly, Jinny's was too.

What was happening?

"Wake up," I begged, gently shaking the women. "You have to wake up. You have to."

They were lifeless. They were alive, but they weren't.

The feds entered my house, guns drawn. Flip, Nancy and Jess were right on their heels. I was sure that wasn't supposed to happen, but the woowoo girls weren't going to listen to anyone even if they were carrying guns.

"Call an ambulance," Nancy told the feds. "There's the

one you're looking for." She pointed to a comatose Jinny Jingle. "She tried to kill all of us, and she kidnapped Cheeto Walters."

The feds surrounded Jinny and made calls to dispatch.

"They're alive," I whispered to Flip. "But they're not here. I think they're in a coma." My voice broke, and I wanted to peel the skin from my body. Images of the hellish landscape I'd sent Jinny to blasted in my head. I could barely breathe. "They were touching Jinny when I wrote her into a story—all of them. I think I sent them into the story with her by accident. Oh my God, what have I done?"

"Was it an island?" Flip whispered as the feds looked around and tried to piece together what had happened.

I shook my head. My words left me. The author of the story controls the action… the players… and the outcome. The consequences had indeed arrived, and they were graver than I could have anticipated.

"What do we do?" I asked.

Jess and Nancy had heard everything. I wasn't sure they understood as well as Flip did, but they clearly got the gist of it.

Flip looked down at her dearest friends. Tears rolled down her wrinkled cheeks. "Where'd you send the hussy?" she asked again.

"To Hell," I said, wanting to curl up into a ball and die.

"Welp," she said, sitting back on her haunches. "I suppose we're taking a little trip then."

"To?" Jess asked.

Before I could answer, the ambulances arrived.

Backing away as the paramedics entered my house and

took our friends and our enemy away, I couldn't hold back my tears.

We watched as the ambulances drove away and the fire trucks arrived. The feds were everywhere and wanted statements. After they were done with us, those of us still standing, moved to the gazebo in my backyard. Seth, cradling his daughter, looked like he'd aged a decade. Thankfully, Cheeto, who had to have been exhausted, had fallen asleep. The seven-year-old little girl had lived through more than I could imagine. It was horribly wrong and unfair. I prayed that she would be okay. I was praying about a lot of things right now. Seth was walking her around the gazebo and softly singing to her. It was moving and beautiful.

"Where are we going?" Jess asked again. "Flip said we were taking a trip."

Flip glanced over at me. I nodded.

"We're going to Hell," Flip whispered.

"Seriously?" Jess asked with huge eyes.

"As a heart attack," Flip replied.

Nancy shrugged. "Already in Hell with menopause. Real Hell can't come close to that. I'm in. Husband's still on a fishing trip. Do you think we'll be gone longer than five days?"

My mouth fell open.

"I'm in," Jess said. "Do you think the ladies will be okay till we get there?"

"They're tough old broads. Joy could terrify the Devil himself," Flip said. "They're gonna be fine."

I decided to believe her. There was no other choice.

"Albinia is with them?" Nancy asked, getting the lineup straight.

"I think so. Not sure," I admitted.

She nodded, then looked to her left. "Lily is in. She wants to thank you for saving Cheeto."

"Umm... okay," I said, unable to absorb the reality of the absurdity.

"Seth's gonna crap," Jess whispered as he walked up the stairs of the gazebo and eyed us all suspiciously.

"What's going on here?" Seth asked softly as to not wake Cheeto.

"You ain't gonna like it," Flip warned him.

"Don't care," he replied. "Tell me."

"We have to take a trip," I explained. "But first I'd like to say something."

He waited.

"Umm... it's far too soon for this," I admitted. "But..."

"But?" Seth asked.

"Nancy, check and make sure this is cool, please," I requested.

Nancy paused, then smiled. "You have blessings and approval."

Seth looked so confused I felt sorry for him.

"Seth, I love you," I blurted out. "I'm sorry I'm springing this on you, but I needed you to know how I felt before..." I let the words trail off.

He narrowed his gaze at me. "I love you too, Clementine, but you know that," he said solemnly. "So, why now? I mean, I'm glad, but I can't help but feel like this is some kind of goodbye."

How could I tell him that he wasn't far off the mark? If I wrote us into Hell, there were no guarantees I'd be able to get us back. Was this foolishness on my part? Probably. But I couldn't leave our fallen friends to the nightmare I'd written for Jinny Jingle. In our Goodness Army, we left no woowoo juju gal behind.

But I didn't know how to say that to Seth. He'd almost lost Cheeto, and I couldn't tell him that he might lose me as well. So instead of giving him a cohesive, adult response to his reasonable question, I gave him a barely audible grunt and a shoulder shrug.

Seth furrowed his brow, then turned to Jess and Flip. "Will someone please tell me where you all are going?"

Seth was a part of my life now, and his daughter was a part of our woowoo. He deserved the truth. Taking a deep breath, I womaned-up and let it rip. "We're going to Hell. We have to rescue Joy, Ann, Sally and most likely my character Albinia. It's my fault, and I have to save them."

"Like Hell as in the real Hell?" he asked, handing off a sleeping Cheeto to Jess so he didn't drop her.

"Yes. We're going to Hell."

"When?" he demanded, looking a little ill.

I glanced over at Flip. She winked at me.

"Right after the feds get out of here, I reckon," Flip said. The FBI were packing up their vans and cars. Most of them had already left. "Ten minutes or so, maybe."

"Fuck," Seth said, sitting down in the heavy teak chair and letting his head fall to his hands.

The story wasn't over, but Princess Cheeto was safe. King Seth and Queen Clementine had quite a way to go before all was settled in their newly found kingdom. Lady Jessica, Lady Nancy and Lady Lily had traded their gowns for armor and were going to slay the dragons with Queen Clementine and the Grand Duchess Flip. The stakes were high and the outcome uncertain. But the woowoo juju clan would not go down without a fight. It was one for all and all for one. Magic made the world go round and good would triumph over evil.

There was no other alternative.

And the story would go on... and on and on.

The end... for now

MORE IN MY SO-CALLED MYSTICAL MIDLIFE SERIES

ORDER BOOK THREE NOW!

**Going to Hell has never been on my bucket list…
until now.**

The fact that I can speak that sentence without laughing or losing my mind is absurd. However, my life has veered into a very tricky tale that rivals any of my books.

The villain has been banished. I've written her right into an infernal doom. Unfortunately, a few of my very dear friends, fictional and real, have been caught up in the horror story and they've taken the trip down under as well.

It's my fault and I can only see one way out…a plot twist of epic proportions. The fairytale is imploding and my imagination has taken flight.

The ending is murky and the stakes are up to me. There is no other alternative.

If I don't get this ending right, my happy ever after might become a happy never after.

ROBYN'S BOOK LIST
(IN CORRECT READING ORDER)

HOT DAMNED SERIES
Fashionably Dead
Fashionably Dead Down Under
Hell on Heels
Fashionably Dead in Diapers
A Fashionably Dead Christmas
Fashionably Hotter Than Hell
Fashionably Dead and Wed
Fashionably Fanged
Fashionably Flawed
A Fashionably Dead Diary
Fashionably Forever After
Fashionably Fabulous
A Fashionable Fiasco
Fashionably Fooled
Fashionably Dead and Loving It
Fashionably Dead and Demonic

The Oh My Gawd Couple

GOOD TO THE LAST DEATH SERIES
It's a Wonderful Midlife Crisis
Whose Midlife Crisis Is It Anyway?
A Most Excellent Midlife Crisis
My Midlife Crisis, My Rules
You Light Up My Midlife Crisis
It's A Matter of Midlife and Death

MY SO-CALLED MYSTICAL MIDLIFE SERIES
The Write Hook
You May Be Write
All The Write Moves

SHIFT HAPPENS SERIES
Ready to Were
Some Were in Time
No Were To Run
Were Me Out
Were We Belong

MAGIC AND MAYHEM SERIES
Switching Hour
Witch Glitch
A Witch in Time
Magically Delicious
A Tale of Two Witches
Three's A Charm
Switching Witches

You're Broom or Mine?
The Bad Boys of Assjacket
The Newly Witch Game

SEA SHENANIGANS SERIES
Tallulah's Temptation
Ariel's Antics
Misty's Mayhem
Petunia's Pandemonium
Jingle Me Balls

A WYLDE PARANORMAL SERIES
Beauty Loves the Beast

HANDCUFFS AND HAPPILY EVER AFTERS SERIES
How Hard Can it Be?
Size Matters
Cop a Feel

If after reading all the above you are still wanting more adventure and zany fun, read *Pirate Dave and His Randy Adventures*, the romance novel budding novelist Rena helped wicked Evangeline write in *How Hard Can It Be?*

Warning: Pirate Dave Contains Romance Satire, Spoofing, and Pirates with Two Pork Swords.

NOTE FROM THE AUTHOR

If you enjoyed reading *You May Be Write*, please consider leaving a positive review or rating on the site where you purchased it. Reader reviews help my books continue to be valued by resellers and help new readers make decisions about reading them.

You are the reason I write these stories and I sincerely appreciate each of you!

Many thanks for your support,
~ Robyn Peterman

Want to hear about my new releases?
Visit robynpeterman.com and join my mailing list!

ABOUT ROBYN PETERMAN

Robyn Peterman writes because the people inside her head won't leave her alone until she gives them life on paper. Her addictions include laughing really hard with friends, shoes (the expensive kind), Target, Coke (the drink not the drug LOL) with extra ice in a Yeti cup, bejeweled reading glasses, her kids, her super-hot hubby and collecting stray animals.

A former professional actress with Broadway, film and T.V. credits, she now lives in the South with her family and too many animals to count.

Writing gives her peace and makes her whole, plus having a job where she can work in sweatpants works really well for her.

Made in the USA
Monee, IL
25 November 2024